Judith Barclay was born and bred in Goodwick, Pembrokeshire. She has a degree in education from the University of Nottingham and started writing seriously after retiring from a career in teaching. She enjoys walking, reading psychological thrillers and has travelled extensively all over Europe, and in Africa and Asia. She has held a lifelong passion for Italy and all things Italian and was inspired to write this book by her research into the history of the mass immigration and integration of Italians into Wales from the late nineteenth century. Judith has twin daughters, Emily and Joanna, and lives in Derbyshire with her husband, Chris.

This is for Christopher, Emily and Joanna.
With my love, as always.

Judith Barclay

THE DA CALVI LEGACY

AUSTIN MACAULEY PUBLISHERS
LONDON * CAMBRIDGE * NEW YORK * SHARJAH

Copyright © Judith Barclay 2025

The right of Judith Barclay to be identified as the author of this work has been asserted by the author in accordance with sections 77 and 78 of the Copyright, Designs and Patents Act 1988.

All rights reserved. No part of this publication may be reproduced, stored in a retrieval system, or transmitted in any form or by any means, electronic, mechanical, photocopying, recording, or otherwise, without the prior permission of the publishers.

Any person who commits any unauthorised act in relation to this publication may be liable to criminal prosecution and civil claims for damages.

This is a work of fiction. Names, characters, businesses, places, events, locales, and incidents are either the products of the author's imagination or used in a fictitious manner. Any resemblance to actual persons, living or dead, or actual events is purely coincidental.

A CIP catalogue record for this title is available from the British Library.

ISBN 9781035882649 (Paperback)
ISBN 9781035882656 (ePub e-book)

www.austinmacauley.com

First Published 2025
Austin Macauley Publishers Ltd®
1 Canada Square
Canary Wharf
London
E14 5AA

I started writing this story some time ago purely for pleasure whenever I managed to find some rare time to myself away from teaching. I have always kept my writing to myself, but recently life has changed and there are a number of important people I need to thank for encouraging me to take my writing a step further.

So, my thanks go to Ruth Durbridge, whose advice and encouragement motivated me to move forward with my work. A new friend, Janet Dewhurst, kindly agreed to read my draft manuscript. made observations and gave me so many objective comments. My thanks go to Helen Wagstaff for her artistic input in developing the front cover image. I must also thank my husband, Chris, for taking the author photograph.

It is true to say that this book would not exist if it were not for Chris and my twin daughters, Emily, for her knowledge of Italian, and Joanna, for her proofreading skills. They not only gave me belief in myself, but also gave generously of their own free time to support me.

Table of Contents

Part One: (Central Italy 1939–1945)   11

Chapter 1: Ernesto   *13*

Chapter 2: Ennio and Ernesto   *17*

Chapter 3: Elena   *25*

Chapter 4: Andrea   *28*

Part Two: (Central Italy, Present Day)   33

Chapter 5: Sebastiano Luce   *35*

Chapter 6: Francesco   *38*

Chapter 7: Ennio and Francesco   *44*

Chapter 8: Sebastiano   *60*

Chapter 9: Massimo   *63*

Chapter 10: Stefano   *66*

Chapter 11: Seb   *90*

Part Three: (West Wales, Present Day)   95

Chapter 12: Cristi   *97*

Chapter 13: David   *108*

Chapter 14: Gillian   *111*

Chapter 15: David   *114*

Chapter 16: Cristi   *124*

Chapter 17: Cristi   *143*

Chapter 18: Cristi and Julie	*157*
Part Four: (Italy, Present Day)	**167**
Chapter 19: Cristi	*169*
Chapter 20: Seb	*180*
Chapter 21: Cristi	*186*
Chapter 22: Signor Luce	*201*
Part Five: The Legacy	**223**
Chapter 23: Cristi	*225*
Chapter 24: Seb	*237*
Chapter 25: Cristi	*239*

Part One
(Central Italy 1939–1945)

Chapter 1
Ernesto

Who would have thought a child's body could be so heavy? He was more used to carrying bales of hay than bodies. Every muscle and sinew screamed pain as he carried the dead weight in his arms up the steep, stony path winding its way through the wheat field to the high, wrought iron gates of the *palazzo*. The boy was deathly white, still breathing, but only just. The wound where his forehead had been sliced open still oozed blood, but it was no longer a rich, bright red. Clear, fresh stream water dripped from the boy's hair, turning his blood into a pale, rose-pink liquid which trickled in rivulets down the groove beside his nose into the corner of his mouth.

Ernesto increased his pace. The extra weight came from the boy's sodden clothes and boots. He wouldn't have believed it possible that such a scrap of a child could weigh so much. Getting the boy back to the *Palazzo Piceno* as quickly as possible was only one of the problems on his mind.

As he struggled on up the hill, trying desperately not to lose his footing on the loose, dry stones, he chewed the soft, sensitive skin on the inside of his bottom lip, his brain working feverishly, trying to come up with what he could possibly say to Signor Fioretti. The boy's father just happened to be the local landowner who held the future of so many workers and their families, including his own, in the palm of his hand.

For more than a century, Ernesto's father and grandfather before him had tended the heavy, clay soil belonging to Silvano Fioretti's family. Ernesto had been born in the farmhouse on the hillside where he still lived, its stone exterior exposed to the blazing, unrelenting summer sun and the freezing, high winds which cut through the valley in winter. The house stood up proudly against the magnificent electrical storms and the torrential rain which lashed the walls and windows for what seemed like hours. Day or night, the extremes of weather in the hills made no distinction. It was the only life he knew—and now, this! He owned very little, but what he did have, he cherished. He could lose everything. How would they survive? No home. No livelihood. No future. Signor Fioretti could be ruthless. How would he react when he saw the state his eldest son was in, delivered by one of his labourers?

Ernesto looked down again at the child in his arms. The boy's breathing was shallow but with short, sharp gasps at irregular intervals. Not normal. *Such a good-looking boy,* Ernesto thought. His own, broad chest was heaving, his lungs fit to burst, but he couldn't slow down. '*Dio, Dio,*' he repeated out loud to himself with each weary footstep until the tall, imposing gates of the *palazzo* came into view at last.

Ernesto and all the other farmhands were familiar with the courtyard at the rear of the grand residence. Here, seated at long wooden tables, the labourers and their families would celebrate the end of *la raccolta*, when the wine flowed, and the tables groaned under the platters of food supplied by the womenfolk. There was always a wide selection of cold meats, fresh salads, pasta and fruit, all grown and produced locally. The night would be full of rejoicing, with music, dancing and fun. A night to forget all the back-breaking work which brought very little reward except for the owner of the land. Today, however, would be the first time Ernesto had approached the house from the front.

'*Dio, Dio,*' he gasped again and again, as his boots scraped along the gravel of the neat driveway, which led directly to the arched double doors in front of him. On each side, rows of cypress trees lined the route, perfectly spaced, a guard of honour watching his struggle.

He stopped a few yards from the steps and looked up at the closed doors. He drew in one deep breath, then shouted as loudly as he possibly could.

'*Signore! Vostro figlio, vostro figlio!*' he screamed. 'Your son, your son!'

Ernesto stood, feet wide apart, holding the inert body of the boy out in front of him in a sacrificial pose. After what seemed like an age, but what could only have been a matter of seconds, the double doors were flung open, and Silvano Fioretti himself leapt down the steps, closely followed by a young housemaid. He snatched the boy from Ernesto's arms without a word, turned away and stomped back towards the house.

'*Venga veloce.* Come,' he commanded, without looking back. '*Presto, presto!*'

Ernesto dropped his aching arms to his sides, shaking out the stabbing pains in his muscles as he released his grip on the boy. Reluctantly, head bowed, he followed the retreating figure of the boy's father into the house.

An hour later, Ernesto retraced his steps down the path away from the *palazzo*. He walked slowly, eyes cast downwards, both hands in his pockets. His shirt was still damp, his heart heavy.

The inside of *Palazzo Piceno* had been grander than he'd ever imagined. The fine marble floors, dark wooden furniture and glittering chandeliers had all mocked him as he'd stood, head still bowed, just inside the vast entrance hall where he had been left to wait. Water from his old boots had slowly created puddles on the floor, creeping smoothly away from the soles. He'd felt ashamed, but why, he couldn't say. He worked hard; he supported his family. He had nothing to be ashamed about, but he couldn't shake off the feeling.

He heard the doctor arrive some time before, but even he had used the rear entrance. How long he stood there, he couldn't tell. All he knew was that slowly but surely, the pains in his arms eased, and his breathing returned to normal. He shifted his weight from one leg to the other, trying hard not to move his feet. He dreaded making more mess, so he just stood in the puddles he'd already made.

'*Avanti!*' He hadn't noticed the door being opened to his right. The voice giving the instruction sounded reasonable, making a request rather than giving an order.

'*Avanti!*' Signor Fioretti repeated, so Ernesto turned and walked towards the open door, smoothing down his thick, unruly black hair with the palms of his hands. As he walked into the grand *salone*, he suddenly felt fear rather than shame. The elegant man now facing him could ruin his life in an instant, and all because of the boy.

Now, making his way home, he needed time to put his thoughts in order before facing the family. His hair and clothes dried quickly in the late afternoon sunshine and, in other circumstances, he would have enjoyed every second of this walk which was so familiar to him.

He would tell Elena all of it, of course. He had no doubts about that. They shared everything, good or bad. She'd tell him what they should do. When dealing with other people, she was the wise one. His Elena could always relate to the emotions of others, men or women, without having to try. She had a natural gift, whereas he just got embarrassed and tongue-tied when faced with other people's dilemmas.

Sometimes, he wished his wife didn't have this "gift", especially when her concern for other people in the village took her away from him for hours at a time. Where Elena was concerned, he was selfish and possessive, and he admitted it. She was the centre of his life, and now, he needed her support and understanding more than ever. He needed her to tell him that he'd done the right thing.

He'd been so deep in thought, he hadn't realised that he'd reached the end of the path at the top of the olive grove just below his house. He emerged from the mass of grey-green foliage into the sunshine, which was still warming the walls of the old farmhouse. He stopped for a few seconds, to take in every detail of his home. He saw the mixture of mellow stone and brickwork, the heavy-arched oak door, weathered and worn for over a century and the paintwork peeling away from the old shutters. He had been born here, and he would, no doubt, die here. Not much to show for a life of hard work, and with this thought and a heavy heart, he moved forward into the welcoming cool air of the kitchen.

Everything was just as he'd left it. He was the one who'd changed. In one short moment of time, he had betrayed his own youngest boy.

Chapter 2
Ennio and Ernesto

Ennio opened his eyes slowly, his long, dark eyelashes flickering rapidly. He had been awake for a while but had kept his eyes closed, trying hard not to think about what had happened. He wanted to put off the inevitable for as long as possible. The angry questions and blame from his father and the disappointment he knew he'd see in his mother's eyes. He had let them down. He had disobeyed the only rule his father had set him. And what about Francesco? Was he dead? He had looked dead, and there had been so much blood flowing away from his head like leftover, water-diluted red wine poured down the sink.

Ennio felt a tear escape from beneath his lashes, brushing it away with the back of his hand before anyone noticed he was crying. His hand was bandaged up with a thick, cream-coloured cloth. There was no pain as he wriggled his fingers, but blood was already seeping through the layers. He hadn't even realised he'd cut himself. *Babbo* was right. The stones in the brook were razor-sharp. Francesco and he had found that out the hard way.

He was tucked up on the old settle against the stone wall. He gazed across the kitchen to where his mother stood, stirring something on the range, her back towards him. Her thick, wiry black hair was tied back with the usual strip of flowery material, fraying at the edges. He preferred it when she wore her hair down around her shoulders, the same strip of material worn as a headband.

Even though he was still a young boy, he knew his mother was beautiful. When he was with his brothers, he acted tough and tried hard to stand up for himself. There was a lot of play fighting and rough and tumble in his life, but alone with *Mamma*, he could be the baby of the family again.

He would sit on her lap, and she would tell him stories about her childhood in Greece. She would also tell him about characters from Greek mythology, gods and goddesses with exciting names: Zeus, Heracles, Poseidon, Aphrodite,

Artemis, Athena and Calypso. Ennio loved his mother's voice, her accented Italian, but above all, he loved it when she sang to him in her own language. He didn't understand a word, but, held closely in her arms, he could feel her breathing, could feel how it changed the more emotional she became.

Now and again, he would risk a glance up into her face, feeling embarrassed when he saw the moisture in her eyes and felt the involuntary sob that would rise up in her chest so close to his head, and escape her lips as she reached the end of her song. Ennio had no doubt that his mother loved his father and their four sons, but there were times when she admitted to all of them that she felt homesick for her homeland.

He closed his eyes again and breathed in deeply. The aroma of fresh bread filled the kitchen. *Mamma* was proud of her delicious bread, baked in her very own oven.

'Back home,' she often told them. 'We had to survive on chunks of bread, sometimes with cheese, a few vegetables, or a bean soup.' Her eyes would take on a faraway look. 'Of course,' she went on matter-of-factly, 'there were no ovens in the houses. Once or twice a week, we would carry our dough to the local baker, who would bake it for us in his oven. We would collect our fresh bread hours later. Baking days were good days. We'd always meet up to gossip and sometimes share food if there was any to spare.'

Now, she had her own oven, and three times a week, she baked her *psomi*, a thick-textured country bread that formed the staple diet of the household. He loved *Mamma* more than anything or anyone, and today he'd let her down. What would he say to her to make everything better? Would she believe his story about saving Francesco? Even in his own mind, it sounded more like an excuse than a reason.

Although he still had his eyes closed, he knew the room had suddenly become darker. He sensed his mother turn away from her oven, and her anxiously whispered, 'Ernesto' confirmed that his father had returned and was standing in the doorway, blocking out the sunshine. No one spoke for what seemed like an age, and then his father's voice broke the silence.

'How is he?' Ernesto asked, his voice sounding surprisingly gentle.

'He's been sleeping. I put him into dry clothes then settled him down, in here with me. He's cut his hand badly, but the wound was clean. I wrapped it up tightly, but blood is still seeping through.'

'Did he tell you what happened?'

'No, not a word. He was in too much distress. And Francesco?'

Ennio held his breath. There was no response from his father. Had he nodded or shaken his head? Ennio was desperate to know, but something was telling him to pretend to sleep for just a little bit longer.

There was no more conversation, so a few minutes after hearing his father leave the kitchen, Ennio opened his eyes properly.

'*Mamma*,' he whispered, preferring to face her alone first before all the questions he knew were bound to come from his father.

'*Caro mio*,' his mother said affectionately, turning and moving towards him. Her face was flushed from the heat of the oven, but it was the concern in her eyes that made him feel even more guilty. 'So, you have woken up at last.'

He pushed himself up into a sitting position with his elbows, taking care not to use his bandaged hand. His mother sat down next to him on the settle and smoothed his hair away from his eyes.

'You frightened me,' she accused. 'Dripping wet and gasping for breath. Ennio da Calvi, don't you ever scare me like that again, do you hear me?'

Her accent got stronger the more agitated she became. She clutched him to her and held onto him tightly. He knew she had forgiven him without question for whatever he had done. All he had to do now was convince his father, and that, he knew, would be a different matter altogether.

The evening meal was a silent affair. His mother told him he was fit enough to join the family at the long, wooden table under the hazelnut tree next to the house. The usual noisy banter between his older brothers was missing. It was obvious that they had been told about his disobedience and were following their father's instructions.

Ennio had no appetite. He kept his head bowed and his eyes on the table. No one had mentioned Francesco, and he was afraid to ask in case the news was bad. *It must be really bad,* he thought, *to ruin the family meal.* Once or twice, he lifted his eyes. Andrea, the eldest son, was shovelling his soup and bread down as usual. Always the first to finish to lay claim to a second helping. Nothing would deter him from his food. Next to him on the bench sat Giorgio, the serious one, always quiet and intense. It seemed to Ennio that Giorgio spent his life worrying instead of enjoying himself.

On this particular occasion, the lines across Giorgio's forehead were deeper than usual, as if the day's events had affected him personally. He looked about to burst into tears. Giuseppe, only a few years older than Ennio and the one usually in trouble, was eating his meal with a self-satisfied smirk on his face. For once, it wasn't him this time having to face the wrath of *Babbo*, who sat upright and proud as usual at the head of the table. The tension was unbearable, and just when he thought he couldn't bear it any longer, *Mamma* started to clear away the plates and dishes. Ennio noticed that although there had been so much tension around the table, very little food was left. Everyone else had still managed to eat a good meal.

'I wish to speak with Ennio,' his father finally announced. 'I am sure you can all find something worthwhile to do. Giuseppe, you start by helping your mother.'

'But it's not my turn, *Babbo*.'

His father, Ernesto, said nothing, just looked at Giuseppe, who in turn glared at Ennio as he stomped off into the kitchen to obey him.

When his other sons had left the table, Ernesto looked at his youngest child. Not for the first time did he marvel at how handsome the boy was. He took after Elena, thank God, with his thick, dark hair, smooth olive skin and good teeth. He hadn't inherited the broad nose and wide mouth of the da Calvi family. The boy was slight and athletic, while his other three sons were more like him—broad-shouldered and strong, hard workers, all of them.

'Come here,' he said quietly, holding out his arm encouragingly. Ennio slid along the bench and stood at the table next to his father, head still bowed.

'Look at me, Ennino,' he commanded gently, using his pet name for his youngest son. When the boy looked up at him sadly, without any trace of defiance, it was Elena's eyes Ernesto saw.

'Francesco will survive. He has a nasty cut on his head and will need lots of attention for a while.' Ernesto swallowed hard, then continued. He knew that what he said to his son in the next few moments would stay with them and be remembered for a very long time.

'*Ennino mio*, I need to explain things to you,' his father went on, knowing in his heart that what he intended to leave out of his explanation would gnaw away at him until the day he died.

As his father started to speak, Ennio's attention was drawn to a swift movement just beyond his father's shoulder. A small, bright-green lizard clung to a log on the woodpile outside the kitchen door. He could see its throat pulsating in the sunshine in stark contrast to the stillness in the rest of its body.

It was this simple image that Ennio always saw whenever he thought about the conversation with his father. It was an image he saw often.

His father was his hero. Although not very tall, Ernesto da Calvi was all dark skin, muscle and sinew. There was no job on the farm that was too difficult or too heavy for him to manage. He knew his youngest son looked up to him far more than his other sons did, although they all respected his position in the family. Above everything, he could not lose this respect, and he would not hurt his youngest child by burdening him with the whole truth. The boy didn't need to know the details of the agreement he had come to with Signor Fioretti in the *salone* of the *palazzo*.

'How are you feeling now, *figlio mio*?' he began, trying hard to put the boy and, if truth be known, himself, at ease.

'I'm OK, but my hand hurts. It's stinging. I'm sorry, *Babbo*, those stones are really sharp like you said, but Francesco—I had to help him.'

'I know that, Ennio. You probably saved his life, but there is something I have to tell you.' He had the boy's full attention now. The innocent face of his son was pale, and there was fear in the soft, brown eyes.

'You were not responsible for Francesco's reckless behaviour today, Ennio,' he stated firmly, wanting more than anything to reassure and banish that fear. 'He should not have been playing in the stream. Like me with you, I know his father had given him clear instructions about those stones. In fact, I now know that Francesco should not have been out in the fields at all. He had been told clearly to play in the grounds of the *palazzo* with his brother. From the look on your face, I take it that this isn't the first time he has disobeyed his father?' The question hung in the air between them, but the boy merely stared straight ahead. He was not going to betray his friend, even if it meant a harder punishment for himself.

To his surprise, his father didn't wait for an answer but went on. 'This is not the first time your friend has got himself into a scrape, but this was far more serious than his other mishaps. So, Signor Fioretti has decided to confine Francesco to the *palazzo* for the rest of the summer, which means he can no longer play with you. At the end of the summer, he will be sent away to a monastery school, where he will be taught and watched closely by the Trappist Brothers. If Francesco disobeys his father, he will be sent away sooner. Do you understand what I'm telling you, Ennio? You will help Francesco by staying away. Bring other friends from the village to play with in the fields.'

His son had gone very still. The fear in his eyes replaced by a look of indescribable horror.

'But he's my best friend!' the boy blurted out. 'He can't go away. He's my friend, my friend!'

The boy's calm deserted him, and his voice rose to a shrill, desperate cry. As Ernesto realised his son was becoming hysterical, Elena appeared in the doorway.

'*Dio*!' she exclaimed. 'What's happening?'

Swiftly she wrapped both arms around her son and held him tightly to her until his heaving sobs subsided. She glared at her husband over her son's head.

'Such a reaction. I didn't even know that he and the Fioretti boy were such close friends,' Ernesto defended himself, shrugging his shoulders.

'That's because you don't keep your eyes open. Where do you think he goes every afternoon? How do you think he entertains himself all day, every day? Francesco is more like a brother to him than his own brothers.'

Taking her eyes away from her husband, she glanced down at the boy still clinging to her.

'Come into the house, *caro*,' she said to her son, gently stroking his hair, her tone changing instantly. 'Things are never as bad as they seem. You'll see Francesco before he leaves, and of course he'll have long school holidays. You'll see. It'll all turn out for the best.'

At the time, she genuinely believed that what she was telling him was the truth.

Long summer days stretched into weeks. The rich, green vine leaves grew abundantly. Very slowly, small green olives appeared on the gnarled, ancient trees that bordered the fields worked by Ernesto and his sons. Every afternoon, at the same time, Ennio turned up under the old cypress tree where he and Francesco always met. There had been no sign of his friend now for the last five weeks. Only once did Ennio walk up to the *palazzo* and peer through the wrought iron barrier, gripping the bars like a caged primate, his hands and arms raised above his head, thrust forward against the cold metal. There had been no sign of anyone. The *palazzo* looked deserted, and Ennio sensed that there was no one at home, but he was wrong. He never saw the shadowy figure of a man watching him from a window high up on the second floor.

As the weeks stretched into months and the long, empty summer days were replaced by the crisp chill of autumn, Ennio's hopes of seeing his friend again diminished. He would still turn up at the *cipresso* now and again, just in case, but he no longer ran through the fields and along the dirt track in anticipation.

His steps dragged reluctantly in the dirt, until for one whole week, he didn't turn up at all, preferring to stay around the house, getting in his mother's way. He worked hard when all the local farmers came to help with the grape picking, and later in the year his father said it was time for him to learn the best way to gather in the olives. There seemed to be so much more to do on the farm than in previous years. Perhaps he just hadn't taken that much notice before, his thoughts more importantly preoccupied with afternoons exploring with Francesco. As far as he knew, his friend had not disobeyed his father, but they had not played together again. The end of the summer arrived, and Ennio knew that Francesco no longer lived in the *Palazzo Piceno*.

Without realising how or when it happened, Ennio became absorbed in the work on the farm, growing stronger and more confident as the years passed by. His tasks filled up every hour of every day. Only when lying in his bed at night, listening to the cicadas in the trees and the barking dogs on the far hillside, did he think of Francesco and often wondered if Francesco ever thought of him. Worryingly, the memory of his friend's face was dimming. He still retained the general impression of thick hair and laughing eyes, but the detail was fading fast.

There had been no goodbyes all those years ago, no long school holidays, no contact at all. Nothing. Sometimes, Ennio believed that Francesco had indeed died that day, and no one had told him, but then common sense would take over and he reasoned that in their small village community, such a major event could not have been kept quiet.

Everyone accepted that the boys from the *palazzo* would receive the best education available, and that meant going away and living at the school their father had chosen for them. Ennio hoped that the teachers were kind, especially to little Federico, Francesco's brother, who suffered so badly from asthma. He pulled the bed sheet up under his chin and smiled to himself. *Not so little now,* he thought. Federico would be fifteen years old, three years younger than his brother.

Ennio turned over in his narrow bed and thumped his pillow to try and get comfortable. They were young men now, living in a country where, for the first time in his life, he sensed uncertainty and danger. Conversations around the table at every evening meal inevitably turned towards the rising tide of political unrest, not only in Italy but throughout the whole of Europe. His brothers sounded very well-informed, forcefully putting forward their opposing points of view, so much so that his parents retreated into a state of concerned silence until his father demanded that they all eat their meal in peace, albeit in a strained, uncomfortable atmosphere.

It wasn't until much later that Ennio understood why his mother sat at those meals in silence, a look of unspeakable sorrow in her eyes. She had, he realised, been watching and listening helplessly to the slow disintegration of her family.

Chapter 3
Elena

Food had always been a part of Elena's life. For as long as she could remember, her family and food had a very close relationship—and what a family! She had four older brothers and lived with her parents and their parents in a whitewashed house beside a rough, shingle pathway that led from the small village of Serifanos down to a fine, sandy beach. There was a small quay, but most of the fishing boats rested on the sand beyond the reach of the incoming tide.

Her brothers all shared the roof space, but in the unbearable heat of the summer months, they slept on the beach under the stars. Her four grandparents shared one room divided only by a heavy, woven curtain. She never once heard them complain. Her parents had a small room behind the kitchen, leaving her to sleep on a mattress in the corner of the living room. Sometimes, she would creep down to the beach with a cushion and a blanket, search out her brothers, and then settle down far enough away from them not to see her, but close enough to feel safe. She would fall asleep to the soothing sound of waves lapping the shore.

Her mother, Evgenia, was an excellent cook, taught by Elena's grandmothers who had their own specialities. The large family rarely ate breakfast or lunch together, just helped themselves to coffee, bread and honey in the mornings and cheese, olives and bread at lunchtime or whenever they could take a break from their work. The men of the family were all fishermen and knew that the best catch was always made at dawn. The haul for the rest of the day was an essential bonus. The old boats had to be maintained, and the ageing nets mended. Elena's father and brothers worked with the other men from the village, never in competition, always as a community.

The women and girls divided their time between washing clothes in the stream that trickled down from the hills behind the village into the sea at the far end of the beach, and the oven at the local bakery. No one had their own oven.

The dough was prepared at home, then carried on a tray covered with a damp cloth, to the bakery behind the church. Most of the gossiping was done when they collected their loaves later in the morning. The ages of the baker's customers ranged from young girls of ten or eleven to the eldest members of the community, most of them in their eighties. No one could have secrets in Serifanos. There were too many female eyes and ears, ever alert to the comings and goings of friends and neighbours.

Late in the evening, Elena's whole family would gather around the long table set up outside the door to the living room, beneath a canopy of vines which stretched the whole length of the house. Sweet eating-grapes hung down in luscious, heavy bunches throughout the summer, and the large blue-and-white ceramic bowl, which lived in the centre of the table, was always full to the brim with grapes, lemons, apricots, peaches and cherries.

Very often, neighbours would arrive unannounced and join the meal, staying to talk until the sun disappeared below the horizon, leaving behind a black, velvet sky and a myriad of bright, twinkling stars. Sometimes the men would get up and dance, not caring that in just a few hours, they would be on their boats again for another hard day's fishing.

To eat with Elena's family was considered a great pleasure, a joy, and this special part of her early life she had brought with her to Italy after her marriage to Ernesto da Calvi, her husband of more than twenty years—twenty good years she was so thankful for—but now, things were changing. There were empty chairs around her table, the absences threatening to overwhelm her with sadness and grief.

She had paid special attention to tonight's meal, and the aroma of lamb and rosemary enveloped her home. She had taken the trouble to make the table look even more inviting than usual, with an array of small side dishes filled with homegrown olives, tomatoes, peppers and zucchini bathed in olive oil pressed by Ernesto himself. Warm ricotta nestled in a large dish next to a long, shallow basket overflowing with chunks of freshly baked bread.

That evening, not all the members of her family gathered to take their place at the table, to help themselves to her freshly baked bread, which they would bite into ravenously after pouring over oil from a small stone pitcher, without saying a word. Shiny traces of oil left their mark around their mouths that no amount of concentrated licking could erase.

'Where is Andrea?' Elena demanded, placing a large, flat ceramic plate in the centre of the table full of the lamb pieces she had roasted slowly over an open fire.

'Up in the town, no doubt,' Ernesto mumbled concentrating hard on the piece of bread in his hand, not wanting to look his wife in the eye. 'He said he had a meeting and would eat with his friends tonight.'

'He's obviously up to something, something he knows we wouldn't approve of,' she called over her shoulder going back into the house to collect a dish of green beans. Ernesto, Ennio and Giuseppe looked at each other silently, all of them recognising the hurt in her voice and not quite understanding why Andrea would choose to eat anywhere but at home.

'Why do you say that?' Ernesto queried when she came back, plonking the dish of beans down loudly and with more force than was necessary.

'Why else would he sneak off without telling me? I don't like the sound of these so-called "meetings" which are more important than his family. I want to know what he's up to!' she finished off firmly, finally sitting down at the opposite end of the table to her husband and reaching for the lamb.

'And I suppose Giorgio has tagged along with him,' she said, more as a statement than a question. There was no comment from the three men at the table, but the uncomfortable silence spoke volumes. As they each helped themselves to various dishes, Elena suddenly slapped both her palms down on the table with a crack.

'What aren't you telling me?' she all but shouted, startling them into staring at her. 'I prepare, cook and care for you all, but my family is incomplete, and you three sit there, being secretive. I will not have secrets around my table, do you hear me?' Her voice had risen with each syllable. 'Now, where exactly are my two sons, and what exactly are they doing? We will all eat the food I have prepared, and you will tell me what's going on, yes?'

She sat down at the table with the look on her face that Ernesto obviously recognised. Implacable determination. She had worn that same look when she'd announced to her Greek family that she had decided to marry the Italian farmer and move away from them to live with him in Italy. She knew for certain that there were things she was not being told, but little did she realise that what her husband would tell her later that evening about his deal with Silvano Fioretti would affect all of them in one way or another and would shatter her strong sense of family forever.

Chapter 4
Andrea

The burden of being the eldest son weighed heavily on his shoulders. Sweat trickled down the back of his neck under his overgrown black curls, and he dried his forehead on the grubby, red cotton scarf he wore loosely around his neck.

The steep, uphill track from the farm to the village was heavy-going at the best of times, but in the breathless heat of a late summer's afternoon it was almost unbearable. Most of the villagers were still indoors, taking an extended break from the heat, which was unrelenting from early morning until well into the evening. They would all start work again at dusk after the sun had sunk behind the horizon.

He had waited until everyone had settled down in the coolness provided by the thick stone walls of the old farmhouse before making his way out to the track up to the village. He wouldn't be missed until the family came together for the evening meal. He felt guilty for deserting his mother when she had worked hard to provide delicious dishes for them all, but recently her love and intensity had begun to overwhelm him more and more.

He was the eldest and was adored. He had been given three names: Andrea, after his paternal grandfather, Thanos, after his maternal grandfather, and Ernesto, after his own father. No one else he knew had three names. So much pride and honour to live up to. The expectation was just too much. He didn't want the life his father led. He didn't want the farm with its back-breaking work for little reward.

Andrea was tall, unlike most of the village folk, who were invariably very short with dark, weather-beaten skin. The whole community was hardworking, and eventually, so much time spent on the land in all weathers took its toll. The desperation to change his destiny from that of the other local boys and young men had intensified in recent months.

He was handsome and strong and had realised very early on, that when he spoke, people around him stopped to listen. He could read and write, thanks to his mother, and could speak clearly, ordering his thoughts before opening his mouth. His parents and grandparents had always included him and his brothers in family discussions around the table, so unlike most of his friends, he was happy to speak out, not deterred when his views didn't coincide with those held by others.

He had attended meetings himself. Held under the trees in the gardens at the edge of the village, they had usually ended when arguments broke out between groups with different ideas, or when the *polizia locale* was spotted by the lookout. No decisions were ever made, because no one was capable of showing true leadership. So, after yet another disastrous, unproductive gathering, he decided to take control himself, even though he was one of the youngest. Now, after a few months, his meetings at the back of the bar were gathering momentum, and he could feel the excitement growing deep in his stomach as he turned right, off the lane into the main street, and the little Bar Pietro came into sight.

As usual, he was the first to arrive, which in itself put him in a strong position. He felt as though the others were coming to *his* meeting, not just to a gathering of young men, all dissatisfied with the small-town life of their parents. He had seen them absorbing the news and information he brought each time to share with them, the promise of change and excitement that was already being experienced by workers in the north of Italy, and indeed throughout Europe.

As he entered the bar, his eyes had to adjust from bright sunlight to the gloom of the interior.

'*Ciao,* Marco,' he greeted the barman.

'*Ciao,* Andrea, *come va?*' the barman glanced up fleetingly before automatically placing a bottle of water and a glass on the counter. Unlike his compatriots, Andrea didn't drink alcohol, not even the fruity red wine produced on the farm.

'*Fa troppo caldo* Marco,' he said walking away towards the back of the room and sitting down, facing the open doorway. *Much too hot,* he thought, as the sweat on his body started to cool, making him shiver slightly in the gloom.

Tonight was the night he was going to propose action. The group had talked, debated and argued for weeks. Talk was all well and good, but it had got them nowhere. Tonight, he intended to find out who would follow him and who wouldn't. From his jacket pocket, he took out three copies of *Avanti* and two editions of *Il Popolo d'Italia*. Six months earlier, he had found the discoloured newspapers lining the drawers of an old wooden cabinet that had been abandoned in the barn the family now used only for storage. At first, he intended to clear the barn and burn its contents, but then he saw his own name at the top of one of the pages. He had carefully lifted the papers out of the drawers and taken them into the daylight to have a closer look.

The dates on the newspapers told him they had been printed two years apart: "*Avanti*" in 1912 and "*Il Popolo d'Italia*" in 1914. He knew enough about politics to realise that these were Socialist newspapers and that the editor of both was the same man. He decided there and then to find out more about Benito Amilcare Andrea Mussolini because he had an inclination, a gut feeling, that they shared more than just a name in common.

He made the decision to leave his home and family during this meeting. Before showing the group his newspapers, he brought them up to date with what, as far as he knew, was going on in the rest of Italy, making sure he told them only what would affect their heightened sense of injustice and dissatisfaction with their lot. His own interest had grown the more he'd read about Mussolini's domestic policies, his public works programmes designed to improve job opportunities, and public transport. The fact that he had also been born the eldest son of a working-class family impressed Andrea.

Mussolini's father had been a blacksmith who had named his son after a Mexican reformist and two Italian socialists.

Unlike Andrea, however, Mussolini had been exposed to his father's significant political beliefs from a very early age, beliefs that created conflict between his parents, resulting in the young Benito being sent away to school. Andrea knew for certain that his parents would never have sent him or his brothers away from home. This was why his decision to leave the village and travel north was so momentous. He was fully aware of Mussolini's rebellious nature, which had resulted in his expulsion from boarding school for stone-throwing, stabbing a fellow pupil and for throwing an inkpot at a teacher. Yet, at a different school, he had worked well and actually qualified as a teacher himself. His emigration to Switzerland to avoid military service was dismissed by Andrea as the actions of an impetuous young man, and the fact that Mussolini was later wounded during front-line trench warfare, albeit accidentally, more than made up for his earlier transgressions.

Above all, Andrea found the ideology of Mussolini's reformed *fascio* fascinating and inspiring. Early fascism, he knew, gained support by claiming to oppose discrimination based on social class, and was strongly opposed to all forms of class war. Didn't Italy need something very different from the current political climate where the workers were all downtrodden and exploited?

According to other articles in the newspapers, it appeared that Mussolini had the power and support to take over interior ministries, foreign affairs, and colonies as well as control over defence and public works. *What an amazing man,* Andrea thought, *to be able to do all this for Italy.* At the meeting, he had been careful to emphasise all the initiatives and programmes planned to combat unemployment levels and tackle economic setbacks. He told the men as much as he knew about the "Battle for Grain", in which five thousand new farms were established and five new agricultural towns constructed on land reclaimed by draining the Pontine Marshes. The promise of thousands of new farming settlements across the country captured their attention and interest. Valuable resources were to be diverted to increase grain production and therefore increase income.

Andrea was convinced that the policies of Mussolini were the way forward for a new and prosperous Italy, and he, along with as many compatriots who would join him, wanted to be at the centre of such a movement. The journey north to Milan was inevitable.

When he eventually returned home, the farm was enveloped in total silence. Pinpricks of light twinkled against the black velvet sky. There was no wind. Complete stillness. Andrea stood gazing into the infinite darkness. This is the memory I want to take with me, he whispered to himself. This, and the smell of Mamma's bread. He squeezed his eyes tightly shut and made his memory.

Part Two
(Central Italy, Present Day)

Chapter 5
Sebastiano Luce

So much had happened in such a short span of time. Of course, recent events had started with the letter from South Africa. Sebastiano had not been into the office for months. Seb, his grandson, kept him up to date with what was going on, and the lovely Giulia, who had been his loyal secretary, called in at least once a week for a chat over a glass or two of *Conero Rosso,* his favourite local red wine. Yet he had known instinctively that something out of the ordinary had cropped up as soon as he saw the expression on Seb's face the day he arrived for lunch, a little more than two years earlier. How time had flown by, but he could remember it as if it were only yesterday.

'*Che cosa c'è?*' he had asked, concerned. 'What's wrong? What's happened?'

Seb led him to the comfortable chairs on the terrace, then handed him the letter with the foreign postage stamp.

'Read it for yourself,' Seb said. 'Let me know what you think.'

The contents of the letter were brief and to the point. Monsignor Francesco Fioretti had requested an appointment with Dottore Sebastiano Luce to discuss an important legal matter. The note gave no indication as to what that legal matter might concern. Two possible dates were given in the hope that at least one of them would be convenient for the "esteemed *avvocato*". The letter bore an official seal of office and the signature of Giacomo Rangello, private secretary to Monsignor Fioretti.

He had read the letter twice, while Seb waited in silence. He had stared at a name he had not seen or heard in decades. Francesco. Little Francesco, who had inherited his father's estate, not because it was his birthright but because there was no one else left in the Fioretti family.

'I'm assuming the request is for you and not for me,' Seb broke the silence. 'Do you know this priest from South Africa?'

'Oh, yes. I knew him as a boy before his father sent him away. He was high-spirited, what you'd call a real boy. His father couldn't cope with him, or didn't want to cope with him, so he was sent away to some school in the north. No one in the village knew where he'd gone, and after a while, people stopped wondering about little Francesco. But surely you recognise the surname "Fioretti"?'

'Yes, of course, but I had no idea where the Monsignor fitted in. Even Giulia couldn't work it out. As far as we could remember, the name Francesco had not cropped up before.'

'Your great-grandfather, my father, dealt with the Fioretti estate. Silvano Fioretti, Francesco's grandfather, was a very wealthy landowner in this region. His son, also called Silvano, inherited the wealth, and with it an unfortunate attitude. He brought his children up to believe that they were special, a different breed from the other children in the village. His wife, I remember, always looked pale and weak. There was a younger boy, I can't remember his name now, but he was never allowed to play outside because he had breathing problems. I believe he died in his teens. Francesco, however, had spirit, but as it turned out, this spirit was something his father didn't like and would not accept.'

Sebastiano folded the letter and put it back inside the envelope.

'I shall come into the office tomorrow morning, with your permission of course, and search out the Fioretti files. They'll be in the cellar somewhere. Please ask Giulia to reply to this letter and offer the first date Signor Rangello suggests. This could be very interesting, Seb. Something to get my teeth into, but I shall want you there with me.'

He remembered feeling energised and excited, sensations he thought he would never have again. He did not really miss his work and the inevitable stress, but the prospect of researching and dealing with a case from way back in his career had made his stomach churn and his chest flutter.

As things turned out, everything he required had been filed away in the cellar just as he had anticipated. All the legal documents and certificates were easy to find, and within half an hour of arriving at the office, he was ready to start work.

Giulia had been delighted to see him and produced coffee in record time, just as he liked it, black and strong with plenty of sugar. A desk in one of the smaller interview rooms had been cleared for him, and on a small side-table, she had put a bottle of water, a glass and a small bowl of pink roses.

It took him just under two hours to get through the paperwork relating to local issues, still amazed at the business acumen of Silvano Fioretti. On the other hand, the man's estranged son had done nothing apart from leaving all his father's other investments in the hands of those who knew what they were doing and in whom he put all his trust.

Now, Francesco was coming home and had asked specifically for Sebastiano, so whatever the issue was, it must be serious.

Armed with as much information as he could keep in his old head, he could not wait for the appointment with the Monsignor.

Chapter 6
Francesco

He had slept surprisingly well, and yet again, Giacomo, his personal assistant, had managed to find a comfortable, moderately priced hotel not too far from the airport. A clear, blue sky had welcomed him as he'd flown into Rome's Fiumicino Leonardo da Vinci airport late the previous afternoon. The flight from Durban had been long and tedious, with just a brief touchdown in Johannesburg not long after take-off. He'd spent the time dozing and eating. Unable to concentrate on any of the films on offer, he just sat watching the little dot of the flight's slow progress north, on the monitor in front of him.

On landing, without warning, his stomach clenched when warm air caressed his face as he stepped away from the enclosed cabin onto the first of the metal steps that would take him down to the homeland he hadn't really seen properly for almost seventy years. Slowly he descended, his vestments waving around his ankles in the stifling breeze of a mid-summer afternoon in Rome. He resisted the urge to sink to his knees and kiss the ground, Pope-like, but did say a short, silent prayer of thanks for a safe journey home.

He walked through passport control without any hold-ups and didn't have to wait long for his small suitcase to arrive on the carousel. Apart from the legal papers in his black leather briefcase, he had packed the minimum amount required for a flying visit. He had no intention of staying longer than was absolutely necessary. Seventy years of exile was a long time. Too long. He was a stranger. Italian by birth, but homeless by circumstance. So much travel, so many appointments, rarely more than five years in one place. If it had not been for his calling, he would probably be regarded as an itinerant. No home, no roots, no family.

As the Leonardo Express whisked him away from Fiumicino to his hotel, his initial exhilaration at returning to Italy slowly dissipated, to be replaced by resignation. He'd left it too late. He would not allow himself to get sentimental about what might have been. He was in Italy on business. He would tie up all the loose ends, sign the necessary paper, and then leave. He'd be back in the township by the end of the week. All links to his Italian roots severed for good.

He was treated with deference at the small hotel. Breakfast, buffet-style, suited him perfectly. He took his time over the almond sweet croissants and savoured every sip of his strong, black coffee. The other guests smiled and nodded in his direction as they entered the small dining room. He acknowledged them with a wry smile of his own and a slight bow of his head, his hair still thick with white, unruly curls. A few weeks earlier, he had made a conscious decision to let it grow. For once, in over half a century, he rebelled against the neat, precise manicure of what he considered to be his finest asset. Pride, he'd been taught, was a sin. *Well, so be it,* he thought, wiping the icing sugar from around his lips and helping himself to a fresh peach. I'm proud of my hair. I'm a handsome man. I don't wear glasses, and I have all my own teeth. If pride is a sin, then I'm a sinner. The broad, private smile on his face drew the attention of his fellow guests who smiled back at him.

'*Un altro caffè, signorina, per favore,*' he called to the waitress.

'*Certo, Monsignor. Subito*!'

He didn't have time to stay longer in Rome. He had only ever seen pictures of the Vatican City, the Colosseum, the Trevi Fountain and the Victoriana. He had read a great deal about Roman history and now and again caught some of the football scores by Italy's top teams. But his destination on this trip was to the northeast of the "Eternal City", and a mere hour after his breakfast, as he settled into his seat on the train slowly pulling out of Roma Termini, his initial excitement and anticipation returned.

At the very last minute, a young man flopped down into the corner seat across the aisle from him. He'd only just made it and was out of breath. For the first few minutes, he fussed with his small rucksack, then took out a flattened panino, which he bit into ravenously, swilling it down with deep gulps of Coca-Cola from a can. After a number of silent burps, the late arrival put his earphones in, covered his shoulders with a well-worn grey fleece jacket, and closed his eyes. By the time the train left, the urban sprawl of Rome behind and was carving its way through the countryside of Lazio, the young man was fast asleep, his elderly companion trying desperately to remember himself at that age, and failing miserably.

The regular rhythm of the train soon had Francesco closing his eyes, his large, tanned hands resting lightly on his thighs. He'd been contemplating this trip for months, and now, it was a reality. He even doubted that he'd recognise the place he was going to after all this time, but more importantly, would anyone remember him?

He must have dozed off. The sound of the train changing speed jolted him awake, and for an instant he felt completely disorientated. Then, the sight of his young companion beating out a rhythm on his knees with the palms of his hand while he listened, eyes closed, to whatever music was playing through his headphones, quickly brought Francesco back to the present. They were travelling through the dark, industrial centre outside Avezzano which he imagined was a far cry from the natural thermal springs on the plains below the town centre of Tivoli nearby with its magnificent gardens.

After a brief stop, the train picked up speed again, forging its way east towards the coast and the Adriatic Sea. Another step nearer to home. Slowly but surely, Francesco could feel his excitement growing. He was impatient now to reach his destination and get on with what he had to do.

For the umpteenth time, he took a small, black leather-bound notebook out of his trouser pocket. Before leaving the hotel, he had made a last-minute decision to pack away his vestments and travel in his own, casual clothes, the pale blue, light, cotton open-necked shirt so much more comfortable than his priest's collar, which was now tucked away in its box together with his crucifix and beads. He was returning home as himself, without the attendant connotations his so-called vocation inevitably created. He checked his appointment time. The *avvocato's* office was in the old building where members of the *Comune* took all the important decisions, which affected the lives of everyone in the village. His father had been the leader of the Council for many years, so Francesco knew exactly where to go at ten-thirty the following morning.

He stared out of the window, alternating between appreciating the open countryside and admiring his own reflection. Where had this recent compulsion to bolster his self-confidence come from? This need to know that he could be admired as a man and not just because he was a priest. Not that it really mattered now. Glancing away from the window, he realised that he had been so self-absorbed he hadn't seen his young companion leave the train at the last stop.

The first half of his journey had passed very quickly, and it wouldn't be long before he reached Pescara on the Adriatic coast. He regretted not having the time to stop off and go to Sulmona, the capital of sugared almonds. How many times in his life had he been given these sweet delights, Italian confetti, as a gift? He had officiated at so many special occasions—weddings, births, confirmations and anniversaries, each one marked with a small, decorated package containing the smooth, pastel-coloured sweets. He was certain that most people had no idea of the significance of the tradition of giving five sugared almonds representing health, wealth, happiness, fertility and long life. In the case of a marriage, five is a prime number and cannot be divided. Perhaps, he could include this in one of his sermons when he got back to South Africa? Or maybe not.

He spent the rest of his journey in a state of impatience, and after changing trains at Pescara Centrale station, his tolerance was tested to the limit. Even the amazing turquoise blue of the Adriatic couldn't disguise the fact that the coastline "express" stopped at every possible station before reaching Civitanova Marche where he had to leave the train.

He emerged from the shaded platform into the full blast of the early afternoon sun blazing down from a perfect, cloudless blue sky. A stout, middle-aged man in a short-sleeved white shirt, cream trousers and open sandals materialised at his side.

'*Monsignor?*' he enquired quietly, dipping his dark head in reverence. 'I am Armando, your driver for this afternoon.'

'*Buongiorno*, Armando. How did you know who I was?'

'*I capelli, Monsignor.* Your hair is very distinctive, and your secretary told me not to expect someone dressed as a priest. *Prego.*' Armando gently relieved him of his small suitcase at the same time indicating a large, shiny Fiat parked under the canopy of a fig tree on the far side of the car park. Armando had left all the windows open, and before stowing the case away in the boot, held the rear door open wide for his passenger.

'I'd rather sit up front with you if you don't mind,' Francesco said, taking off his jacket and throwing it onto the back seat next to his briefcase before settling into the passenger seat and closing the door.

'*Si, si, certo,*' Armando replied quickly, a surprised expression on his face.

The road inland away from the coast was quiet at this time of day. Shops and offices were closed until late in the afternoon or early evening. *No sensible*

Italian worked in the heat of the day, unless you were a taxi driver, Francesco thought. Smiling broadly, Armando offered him some chilled mineral water, which he accepted gratefully.

'Do you live on the coast?' Francesco asked, happy to have someone to chat to after the emptiness on the train.

'No, *Monsignor*. I live just outside Macerata.'

'Do you have a family?'

'*Si, si*. I have my wife Paola and two girls, Isabella and Flavia. My mother also lives with us. I am surrounded by women!' he laughed, and although sounded hard done by, Francesco could tell by the indulgent smile on his face that Armando was more than happy with his home life. Even in his car, Armando had the constant company of one female in particular. Pictures, cards, stickers and a mirror hanging, all depicting the Virgin Mary in one pose or another, and once again, the now familiar lack of emotional response to such religious paraphernalia, as Francesco had come to regard them, threatened to overwhelm him.

'…visiting family and friends?'

He'd been so wrapped up in his own gloomy thoughts he'd missed Armando's question.

'*Scusi*, Armando,' he said, turning in his seat to give the driver his full attention. 'What did you ask?'

'Are you here to work or just visiting family and friends?'

'I have some legal business with the *avvocato* first, then I have one friend I must visit without fail.'

'He'll be pleased to see you, I'm sure, *Monsignor*.'

'He doesn't know I'm coming, Armando.'

'Ah, a surprise.'

'More of a shock, I'd say. We haven't met for more years than I care to remember, but at one time we were like brothers. Maybe we can be again, if only for a short time.'

Armando nodded, then fixed his eyes on the road ahead.

It was a twenty-five minute journey from the coast to the medieval hilltop village where Francesco had been born. He wanted to walk the last mile or so to his final destination, so he asked Armando to drop him off outside the *carabinieri* building on the main road. Although all his expenses had been pre-paid, Francesco handed over an extra twenty euro note to a very surprised Armando.

'Here is my card, *Monsignor*. Your secretary didn't know the exact time of your departure, so please call me when you are ready to leave, and I will collect you. Your briefcase and your jacket, *Monsignor,* and here is your suitcase. Enjoy your stay, and I hope you and your friend have a good time.'

'*Grazie mille*, Armando. *Arrivederci.*'

'*Prego, Monsignor. Arrivederla.*'

Long after Armando had pulled away from the kerb and disappeared over the brow of the hill on the road to Macerata, Francesco stood alone, slowly taking in his surroundings. He had been sent away from this place, torn from all that was familiar and safe. No one had given a moment's thought to the feelings or opinions of the young boy, bundled away from everything and everyone dear to him. Over the years he had been unable to get rid of the belief that he had been cast adrift from his family for the simple reason that he'd been unwanted from the start. Rightly or wrongly, this was how he felt, and nothing had ever happened to change his mind.

Now, he was back. The heat of the sun high in the sky beat down on his head. He stood with his suitcase and briefcase at his feet, his jacket draped carelessly over both. The main street was empty and silent. Nothing stirred. The *Api* garage opposite the *carabinieri* offices and the small *Punto* supermarket next door were both closed and shuttered against the relentless heat. Francesco wiped his forehead and face with a clean handkerchief and smiled to himself. *For us, this was the best time of the day*, he thought.

All the grown-ups indoors, eating and resting before working again in the cool of the evening.

Our escape time.

Exploration and adventure.

Freedom.

He shook his head, his smile replaced by a frown. He gave himself a few more minutes to stand in the stillness and the silence before running both hands down the sides of his trousers to dry off the sweat. Then he picked up his case, his briefcase and jacket and turned to walk down the narrow road he knew would take him to the farmhouse.

Chapter 7
Ennio and Francesco

It was too hot. Even the breeze that constantly rustled the leaves of the vines was stifling and dry. Only in the back bedroom could he get away from the dazzling sunlight and find some relief. He never opened the shutters, and by the time the sun had risen high in the sky, it had moved round to the front of the house.

Ennio started work before six o'clock every morning and finished just after ten. He was slowing down. What used to take him an hour now took two or more. He didn't worry. He had nothing better to do. What didn't get done today he would do tomorrow or the day after.

Today had been particularly difficult. Working on the slope of the hillside had aggravated the arthritis in his left hip. At times, the pain had been unbearable to the point where he just wanted to give up. Why did he keep putting himself through the pain and making such an effort? As he lay on top of the bed, he answered his own question. If he didn't carry on working the land, what else was there?

'*Niente,*' he said, staring at the ageing paintwork between the oak beams above his head. '*Lavoro o niente.*' Work or nothing. As his eyelids closed, he saw quite vividly all the members of his family standing smiling at him—Mamma, Babbo, Andrea, Giorgio and Giuseppe, all frozen in a time long since passed. Just as quickly as they appeared, they vanished as sleep overtook him.

He had no idea how long he had been asleep, but the sound of footsteps crunching on the gravel outside the shutters alerted him to a visitor. He hadn't heard a car's engine, and although the farmhouse was not exactly remote, people rarely approached it on foot. Slowly, painfully, he swung his legs round and sat on the bed for a moment, straightening and stretching his back and shoulders. He put his weight on his good leg first, then stood up, groaning in the back of his throat as he carefully put weight on his left leg and limped heavily out of the room.

He mentally prepared himself for one of the numerous North Africans who turned up every so often to sell goods out of an oversized holdall. The last woman, he recalled, had been so persistent and aggressive.

'I need money to pay for surgery,' she had told him, pointing to an unsightly, pink jagged scar on her face. 'Would you deny me surgery when you have all this?' she had demanded, waving her arms towards his vines. Ennio had felt himself weakening. He had felt sorry for her, but his overwhelming feeling was the desire to get her away from his home. But then, he had looked at her again more closely. She was well-dressed (much better than he was) in colourful cotton. Her open sandals were fashionable and made from soft leather. Even her holdall was of the highest quality. She also spoke perfect Italian. He still felt sympathy for her scarred face, but this woman seemed to have found a very successful way of exploiting her disfigurement. He had refused to buy, firmly but politely.

'Grazie, signora, ma non ho bisogna di niente.'

She had responded angrily and glared at him before marching off, cursing him under her breath. He had watched her go, making sure she went through the gates and back up the hill. He hated any form of confrontation, and the encounter had left him shaking and feeling vulnerable.

Now, as he moved through the kitchen to the front door, he braced his shoulders ready for whoever was on the other side. He paused in the middle of the room, waiting for the knock, but it never came. Seconds turned into minutes. He ran his fingers through his hair to tidy it up a bit, then slowly opened the door to the sunlight. The space outside the door was empty, so he took one step forward and glanced to his right. No one. He turned his head to the left and there, gazing out over the hills, his back towards the house, stood a white-haired man, his feet apart, his hands dangling loosely at his sides. At his feet lay a small suitcase, a black briefcase and a jacket. But what struck Ennio the most was the man's stillness. He stood like a statue, looking up the valley to the rolling hills in the distance. Ennio's stomach muscles clenched. The man was not local, and yet he knew him. What was it? Then, in a split second, he knew. The hair. Only one person in his life had such glorious hair. With tears in his eyes, his throat tight with emotion, barely able to speak, he whispered, '*Francesco. Francesco mio.*'

The late afternoon sun had created a pale, golden halo effect shining through the curly hair of the man staring out over the countryside. But as if suddenly aware that he was no longer alone, Francesco turned slowly towards the house. Standing on the threshold was the reason for his return after all this time. In an instant, the years fell away. Still small, still scruffy, still his best friend—Ennio. Ennio da Calvi—his soulmate.

He didn't know who made the first move, but they closed the distance between them, and without a single word, they clung to each other as if their lives depended on it. They stood holding each other tightly, absorbing the uncontrollable sobs that wracked them both. It seemed as if sixty years' worth of crying was released in those first few seconds. Finally, they moved apart, not letting go, just putting enough space between them so they could look at each other.

'Ciao, Ennio.'

'Ciao, Francesco,' Ennio managed to whisper, wiping tears from his cheeks with the back of his hand. Francesco took in two things at a glance. The rough, gnarled old hands of a man who had spent his life working the land, and the flash of a vivid, white jagged scar, damaged tissue not weathered by the elements. His friend must have cut himself very badly at some time in his life.

'*Sei qui Francesco?* Really here after all this time? You look wonderful.'

'*Si, sono qui.* Yes, I'm here, and you haven't changed a bit,' Francesco laughed, pointing to the fraying tear at the knee of Ennio's work pants and at the gap in his shirt where there should have been buttons. 'It's good to be here,' Francesco went on, his tone suddenly more serious. 'I only have two days. Can I stay with you?'

'You have to ask?' Ennio replied indignantly. 'You know my house is a simple one, but what's mine is yours. I'll get your case, and we can sit and have a drink. I can't believe you're really here, standing with me, older but not much taller,' Ennio laughed out loud. 'You always were a shorty.'

'And you were always a shorty, too.'

Their laughter rang out over the hillside, disturbing the family of swallows resting in the hazelnut tree before beginning their evening ritual of swooping along the stream catching unsuspecting insects.

'And I can get my own case,' Francesco said. 'You're not going to fuss over me. I'm not your guest. We do things together, just as we always did.'

Francesco walked back to the edge of the path and picked up his cases while Ennio, in spite of Francesco's protest, grabbed his jacket before walking by his side into the coolness of the farmhouse kitchen. A comfortable, all-enveloping silence wrapped itself around them. Francesco sat down on one of the wooden chairs, making himself at home straight away, his palms resting flat against his stomach, his eyes closed. He could hear the rustle of a light breeze whispering its way through the leaves of the vines. He had forgotten what total contentment felt like. This was it for him. Peace, quiet, the promise of good food, excellent wine, and the company of his dearest friend. *Perfetto,* he thought. Perfect.

While Francesco freshened up after his journey from Rome, Ennio prepared the simplest yet most delicious pasta dish for their evening meal. His mother had taught him and his brothers all those years ago how to make fresh pasta. He never bought packets of the anaemic-looking shapes from the supermarket. *Mamma* would have been horrified. He grew his own tomatoes, onions and peppers near the house, and throughout the year, he had an abundance of herbs to choose from—rosemary and thyme sharing their perfume in the still warm air with sage, parsley and mint. Basil and oregano grew continuously in pots beside his front door.

It didn't take him long to put the simple yet filling meal together. Not a grand homecoming feast, but the good, rustic food he knew Francesco would enjoy. He also felt pleased that he had taken the decision to have a shower installed in the bathroom. He'd made so few changes over the years to the house he still thought of as his parents' home as well as his own.

He needed very little. A comfortable chair, a comfortable bed, simple food and a good fire for the winter months. He had a radio, but no television. His one and only vice was books—if a copious amount of reading could be called a vice. Paola, the librarian, knew what he liked to read, and every week, she sorted out a selection for him to choose from. He never felt alone when he had a book in his hands. Loneliness crept up on him unbidden when his eyes grew tired, and the book had to be closed. The thought of going to sleep and not waking up had started to appeal to him more and more in recent months, so he made sure his humble home was clean, tidy and in good order in case such an eventuality occurred. He couldn't bear the thought of strangers going through his home and his belongings, then gossiping about the poor conditions the old man had lived in. His *mamma* had kept an immaculate house, and so did he.

The neat, clean farmhouse kitchen with its large table covered in a starched, white cloth with a deep, handmade lace border was not lost on Francesco. Small bunches of lavender hung from the thick, oak beams. Gleaming pots, pans and kitchen utensils hung from hooks above the old cooking range next to the pizza oven. Earlier, as he'd walked behind Ennio to his room, he'd glimpsed for the briefest of moments, a memory of Signora da Calvi, standing stirring something on the range—her thick, black curly hair held back by an old scarf. A red, floral dress, belted at the waist, showed off a shapely figure even a nine-year-old boy could admire. He had blinked consciously, and the image left his mind as quickly as it had arrived as Ennio commented, 'Not what you're used to, I'm sure, but the bed is comfortable and aired. Do you need towels?'

'You sound like a chambermaid,' Francesco laughed. 'And yes, I could do with a bath towel if you have one to spare.'

Ennio had given him a withering look which said, *you should know better than to ask that*, and from a large storage trunk in his own room, he took out two large white towels and a hand towel and thrust them at Francesco.

'I hope you wash yourself more these days than you did when we were boys,' Ennio quipped, recalling the trouble Signora Fioretti had had trying to get Francesco to have a wash, eventually giving up chasing him around the *palazzo* just to get her son into a bath or anywhere near a bar of soap. 'Don't they say that cleanliness is nearer to godliness?' Ennio went on.

'If that's the case, then I've had it,' Francesco replied. 'I've had enough of both to last a lifetime,' he scoffed, turning away to open his small case and take out a toilet bag.

'We'll eat in an hour,' Ennio announced, immediately sensing an aura of disquietude around his guest. 'Francesco,' he went on, 'I can't tell you how good it is to have you here with me, in my home.'

'*Grazie.*' And with this word of thanks, he returned to the kitchen determined to provide the tastiest pasta and sauce he'd ever produced.

Now, over an hour later, when Francesco opened his eyes, he found Ennio gazing at him intently, a contented smile turning up the corners of his lips. The sun had disappeared completely, leaving a balmy evening just right for sitting outside with a good wine and a good friend.

'Ah,' sighed Francesco. '*I pipistrelli.*' His eyes followed the many small, harmless bats that were flitting around the house and across the fields. He recalled watching the little black animals flying around the *palazzo* so many years earlier, but his mother had been afraid of them, and his father considered them to be vermin. Estate workers were under orders to treat any of the little creatures they saw in the same way they treated the rats in the storage buildings. But here, at the da Calvi house, the little bats were free to fly and make their homes in the old barns dotted around the hillside.

'They keep me company every evening,' confided Ennio. 'I watch them until it gets too dark for me to see.'

'That meal was *ottima*. I enjoyed every mouthful. I have a cook back in South Africa. She's kind, willing and helpful but mothers me a bit too much, if I'm honest.'

'So, what's the problem?' Ennio interrupted.

'The woman can't cook. That's the problem,' growled Francesco.

'Get rid of her, then.'

'Not an option, *amico mio*. If I get rid of her, she'll have no job. No one else will employ her, and she has four children. No. I can tolerate her cooking if it means her family can get by.'

Silence descended between them once again. *Not so comfortable,* thought Ennio. Somehow, tonight, the air had to be cleared, questions asked and answered, gaps to be filled. He knew without being told that what wasn't said this evening would never be said. Time was running out for both of them. As if reading his mind, Francesco broke the silence.

'We need to talk. No! *I* need to talk,' he said firmly, swirling what was left of his wine around the sides of his glass. For a moment, he just stared at the rich, deep-red liquid produced from Ennio's own vines. He had already drunk two large glasses of *Rosso Piceno,* but before he started on the small glass of *vino cotto,* the sweet dessert wine Ennio had put in front of him, he needed to get matters off his chest.

'So much time has been wasted already, so I will tell you straight my side of the story. You deserve the truth, Ennio. There must be no misunderstandings left between us.'

Ennio nodded uncertainly. He wanted, no, needed to hear what Francesco had to say, but a part of him was apprehensive, even afraid. He was too old and set in his ways to hear about events which could easily unsettle his life, simple as it was.

'Before I start,' Francesco went on, 'you must believe that you are my best friend, always have been, and always will be, come what may. Distance in miles changed nothing for me. My one huge regret is that I was not strong enough or determined enough to come home before now. I almost managed it once…but I'm getting ahead of myself.' Putting his glass to one side, he pulled his chair closer to the old wooden table under the kitchen window. Darkness had fallen. No lights showed on the hillside opposite the house, only the lamp above the door, shed a glow over the two old men. It was as if they were both in the spotlight. Cicadas created the only sound in the night.

'I was sent away. My father didn't want me mixing with people from the village. By people, he meant you and your family. The accident in the stream gave him the ideal excuse he needed. I had a concussion and a deep cut on my head. Lots of blood but nothing life-threatening. They kept me in bed for four days, not to give me time to recover, but to give my father time to make arrangements for me to be sent away.'

Ennio recognised resentment, even anger, in Francesco's matter-of-fact tone but the hand held up towards him stopped him from questioning or commenting.

'Let me continue, Ennio. Ask your questions when I've finished.' The authority in Francesco's voice was unmistakable. 'I was taken away from the *palazzo* before daybreak on the fifth day. All my things had been packed, and I was bundled, half-asleep, into the back of my father's car. We went north, and after what seemed to me to be many hours, I was deposited in a monastery school in the middle of the countryside as far as you could get from the nearest town.'

'My father nodded to me and left with no explanation, no encouraging words, nothing but a nod. Can you believe I didn't even get to say goodbye to my mother or to little Federico? What must he have thought of me? Needless to say, I survived. Harsh lessons, a rigid daily regime, every second dedicated to the glory of God. No doubt about it, I was indoctrinated in that institution, and my only excuse is that I had nothing else.'

'I was isolated from my family, my best friend and the rest of the outside world. It sounds dramatic, but that was how it was. Unbelievable cruelty, Ennio, but I came through it. I was ordained as a priest at the age of twenty and was released back into society. War had unleashed chaos in Europe, and for the briefest time, I thought I could come home, but I had reckoned without my father's still considerable influence.'

'I was sent to Brazil, then on to Argentina. I spent years working with the poor in Asuncion in Paraguay, then decided once and for all to come back to Italy. During my time in South America, my mother died, but no one at the monastery passed on the information. My poor little Federico suffered a severe asthma attack and passed away soon after my mother. Again, I was not told. Only when my father died did they speak to me, not out of sympathy but to inform me that he had made adequate provision for my future in the priesthood attached to the Benedictine Brothers who had been given sole charge of my upbringing and, as it turned out, my career.'

'Finally, I made arrangements to come home. I got as far as *Roma*. Can you believe it? *Roma*. One step away from home. But I should have known. I didn't even get to leave the airport. I was met in the arrivals area and given written instructions and a one-way ticket to South Africa. I was to present myself to the Catholic Archbishop of Durban the following day. I have been in South Africa ever since. I have no excuse for not writing, for not telephoning, for not getting in touch with you, and I ask for your forgiveness, Ennio *mio*. Oh, how I envied you.'

'Envied me?' Ennio burst out incredulously.

'*Si, si,*' Francesco answered earnestly. 'I lived in the *palazzo,* but even as a child, I knew it wasn't how a home should be. Your house was a real home. My poor mother was sickly, a complainer, relying totally on my father obeying his every word. Your *mamma* was fun, lively, a good cook and so very kind to me. Poor Federico had a weak chest, always ill, so couldn't run around and play. Your brothers were handsome and strong, and your father always had time to speak to you, to us. My father was always in Milan on business. He had a girlfriend there. I wanted your way of life, Ennio, with you. I wanted to be another brother, and I think this, above all things, my father found unacceptable. It was the one part of his life that was a failure.'

Ennio frowned, not knowing how to respond to Francesco's outburst, which was so unexpected and out of character—at least, the character he remembered. The temperature had dropped suddenly, and Ennio rubbed the backs of his arms.

'You are here, Francesco. I have nothing to forgive. But you need to forgive yourself. We are much too old for recriminations, to hold any kind of grudge. The past is the past. Let's just enjoy this moment together. Drink your wine. Do you have an early start in the morning?'

'My meeting's not until eleven o'clock.'

'So, we will have time. The fields, the stream and our wood are all expecting us as soon as we've had breakfast. Now, drink your wine. Another ten minutes, and it'll be too cold to sit here.'

Francesco smiled. He finished his wine and got up slowly. God! His legs felt stiffer than ever, the pain shooting down from both hips to his calf muscles. He knew his ability to move around was getting worse. Another few weeks and he would not have been able to make the journey home.

'*Buona notte, Ennio, e grazie mille.*'

'Goodnight, Francesco. Sleep well, and it is I who thank you for remembering me.' He pushed back his chair and stood up, watching his friend walk slowly back into the house before starting to gather up the empty plates and glasses.

In the bathroom, Francesco swallowed the numerous tablets he'd had to take for the last six months, leant on the washbasin and stared at his reflection in the mirror. The lines of strain around his eyes had disappeared. His heart felt lighter, and the heavy burden he'd carried on his shoulders for years no longer weighed him down. He had unburdened himself tonight, but not totally, he conceded. There was one important matter he had not shared with Ennio, and he had until the early morning to decide what to do about it.

He enjoyed train journeys. Considering the amount of time he spent on trains travelling between cities, towns and villages, this wasn't a bad thing. So many of his parishes had been off the beaten track. He would arrive at the nearest town by train only to be met by a church official who would take him the rest of the way by car if he was lucky, but more likely by a rusting van, truck or, on one memorable journey, by mule.

He remembered travelling south from Paris with a small group of young men, just like himself, all preparing for ordination. They had attended a number of seminars at an ancient monastery near Versailles and were finishing off their stay in the Papal city of Avignon. The train had been full of travellers, mostly men who looked as if they were in search of work away from the capital. After a laboured departure from the gloom of the station, the train had started to pick up speed.

Urban sprawl gave way to open, green countryside, which seemed to stretch for miles. Almost imperceptibly, the colours and light changed. Greens gave way to shades of ochre, and vibrant burnt orange gave way to mellow, mustard yellow. At the time, he remembered thinking how much that one particular journey reflected life: the slow start, the increase in speed, youthful activity gradually making way for the slower pace again of later life. Even then, there was a touch of melancholy about him, a trait he'd never been able to shake off, only camouflage with the persona of bonhomie he presented to those around him.

This journey would be different. There would be no drastic change in the countryside speeding past the window. He'd come to the end of great changes in his life. All he wanted to do was get back to his familiar routine for the short time he had left.

His parting from Ennio had been far more traumatic than he'd anticipated. He had planned to call Armando and ask to be collected from the *piazza* in the village at midday. His meeting with the lawyer would certainly not take longer than an hour, and he would have already said his goodbyes to Ennio with a hug and manly pat on the back with the promise to return in the near future—a promise both of them knew to be worthless. However, Ennio had other ideas!

Dogs barking on the hillside opposite had woken Francesco up that morning almost, it seemed, as soon as he'd fallen asleep. The aroma of fresh coffee spurred him into action, albeit very slowly. Ennio was already up and about and was, no doubt, impatient to get the day started. Their limited time together was already slipping away.

'*Buongiorno,*' he greeted Ennio, who was carrying cups and plates outside into the weak sunshine.

'Did you sleep well?' Ennio asked. 'Not easy in a strange bed, I guess.'

'The best night's sleep I've had in a long time,' Francesco replied, realising that he was not exaggerating. He had slept soundly once he'd managed to drop off.

'We have lots to do and see this morning before your meeting,' Ennio went on, as he walked back into the kitchen to collect an old wooden tray laden with what looked like homemade bread, fresh butter, jam and honey. Catching Francesco's glance, he nodded at the tray. 'I buy very little from the supermarket. This way, I know where everything comes from.'

Francesco joined him at the table and reached for a fresh peach from the fruit bowl.

'All yours as well?' he asked, gesturing to the plums, grapes, apples, peaches and pears.

'Of course,' Ennio answered proudly. 'Sometimes I have to wait a while longer for the apples and pears, but this year has been a good one for ripening. Even the almonds and hazelnuts are just about ready. The only essential thing I can't manage is the coffee, but then, nothing's perfect.'

Except this peach, Francesco thought, biting into the delicious fruit, the juice running down his wrist.

'Here, take one of these,' Ennio said handing him a napkin.

'How come you're so domesticated?' Francesco asked, wiping away the sticky liquid.

'Coffee?' Ennio asked, ignoring his comment, holding out a large, brown ceramic jug.

'Please. No milk for me,' Francesco said, still waiting for an answer to his question.

'Me, domesticated? I suppose I am. I've never really thought about it.' Ennio frowned deeply, his mind skipping back in time in an instant. 'We had some difficult times,' he went on hesitantly. He decided he might as well fill in the lost years between them but without too many painful details. He took a sip of his strong coffee before speaking again.

'Andrea, Giorgio and Giuseppe all left home and went their separate ways. *Mamma* was never the same after they all left the farm, and *Babbo* didn't know how to help her. Although she still had me, I knew I wasn't enough. The hole my brothers had left in the family was too big. I took over the house when she started to fail.'

'One winter, she caught a chest infection. Most people would have recovered, but she just didn't have the will to fight it and died after only a couple of weeks. Babbo and I ran the farm for a few more years after, but as he said himself, "Without *Mamma*, I'm nothing, *Ennio mio*. Forgive me". I didn't really think much about what he said. He'd been morose and silent for a long time. He ended his life in the old barn at the top of the field. Inevitable, I suppose, thinking back, but depressing at the same time—mortal sin and all that. It took the local people a long time to come to terms with my father's suicide and even longer to be able to look me in the eye. Some of them avoid me even now.'

Francesco stopped eating his peach and shook his head. He could see Ennio had both hands clenched tightly into fists. How did two bright and lively young boys end up with lives so full of sorrow and pain?

'We should have been together to face all these things,' Francesco said quietly, thinking that while he was preaching the word of God to strangers in far-off countries, his best friend was having to face his own demons alone.

'Anyway,' Ennio went on in a lighter tone, 'I have tried hard to keep up the standards *Mamma* set, and considering the way you are staring at my bread and honey, I've succeeded.'

It was obvious to Francesco that Ennio's swift resumé of the past sixty years was finished, begging no questions.

'So, what plans do you have for us after breakfast?' he asked instead.

'We leave the dishes and head for the stream. OK with you?' Ennio asked.

'Anything you say. Today, you're the leader. You lead, I follow.'

'Do you remember what happened that day?' Ennio asked as they watched the shallow waters of the stream trickle its way down the valley, meandering around the sharp stones standing in its path. During the winter, the little stream became a forceful torrent with scant regard for any obstacle in its way. But the summer sun had imposed its will, and slowly but surely, the torrent had been tamed.

'Not a thing,' replied Francesco absently, far more intent on listening to the gentle gurgle of the water lapping at his feet. He didn't want to speak. The tranquillity of the moment was enough for him. He stood in the water at the edge of the stream, his arms hanging loosely at his sides, lifted his face to the sun and closed his eyes. After what seemed like an age, but was in reality only a matter of seconds, Ennio whispered, 'Francesco, are you OK? What are you doing?'

'I'm making a memory, *amico mio*,' came the brief response. 'Let's go on now. Where are we going next?'

Together they walked slowly across the fields, stopping at regular intervals to look back, or, in Francesco's case, to catch his breath. The muted rumble of a distant tractor engine had replaced the sound of the barking dog on the hillside opposite the farmhouse. No other sound reached their ears.

'Look at the sky, Francesco. Deep, clear blue. Not even a single jet stream this morning. They must know you're here.'

Surprisingly, the *Palazzo Piceno* looked in fine condition. Even the gardens were neat and well-maintained. 'Another life, another time,' Francesco commented, reluctant to linger in front of the tall gates that protected what had once been his family home. Ennio thought his friend would want to see what was happening in the imposing building and how it was being cared for. But no! With a firm nod of satisfaction, Francesco walked on, ignoring the words embedded in a tablet of smooth, black granite in the wall beside the gate.

'I like *your* house,' he said, twisting his head round to speak to Ennio who was now following him down the stony path which would eventually lead them back to the farmhouse. 'Just time for another coffee,' Francesco said, 'then I need to get to that meeting.'

While Ennio made a fresh jug of coffee, Francesco went back into his bedroom to get changed ready for his meeting. He decided to wear the same clothes to travel in, at least for the first part of his journey. When he reappeared wearing his priest's collar and vestments, he couldn't help but notice the expression of sadness that passed fleetingly across Ennio's eyes. Perhaps he had imagined it, but he didn't think so. He sat down again heavily, without saying a word, and reached across the table for the coffee.

'I knew there was something missing,' Francesco blurted out suddenly, stopping mid-pour, the coffee jug tilted over his cup. 'The smell. I can't smell the pigs.'

'That's because there aren't any,' Ennio said, holding out his cup for Francesco to finish pouring. 'They were all moved out to the flatlands along the coast many years ago. Only Dino Conti keeps a couple on the quiet at his place up the hill.'

'Dino Conti,' Francesco repeated. 'Wasn't he the boy with the withered arm?'

Ennio nodded. 'Mm,' he said. 'He always tried to hide it up his sleeve, but now that he's old, he doesn't bother.'

'I was warned off him by my parents. My mother believed it was a sign of evil, the mark of the devil. I wasn't to go anywhere near him,' Francesco went on, staring down into his coffee cup, watching the dark liquid swirl around as he twisted the cup between his hands. For a minute or two, a brooding silence hung between them, both wrapped up in their own thoughts.

'Time to make a move,' Francesco broke the spell, putting down his cup and pushing himself upright in one, slow movement.

'I'll get my jacket,' Ennio said, walking towards the house, 'and my keys.'

Francesco took a final look down the valley and up at the hills surrounding the old farmhouse. He wanted to cry, but took a deep breath, braced his shoulders, stood up straight and whispered his farewell before collecting his bags from the bedroom.

Ennio parked the old Fiat he was driving on the piazza in front of the bank directly opposite the Comune. At least twice during the climb from the farmhouse to the village, Francesco had been convinced that the ancient vehicle wouldn't make it. But here they were in the busy square, and he would have to say goodbye to his old friend. In public, they would have to keep their deeper emotions in check. *Much better all round,* he thought. Ennio joined him at the rear of the truck and pointed across the street to the avvocato's office, which was tucked in between the village school and a newspaper stand which doubled up as an information kiosk.

'Right on time,' Ennio said. 'I'll wait for you here outside the bar. No hurry,' he said, walking away before Francesco had a chance to say a word. The moment for goodbyes had been put on hold.

The meeting went well. Francesco was happy to sign and initial the papers the avvocato had prepared for him in triplicate. There didn't appear to be any legal difficulties, and he felt more than content with what he had decided to do. Getting back to South Africa was now a priority, his links to Italy finally severed for good.

'Grazie mille, signore,' he thanked the ageing lawyer.

'A Lei, Monsignor,' Sebastiano Luce responded with a swift bow of deference. 'It has been good to see you. Any previous business was conducted between your father and mine, of course, but I do remember you as a young boy. Your wishes will be carried out to the letter, I can assure you. My own grandson has the highest principles and will handle your estate personally from today.'

'I am most grateful for your consideration but must leave you now. The train for Rome leaves at three, so I need to get out to the coast in plenty of time.'

'Do you have transport, *Monsignor?*'

'It's all arranged,' Francesco replied, passing through the heavy double doors held open for him. *'Arrivederla, signore.'*

'Arrivederla, Monsignor, e grazie.'

Francesco left the coolness of the lawyer's office and emerged into bright sunlight. The heat was overpowering, and almost immediately he could feel his robe start to stick to his back. The old white Fiat Punto, engine running, stood at the kerb right outside the office with Ennio sitting behind the wheel, ready to drive off as soon as Francesco got into the passenger seat and closed the door.

'I've put your other case in the boot!' he shouted as Francesco walked round the back of the car to get in on the other side.

'What's all this?' Francesco asked waving an arm around the inside of the car, settling into his seat and fixing the safety belt across his chest.

'I borrowed it,' Ennio replied, as he carefully pulled away from the parking spot and joined the one or two cars still on the road at the beginning of lunchtime. Most of the offices and shops were already closing, not reopening until late afternoon or early evening. Sensible people were indoors, out of the heat. The village was quiet, the road virtually empty.

'A good time of day to be driving,' Ennio commented. 'We should be at the coast in plenty of time.'

Francesco just stared at him, at his strong nose and chin in profile. The swarthy skin Ennio and his brothers had inherited from their parents was now deeply lined and well-weathered. He had shaved carefully, Francesco noticed, and was wearing a tie. His friend had made an effort. An effort just to say goodbye.

Francesco turned his head and gazed unseeingly out of the window. Earlier in the day, just as dawn was breaking, he had decided not to tell Ennio about his failing health, nor about the real reason for his visit. Best to leave things as they stood. The countryside on either side of the dual carriageway was uninteresting, mainly flat fields and industrial units. The character and sense of history of the region remained in the narrow streets and buildings of the medieval hill towns and villages above the valley. New industrial units were springing up everywhere, necessary but soulless.

Ennio drove carefully yet confidently, and before too long they would reach the mainline station and the express train to Rome. They walked from the station car park in silence. Only when they were standing on the platform did Ennio speak.

'This time, we get to say goodbye.'

'And this time, it really is goodbye,' Francesco said quietly, his voice hardly above a whisper. His train was already in the station. Ennio had insisted on carrying his suitcase and now seemed reluctant to let it go.

'We have come full circle,' Ennio spoke hoarsely, his voice cracking, his words indistinct. 'We have come together again, even though we have travelled in different directions.'

'We certainly have,' Francesco agreed, satisfied in that instant that his decision not to burden his friend with details of his illness was the correct one. Slowly, Ennio released his grip on the handle of the suitcase and held it out to Francesco, whose fingers were soft and warm, so different from his rough, calloused hand, and yet, the brief brushing of fingers and the swift locking of eyes said everything.

'*Arrivederci, Francesco.*'

'*Addio, Ennio mio.*'

They both knew they were really saying farewell.

An instant. A moment frozen in time. Eyes looking out of the train window saw just an old priest enveloping his companion in a fierce hug which seemed to go on forever.

Suddenly, the two men broke apart, and without another word, Francesco, the priest, boarded the train. Ennio stood on the platform alone, long after the train had pulled away from the platform and disappeared around a bend in the line. The sun's dazzling rays reflecting off the deep aquamarine of the Adriatic, for once, made no impression on him, as with blurred vision, he walked hesitantly back to the car.

Chapter 8
Sebastiano

Three days later, after his meeting with Francesco Fioretti, Sebastiano found himself driving down the *strada bianca,* the small, gravelled lane, on his way to the old stone farmhouse he had not visited for so many years. Near the bottom of the hill, he turned left and drove between rusting gates hidden in the undergrowth, the tyres of his small BMW crunching on the gravel at the rear of the house.

He closed the car door gently, not wanting to disturb the all-enveloping silence which shrouded the hillsides around him. He did not bother to lock his car. There was no need. He made his way down the side of the house, inhaling the scent of white jasmine which clung to the mellow stone wall. He was met with a view which was, if anything, more beautiful than his own.

The sweeping hills of his region never ceased to amaze him. To his left, he saw a field of sunflowers, not yet in full bloom, and a small orchard with plum, apricot and cherry trees. The rows of vines which disappeared down the slope below the fruit trees were already heavily laden with unripe grapes for table wine and for the local speciality, *vino cotto.* Another two or three months and they would be perfect for the *raccolta*, the grape harvest.

As he walked around the corner to the front of the house, Sebastiano saw the man he had come to see standing at the far end of the *terrazzo*, wiping down the slats of some shutters that had seen better days. Sebastiano realised that his arrival had not been heard, and the old man only stopped what he was doing and turned around when he was greeted with Sebastiano's clear shout of *'Buongiorno, signore*!' Putting the cloth he had been using into the bucket by his feet and wiping his hands down the sides of his trousers, the old man walked towards his visitor, a defensive frown creasing his forehead.

'Buongiorno, signore.' he said in a soft voice full of uncertainty.

'*Buongiorno, Ennio. Come va?*'

Not until he was much nearer did Ennio seem to recognise his visitor.

'Sebastiano. What are you doing here? I've not seen you for many a long year.'

'You look well, Ennio,' Sebastiano lied.

'Not so well, *Dottore*. Too old to be looking after this place. Come and sit down. Some wine?' he asked, already making his way into the house without waiting for a reply.

Once they were settled in the two old chairs on the *terrazzo* under the portico outside the door to the kitchen, with a glass of red wine each and a bowl of olives on the table, Sebastiano explained briefly the reason for his visit.

'I need you to come into the office, Ennio. There are some papers to do with your property that need signing.'

Ennio lifted his head abruptly from his wine glass and looked enquiringly at the *avvocato*.

'Is there something wrong, Sebastiano? I thought everything was put in order years ago when I was left alone to work the property.'

'Everything is perfect, Ennio,' he said reassuringly, 'but one or two things need updating, and I need to explain some changes. Will you be able to come up to the village tomorrow morning? If not, I shall bring all the papers here to you.'

'That's very kind of you, *Dottore*, but I shall come up to you. What time would be best?'

'Shall we say ten-thirty? The business will take about an hour. You know how it is; every page is signed in triplicate. This wine is excellent. Your own, I take it?'

'Of course. This particular bottle is five years old, nearly ready for my taste. You must take some with you.'

Sebastiano finished off his wine and rose to leave, hesitating for a moment to take in the view, remembering the time when the da Calvi family made the home so joyful.

'I love it here,' he said suddenly, without thinking. 'Always have.'

'So do I, *Dottore*. So do I,' Ennio whispered standing by his side.

The meeting the following morning took much longer than an hour. Ennio had agreed to have the younger *avvocato* present while Sebastiano went through the necessary documents, taking time and trouble to speak clearly and slowly and avoiding wherever possible lapsing into "legalese". He stopped at regular intervals to ask Ennio if he understood, or if he had any questions, but it soon became evident that the old farmer was so shell-shocked by what he was hearing that he could hardly speak.

When Sebastiano finally came to the end of the documents, he recommended strongly that Ennio make a will, the alternative being an easy gift to the state.

Eventually, after many minutes of silence, Ennio spoke, his voice clear and decisive.

'I know that everything you tell me is true, *Dottore*, but I am having difficulty believing it. I want you to draw up a will for me. Somewhere out there, I know, there is a da Calvi. I will pay you to make a search. This person will get everything when I die. When will the papers be ready for me to sign?'

Sebastiano glanced at his grandson, who would have the responsibility of drawing up the will.

'One week from today,' Seb told the old man.

'I shall come back at the same time, ten-thirty,' Ennio agreed, rising slowly from his chair. 'Thank you, Sebastiano, for your time and patience. As you can imagine, the information you have given me this morning has stunned me. Perhaps, when all this official business is done with, we'll have a chance to talk about Giuseppe.'

Sebastiano smiled and nodded. 'I shall look forward to it, Ennio.'

The chance, unfortunately, never came.

Chapter 9
Massimo

The groan came from somewhere deep down in his throat and got caught between clenched teeth, his lips tightly pressed together. The pain in both his knees was excruciating and was getting worse by the day. He sank down heavily onto the red plastic chair, closed his eyes, and willed the agony to subside. Slowly, he let his shoulders relax and started to breathe evenly again.

He hated the way he now had to live his life. Age had caught up with him at last. He hated even more having to leave the house earlier and earlier each day to make sure he arrived at the bar on the *piazza* before his friends. The last thing he wanted was for them to see how immobile he had become, and how much of a struggle it was for him to join them for their morning "putting the world to rights" sessions.

Over the last fifty years, only severe weather had prevented the old men from meeting at the same time and in the same place. He was always the first to arrive and made sure he had just a drop more coffee to finish off before he was the last to leave. At one time, there had been eight or nine of them. Now, they were down to four, and before too long he knew they would be down to three.

His legs started to feel better, responding to the warm sunshine spreading through his grey flannel trousers. He needed a new pair, thinner for the summer, but what was the point? His well-worn, scuffed shoes might just last until the autumn. He would not need to replace them. Gently, he massaged both knees, rotating the calloused palms of his weathered, old hands around each kneecap. Age spots and thick, blue knobbly veins vied for position on the backs of his hands. His nails were chipped and jagged, breaking and peeling off regularly, and no matter how hard he tried, he could not get all the dirt out from the grooves between his nails and the wrinkled skin of his fingers. Looking after himself had become too much of an effort. He was ready to give up.

Massimo lifted his head and gazed around the *piazza*, which was already busy even at nine o'clock in the morning. The Friday fresh fish van was doing a steady trade as usual, and he recognised many familiar faces going into the popular *Punto* supermarket. The smell of fresh bread was coming from *Da Clara's* shop where, sometimes, he would treat himself to a small slice of apricot flan. He never bought his bread there, preferring to walk a few metres further along the main street to the unsigned artisan bakery belonging to the one-armed Giacomo. There, he could chat with the baker and buy half a loaf of fresh crusty bread. He would waste too much if he bought a full loaf., At other times, he would treat himself to half a dozen small, almond *biscotti* to dip into his espresso late in the evening when he was at home on his own.

His companions were not due for at least another fifteen minutes, so he settled back into his chair as comfortably as he could to watch the world go by, a pleasure he knew for certain would soon come to an end. He knew he would not see another summer. Everything was so familiar—the sights, the sounds and even the changing smells of the *piazza*.

Only once had he ventured away from home and that had been a disaster. The worst period of his life. An unforgettable experience which still gave him nightmares seventy years later. Disturbing images of horror, creeping up and invading his dreams when he least expected them.

He shook his head sharply to dislodge the unwelcome thoughts, and instead focused on the people who went into the *Comune*, coming up with his own reasons why each one would be visiting the local council offices. Massimo Sauro was one month short of his eighty-ninth birthday, and he calculated that he had been inside that building four times in his whole life. He hated bureaucracy and all it implied, especially in his own country—paperwork gone mad. He shook his head again and smiled to himself. At least, it gave them all something to argue about every morning, official paperwork and the fascinating tapestry and fragility of Italian politics.

Massimo cast his mind back to the last time he had walked through the heavy wooden doors into the stone building opposite the bar. He had not gone into the *Comune* offices, exactly, but had visited the *avvocato* whose offices were on the ground floor. He would not even have done that unless he had been prompted. It must have been about two years before, he mused, when on his way to the bar, he had bumped into Ennio da Calvi coming out of the old building. They were acquainted, of course, both born and bred in the town, but Massimo was older, Andrea's age.

It was the thought of Andrea which had made him stop and speak to Ennio, if only for a few moments. The youngest da Calvi, he knew, was reclusive, and Massimo had not been sure about how his friendly gesture would be received. He need not have worried. He remembered again how easily the conversation had flowed between them, mainly about the weather, their health and the inevitable aches and pains of getting old. Then, out of the blue, Ennio had told him that he had just been in to make his will.

'Have you made your will?' Ennio had asked him bluntly.

'I've never thought about it,' he had replied honestly. 'There's only my sister left,' he had added.

'Then you have to decide, Massimo. Do you want your sister to have whatever you have to leave behind, or do you want the state to benefit? I know which one I'd choose.'

Massimo had looked directly into Ennio da Calvi's face. Even in the faded, milky eyes and under the yellow-tinged skin, he had seen just a slight, yet definite resemblance to the man's older charismatic brother, and in that instant, Massimo made a decision.

'What you say makes sense, *signore*. I must do the same and make a will. I don't have much, but I'll be damned if the state will get its hands on it.'

'*Bene,* Massimo. I can recommend Dottore Sebastiano Luce,' Ennio said, pointing back over his shoulder to the offices he had just left. 'Not the young one. You want the old one. He only comes to the office when he is needed, so you will have to ask for him and make an appointment. They make it very easy for old men like us,' he had smiled.

'I'll do exactly that,' Massimo had said. '*Grazie mille*, Ennio.'

'*Arrivederci, signore,*' Ennio had replied and walked on very slowly, not once glancing back.

Two months later, Massimo heard that the youngest da Calvi had died, and on the Friday of the following week, a day after the funeral, he made his will and spoke at length to the *avvocato* about things he had never told another living soul.

Chapter 10
Stefano

Five years younger than Seb Luce, Stefano was first and foremost an academic. His forte, he had found early on in his studies, was research. He relished the challenge of delving deep into a topic and discovering the smallest detail he could possibly find. He had a degree in law, and although he was part of the Luce family firm, he preferred to work alone. He was happy in his own company and liked nothing more than sorting out legal dilemmas and finding solutions. He felt comfortable with a pen, paper, charts and diagrams, but more and more he relied on his mobile phone, tablet and laptop to speed up his research.

It had taken him much longer than he had anticipated to find and go through the documentation relating to the Leftakis family. Travelling in the rural areas of Greece had been hot, dry and difficult. The certificates he needed had not been where they should have been, and so he had had to start again and follow a totally different paper trail. The language had posed another problem, but he found all the people he had to deal with very friendly and patient.

Eventually he had satisfied himself that he had gathered all the necessary information available and was in a position to tell Seb that the Leftakis family had indeed come to the end of the line, so they could eliminate the Greek stem from their investigations.

He felt far more confident with his next assignment.

'I might need you to go to England, Stef,' Seb had greeted him one morning a week after his return from Greece. He had spent a good two days compiling his report on the trip before taking a break trekking and cycling in the nearby Sibillini mountains.

'Come into my office, and I'll go through the information I already have with you. Bring your coffee with you.'

Both men settled on the comfortable chairs, putting their coffee cups down on the low table between them.

'As usual, I haven't got that much to tell you except that we're dealing with the same family but on the Italian side this time.'

Stefano sat back, his left ankle resting casually across his right knee, displaying a very tanned and hairy leg between a plain, black sock and the bottom of his tailored black trousers. Just like his boss, he knew he dressed in an understated style. He favoured silk for his shirts and top-quality soft leather for his shoes and jackets. He enjoyed spending money on himself, his clothes, his hair and his sport. He was a triathlete and had the fitness to prove it.

'Just after the da Calvi estate came into our hands,' Seb continued, 'we had a visit from Massimo Sauro.'

'I know Massimo. Once, I made the mistake of sitting on his chair outside the bar on the *piazza*. He didn't say anything, just stared at me until I moved. He smiled at me then and said he'd sat in the same place for more than forty years, so he was sure I'd understand. Then he bought me another espresso.'

'That sounds like him. He made an appointment with my grandfather, who passed me some information Massimo gave him, which could be relevant to the next line of our research. So, this is what I've got so far.' Seb glanced down at the file resting across his knees.

'It would appear that Giorgio da Calvi followed his older brother Andrea north to join Mussolini's forces somewhere east of Milan. Andrea made it and got killed for his trouble, but according to Massimo, who was also in the group, somewhere along the route, Giorgio took a diversion. That's your first task, to find out where he went and what happened to him. You'll probably have to go back to 1939 or even 1938 to get more background information on the two brothers. Massimo can remember the smallest details of fighting and bloodshed but hasn't got a clue about places or dates. It's up to us to fill in the gaps.' Seb sipped his coffee, grimaced, and put his cup back on the table.

'The second challenge is to find out what happened to Giuseppe da Calvi. We know a bit more about him, not least that he was my grandfather's closest boyhood friend.'

'So, no pressure there, then,' quipped Stefano.

'After the war,' Seb went on as if Stefano had not spoken, 'Giuseppe went off to look for Giorgio. It's possible he followed the same route as his brother, but we don't know that for sure. As usual, Giulia has put together, as far as possible, a comprehensive file on each brother. It would be good if we could wrap this up as soon as possible. The whole thing is weighing me down a bit. I'd say it's the largest estate we've ever had to deal with—and that's saying something!'

'Leave it to me, Seb. I'll read through the files today, work out my starting strategy and travel arrangements and then be on my way. Today's Monday, so I'll be off first thing on Thursday morning. As agreed, I'll update you every two days unless something important or urgent crops up. Thanks for the coffee, even if it has gone cold. It's the one thing I refuse to give up even when I'm training. I'm convinced a daily hit of caffeine helps me perform better.'

The two men shook hands at the door.

'Let's hope we have a more positive outcome this time,' Stefano said, walking into the outer office. Giulia stood up, holding two coloured wallets in her hands.

'All the information is also on our system, Stef, so you can download what you need in your own time,' she told him.

'I'll do that, but there is still something I love about paper, being able to underline and make my own notations. It's not quite the same on a screen. No doubt I'll convert completely at some time in the future, but not yet. Love the flowers, by the way, Giulia. The colour matches your eyes perfectly.'

Seb and Giulia could still hear his distant laughter as they both looked at the bright orange marigolds arranged beautifully in the vase on the corner of her desk.

Stefano started as he usually did by gathering as much information as he could from local sources. He joined Massimo Sauro for a coffee on the *piazza* the following morning, but the old man couldn't tell him any more about Giorgio da Calvi than he had told the *avvocato*. He only repeated over and over again that the younger da Calvi boy had had more sense than his brother and had gone his own way, far away from the horrors awaiting the rest of them. Stefano had thanked him for his time, apologised for dredging up unpleasant memories and left him in peace.

Before resorting to online documents, he drove to Macerata, the regional capital, after lunch, to meet Gianni the archivist whose office was just off the main *piazza* in the centre of the town. Beneath his office, thousands of historical papers, documents and certificates were stored in temperature-controlled conditions. Stefano had worked with him on a number of cases, so he knew exactly where he was going. After an espresso and a small *torta di frutta,* he settled down at an old desk surrounded by files and folders that had not been touched in decades. Gianni had sorted out the papers he had requested according to the relevant *Comune*, so the research could start in earnest.

Stefano was in his element. He loved the bare stone walls that had been there for centuries, the files that demanded he blow on them to disperse the dust before he could open them to delve into their secrets. Above all, he revelled in the cool silence enveloping him. He was alone with history, and he felt privileged.

After sitting still with his eyes closed, absorbing his surroundings for at least five minutes, he finally jerked himself into action. He bent down and took a pencil and notebook out of his briefcase, ignoring his tablet for the time being. He took pleasure in the musty smell of the papers in front of him and felt happy with the soft scrape of pencil lead on paper as he jotted down the notes he needed to take his research forward.

It took him just under three hours to get enough information to start him on his journey. He checked out as far as possible the movements of local men from 1938 onwards. There were copies of travel and work permits to read through, together with identity card renewal documents. He was fascinated by the old train timetables and had to discipline himself not to get sidetracked. He could always come back another time and indulge himself further. Now and again, he would come across familiar names, men who still lived in the village, and he wondered if they were aware that various parts of their lives were documented for posterity in the vaults of the regional centre.

Making doubly sure he had all the necessary information, Stefano reluctantly packed away his things. The tips of his fingers were grubby and stained from the dust, and the smell of decay loitered in his nostrils and on his clothes. He left the files and folders as he had found them, piled neatly on the table, and made his way up the narrow stone staircase to the public area at street level.

'*Grazie mille,* Gianni,' he called over to the archivist who was dealing with another visitor.

He was already outside on the steps by the time his friend answered.

Stefano checked the time on the clock of the *campanile.* Twenty past three. The streets were quiet and deserted. He walked briskly back to the bar where he had enjoyed his espresso earlier and ordered a ham and mozzarella *tramezzino* and a bottle of sparkling mineral water. Outside on the terrace, he mulled over what he had found out and tried to formulate his next steps. He was already looking forward to his forthcoming trip to England and felt quite excited by the prospect. The butterflies of expectation were already fluttering in his stomach.

By seven o'clock that evening, he had transferred all the details he needed from his notebook onto his iPad. He managed to précis a great deal, leaving him with just the essential bare bones. He packed his case with two weeks' worth of clothes and toiletries, bearing in mind that the English summer weather would not be as warm or predictable. He checked the train timetable online, jotted down the possibilities, then left his apartment for his favourite *ristorante*. From experience, he knew that, more than likely, the food where he was going would not quite reach the standard he was used to.

Mid-morning on the Thursday after his meeting with Seb, Stefano was well on his way north. His train was on time for once and, rather than have his head buried in a book, he took the time to gaze out of the window and watch the countryside go by. At first, the train followed the stunning Adriatic coastline as far north as the prestigious port of Ancona. Stefano knew it well with its restored 11th century San Ciriaco Cathedral, the pentagonal *Lazzaretto*, a former quarantine station built to protect the city from the risk of contagious diseases arriving on the ships, but Stefano's favourite had always been the *Fontana del Calamo*, a fountain in the city centre with bronze masks of mythical figures. He reflected on his many previous visits, and still believed that Ancona was an underestimated city, rarely favoured by the many tourists who flocked into Italy every year.

Not long after passing through Ancona, the train turned inland, and Stefano was soon having to change trains in Bologna before continuing his journey towards Milan. The Italian countryside looked very dry, and he could see the heat shimmering above the neatly ploughed fields. The rich aquamarine of the sea soon gave way to pale brown and yellow expanses of farmland with young crops just starting to peep through. In a matter of weeks, there would be wheat and sunflowers hiding the bare earth. His journey was uneventful, and he reached his destination without any delays.

The one definite piece of information he had gleaned from Massimo was that no one recalled seeing Giorgio da Calvi after the group left the town of Reggio Emilia.

'If you want my opinion,' Massimo had told him, tapping the crooked fingers of his right hand on the table in front of him, 'young Giorgio had a change of heart. He wasn't as strong or as passionate as his brother, so I reckon he went off on his own rather than join the fighting with the rest of us.'

'Where would he go, do you think?' Stefano had asked, more in hope than expectation.

Massimo had given the question some thought, and Stefano had waited in silence until the old man's mind returned from his memories to the present.

'I'd try the town of Bardi if I were you. It's in the right region, and I know for a fact that, even before the war, lots of men left that region to find work in England. Yes. Start with Bardi. They'll have records there. Maybe our Giorgio joined up with others going west rather than north. *Buona fortuna, signore.* Good luck to you.'

The mention of England fitted in with the scant details Seb had given him, so he had researched the town of Bardi and decided to make it his first port of call.

He was tired. As usual with a new case, he had launched straight into his research without pacing himself. The travel, all the reading, conversations and analyses eventually caught up with him. So far, he had enjoyed every minute of the da Calvi case and felt that he had made good progress. He knew exactly what his next step was going to be but needed to recharge his batteries before moving on.

His room was delightful. At the end of a long day, he had had a problem finding somewhere to stay in Bardi itself, so he found a taxi and asked the driver to take him somewhere decent to stay just for the one night. Twenty minutes later, he had been dropped off outside an old farmhouse nine miles outside the town. He had received a warm welcome and was shown to a large airy room on the first floor. '*Ca' Mariella*' was an *agriturismo* at the end of a winding farm track.

Surrounded on three sides by tall cypress trees, the mellow stonework of the building glowed in the evening sunshine. His *matrimoniale* bed was huge with two high, ornately carved, wooden headboards. The walls were painted white, and he glanced at the mish-mash of paintings on three of the four walls. Above the bed hung the obligatory crucifixion scene in a heavy, tarnished gold frame. The painting had faded badly, but obviously had significance for the family.

Stefano took off his jacket and draped it casually over the back of a well-worn armchair tucked into the corner behind the door. He unlaced and took off his shoes and socks, then flopped down on top of the thick eiderdown on the bed.

No modern duvet here, he thought to himself as he relaxed and closed his eyes. He was not particularly hungry. At home, he never went out to eat until after nine, so he had at least a couple of hours to put his thoughts in order and have a short nap. The room was warm, so he stripped down to his underpants, stretched out on top of the bed and cast his mind back over the last few hours.

The hill town of Bardi was in the Ceno valley not too far from Modena and Parma in the north west. The town itself was dominated by an imposing ninth-century castle, perched on a rocky outcrop. According to legend, the town got its name from Bardus, the last elephant in Hannibal's army who died there on the long march to Rome. Historically, however, the name derived from the Lombard nobility who settled in the area in the seventh century. Stefano decided he preferred the imagery of the Hannibal story, and although he would have loved to have found out more about the town's ancient history, on this particular visit he needed to focus on far more recent events.

In his research, he found that in the 1870s sixty percent of the population of Italy worked on the land. Farm workers did not own their own plots, nor did they pay rent. The landowner paid the taxes and bought the seed and stock. The farmers did all the hard work and were then given a small share of the profits. This was the *mezzadaria* system. So, if ever the government raised the taxes, profits would fall. The Roman Catholic labourers had large families to support, and when the inheritance tax laws also changed, the head of the family, when he died, was required to leave at least half of his plots to be divided equally between all his children. Inevitably, farms grew smaller and smaller, and poverty increased. There were no alternatives, as industrial growth was at a standstill, and besides, the majority of people were illiterate. Emigration appeared to be the best solution. Italians had been emigrating in small numbers since the seventeenth century, but by the end of the nineteenth century, at least ten percent lived abroad.

Stefano had been surprised to find that the majority of people who emigrated to England came from the north of Italy, but as time passed, more and more left their homes in the south. By the twentieth century, more than two million Italians had left their homeland to escape from disease and starvation. The lack of food and the inability to pay for whatever was available led to sickness and death. In the north, people contracted *pellagra*, which resulted in insanity and death. In the south, the threat came from malaria, which spread inland from the coast, helped, no doubt, by deforestation, erosion and flooding.

Stefano tried hard to imagine his beautiful country in a state of desperation with very little hope of rescue. The majority of people at that time did not have a vote, democracy did not exist, and, for them, education was non-existent. He already knew that there had been many different socio-economic reasons for emigration by so many, and he also knew that cheaper rail travel and steamship journeys made the decision to leave that much easier.

Early records showed that there had been Italian cafés in Paris as early as the middle of the seventeenth century, and wherever Italians settled, there would be ice-cream sellers and musicians, usually itinerant organ grinders. Very few were employed in agriculture. He had already discovered that so many people from Bardi had chosen to go to South Wales rather than England, exchanging rural life for commercial and industrial opportunities, and many locals still had close ties to family members who had left the town before and immediately after the war.

Not every son of Bardi ended up in a factory, however. A side note to one of the documents Stefano found confirmed that a local man, Aldo Berni, with his brother, Frank, established a famous chain of restaurants in England after the Second World War—a business that remained successful right up to the end of the 1970s. A sharp knock on the door interrupted his musings and had him scrambling around for his trousers and shirt.

'*Avanti!*' he called out, feeling light-headed from being roused so sharply from his sleep. He must have dozed off while mentally going through his research so far and, without realising it, he had slept for nearly three hours. It was already nine-thirty, but still very warm in the room.

'*Mi scusi signore, ma vuole qualcosa da bere? Fa molto caldo.*'

'Yes, I'd love a cold drink, and you're right, *signora*, it really is very warm.'

'I can get you something to eat, too. Some cold meat and salad, perhaps?'

'That would be perfect, *signora*. It's too late for me to go back into the town.'

'*Dieci minuti, signore.* You can join us. Come through to the kitchen when you're ready.'

Mariella closed the heavy oak door and made her way back through the house, her sandals slip slapping on the old terra cotta tiles. Ten minutes later, Stefano joined her and her husband, Mauro. They were outside on the terrace, and from where he stood in the open doorway, he could see a long wooden table laden with a choice of cold meats, olives, sundried tomatoes, salad leaves and a variety of cheeses. Homemade bread stood on a board next to a jug of freshly squeezed orange juice. A large stone pitcher of wine stood in front of Mauro, ready to be poured. Stefano was delighted to have the chance to spend time in their company and chat about their town.

The breathless night was warm. The heat enveloped the stone buildings, the stillness pierced only by the cacophony of sound made by the cicadas in the trees. The scent of jasmine hung in the air, and the whole effect reminded Stefano of the relentless heat he had endured weeks earlier in Greece. But at least, here, he could speak and understand the language. Here, he felt at home, and was soon helping himself to the numerous dishes on offer. The bread had been made that morning, and the cheese and wine were both strong, just the way he liked them.

After chatting about their respective regions—the similarities and differences, Italy's economic state in relation to the rest of Europe, but more importantly, the prospects of the two football teams from Milan in the coming season—Stefano told them the reason for his visit to Bardi.

'There were four sons in the family I'm trying to trace,' he began, breaking into another chunk of bread and smothering it in olive oil and salt. 'I already know that the eldest was killed fighting with Mussolini's army, but it's the second son I'm most interested in now. Instead of going with his brother to fight, I understand he broke away from the group and more than likely joined up with others trying to make their way to England. I am hoping that he made the right choice. At least, that is what I think happened to Giorgio, but first I must find him to be absolutely sure.'

'Most men from here went to Wales, not England,' Mauro said quietly. 'Word spread that there were jobs to be had other than working hard on the land for next to nothing. Our community almost died at that time,' he went on, shaking his head, his eyes fixed ahead on nothing in particular, his wine hardly touched.

'Before you go anywhere,' Mariella said softly, breaking the brief silence that had descended over the table, 'you must visit the chapel. You need to check to see if the name of the man you are looking for is listed on the wall. So many men from here and from the villages nearby were caught up in the disaster. So many. So far from home. So far.'

Both Mariella and Mauro frowned and shook their heads slowly. Stefano took another sip of his wine, then replaced his glass on the table. He knew the value of hearing stories from people associated with events. Their accounts always had far more life and immediacy than accounts in books.

'This is obviously difficult for you,' he said in a gentle tone, 'but do you think you could tell me about the disaster? It clearly has great significance for you and the town.'

He took another sip of wine, watching the insects darting around the lamps that bathed the terrace in a soft glow.

'I could tell you what happened,' Mauro said, 'but it's late, and I'm sure you'll find more facts and information on the internet. But if you want to *feel* what the disaster means, then you must go, as Mariella said, to the chapel in the town. We'll tell you how to get there.' With both palms flat on the table, Mauro stared down at his empty plate. 'Those men needn't have drowned. They shouldn't have been on that ship. It was all so unnecessary.'

'What was the name of the ship?' Stefano asked quietly.

'The *Arandora Star*. Perhaps, the man you are looking for was one of the victims; you never know. Check the lists on the walls of the chapel. That's the best idea.'

'That'll be my first job in the morning. To be honest, I didn't really know where to start. I'd better get some sleep,' he said, getting up from the table. 'It's almost midnight. The meal was delicious, *signora*, and very welcome, *grazie*. *A domani.* I'll see you tomorrow.'

'Breakfast will be ready when you are, *signore*. The weather is going to be very warm again, so we shall eat outside as usual. *Buona notte.* Goodnight.'

Mariella smiled at him as he left the terrace.

Mauro said nothing.

Although it was after midnight, Stefano settled back on the bed, his laptop open on his knees. He googled *Arandora Star* and, for the next hour, became totally absorbed in the wealth of facts and data his search threw up, amazed that he had never come across the information before. At half past one, he closed his laptop, put it on the floor next to the bed and slid down under the crisp, white sheet, which was the only cover needed in such heat. He fell asleep almost immediately, happy in the knowledge that he now knew exactly what his first move was going to be the following morning.

Birdsong outside his window woke him up from a very deep sleep. It was five thirty-five, and without giving it a moment's thought, he swung his legs over the side of the bed, stood up, and stretched his arms as far as they would go into the air above his head before heading for the shower, his mind already buzzing. He had so much to do in the town, but with little time to do it all. There definitely was no time to linger under the jets of warm water. He needed to plan his day, hoping that by late evening he would find himself in England, or if logistically possible, in Wales. He felt he needed to follow the Bardi link, at least as a first step.

Dressed in a clean, blue short-sleeved shirt and his favourite designer jeans, Stefano logged on to the memo pad he had used in the early hours of the morning. He quickly checked out his options and timings before joining Mariella and Mauro for breakfast.

To get to Wales, he would have to fly into Cardiff Airport. The options from Bardi were limited, to say the least. Bologna was the nearest airport, but there were no suitable flights. Genoa was a possibility, but again, no flights. Almost as a last resort, he tried Milan *Malpensa* and found a flight to Cardiff leaving early that afternoon.

The distance from Bardi to Milan was just under two hundred and thirty kilometres. He would need at least three hours, which meant leaving by eleven o'clock at the latest. Should he drive himself or take a taxi? Hiring a car and leaving it at the airport would take up too much time. He was sure that Mauro could find him a reliable driver, possibly the same man who had brought him to the farmhouse. He opened another window on his laptop, and fifteen minutes later completed his flight booking. He could use the app on his phone to check in so didn't have to bother printing out the boarding pass. Next, he checked out Cardiff, the airport and the city centre.

He decided to book himself into what looked like a modern hotel on the waterfront, about a forty-minute drive from the airport. If all went to plan, he would arrive at the hotel at some time in the early evening. He smiled to himself as he closed his laptop. He could just imagine Seb's face when he submitted the expenses for this trip!

At seven o'clock, after packing up his things, he made his way out into the early morning sunshine. Mariella followed him out, carrying a jug of more freshly squeezed orange juice. She had already put the bread, a few *panini* and a plate of sweet, almond croissants on the table. A large, blue ceramic bowl held peaches, oranges, apples and plums.

'*Buongiorno!*' she greeted him enthusiastically.

'*Buongiorno, signora,*' he replied.

'*S'accomodi.* Sit down and help yourself, *signore.*'

She left him but was soon back with a pot full of strong coffee and a jug of milk, surprising him by saying, '*Il latte è caldo, signore.*'

Stefano helped himself to a warm bread roll, butter and jam. The coffee was very strong and aromatic, but he was not too sure about adding the hot milk. He liked his coffee black but tried the milk anyway, deciding that he was much too fussy. He poured himself a second cup and finished off the milk, feeling quite pleased with himself for trying something new. The almond croissant was full of thick custard, another one of his favourites. He would definitely be sorry to leave the farm but knew his waistline would suffer if he stayed much longer.

He was just finishing off his glass of chilled orange when Mauro appeared in the doorway.

'*Buongiorno, signore.*'

'*Buongiorno,*' Stefano replied, then asked about the possibility of finding someone to take him to Milan. He told Mauro what time he needed to leave the town and was pleasantly surprised when Mauro said he would arrange for him to be picked up after breakfast, taken into town and then picked up again outside the memorial chapel just before eleven o'clock. The driver, who was called Michele, would be the same one who had brought him the night before, and it came as no surprise to find out that he was, in fact, Mauro's brother-in-law.

'*Mi scusi, signore.* I shall call him now before he has other customers.'

Stefano was just finishing his breakfast when Michele arrived, driving a much more up-to-date Lancia rather than the ageing Fiat from the day before.

'*Buongiorno, signore,*' he greeted Stefano before sitting down at the table and helping himself to a cup of tepid coffee and an almond croissant.

'I will take you into town and will wait until you finish your visit to the chapel and the cemetery. Today, you're lucky. There are no problems on the road to Milan. No accidents so far and no road works, I've checked. We should have a good trip.'

Stefano thanked him, excused himself and then went to collect his things from his room. He paid Mariella in cash, adding a generous bonus for making him feel so welcome, said goodbye to Mauro, then walked out to the car parked under the canopy of a large mulberry tree. Michele said very little on the short drive into Bardi, but as he dropped Stefano off near the chapel, he carefully went over the arrangements he had agreed with Mauro just to make sure he had understood correctly. He assured Stefano that he knew exactly where he was taking him later, and that it was quite safe to leave his bags in the car. Although they had arrived at the chapel very early, Michele had made arrangements for the doors of the chapel to be open. The joys of local knowledge.

As he approached the cemetery, the heat of the sun was already quite fierce, and he was thankful to be wearing his lightweight linen jacket. He climbed the dozen or so steps up to the tall, wrought iron gates, gave one of them a gentle push and walked through. A paved path stretched out in front of him, leading to an archway. On either side were beautifully tended graves with a kaleidoscopic variety of colourful, freshly cut roses already in full bloom.

Stefano glanced to his left and at the end of another short path saw a row of pristine, white mausoleums, the resting places for members of local families. The eighth structure along, however, was quite different, immediately attracting his attention. Pale pistachio green in colour, topped by a pediment, was the chapel he had come to see. Above the entrance was a striking, black painting of a ship, both funnels still in view but with its bow plunged beneath the waves. A grey, metal plaque under the painting bore the inscription *"Vittimi Arandora Star"*.

Stefano stood motionless on the threshold, breathing in the atmosphere and the overwhelming feeling of reverence and respect the little chapel commanded. It took a few silent seconds for his eyes to get accustomed to the cool darkness inside. Dust motes danced in the weak rays of the sunlight creeping through the stained glass of three small windows directly opposite the doorway. Above the central window was the same simple image of the sinking ship. In front of him were two wooden pews and a low lectern supporting a large, open volume for visitors' names and comments. There was a small, marble altar with candles in wrought iron holders and more beautiful roses. The air inside the chapel was heavy with the scent of age, candle wax and flowers.

Stefano glanced to his left. There was a small collection of very old photographs, but most of the wall space was taken up with lists of names. The wall to his right looked just the same. The names of the *vittimi*. The names he had come to see. Below each list stood a vase of fresh, perfectly formed rosebuds and a small light. He moved to stand in front of the wall to his left and shivered a little, not sure if it was because of the chilly air or because of the significance of what he was looking at. What struck him immediately was the repetition of names. There were two from each of the Fulgoni, Sidoli, Rossi and Conti families, and there were five from each of the Rabaiotti and Gazzi families.

Mauro had told him that out of the 446 victims, one in ten had come from Bardi and the surrounding villages. The absence of the name Giorgio da Calvi came as no surprise. Giorgio had not been a local man, simply a traveller passing through, so his name would be absent from the list. Yet, for some reason, Stefano was still convinced that Giorgio had joined up with some of the local men who had left Bardi in search of a better life.

Slowly, he wandered from list to list: Minotti, Marenghi, Menozzi, Giovanelli, Pellegrini and Cavalli among many more. He recalled from his online research that there were similar memorials in London, Liverpool and Cardiff and that there were graves in Ireland and on some of the smaller Scottish islands, where bodies had been washed ashore mostly without any form of identity. He sat down for a few moments in one of the narrow pews and took time to think about the events leading up to the *Arandora Star* tragedy and the reason why he was sitting alone in this chapel in total silence.

Stefano had learned that in June 1940, the Italian leader, Benito Mussolini, had entered the Second World War on the side of the Germans. There had been an immediate response from Winston Churchill and the British Government. All Italian males between the ages of eighteen and seventy living in Britain, without British citizenship, were to be rounded up and interned.

Stefano was appalled that people could be treated in this way. Many of the Italians who had left Italy at the end of the nineteenth century had integrated so well into the British way of life that they had never felt it necessary or important enough to apply for citizenship. So it was that thousands found themselves being taken to internment camps in various parts of England, Scotland and Wales. Women were left to fend for themselves, children were left without a father and many Italian businesses were taken over by "legal" residents.

With so many Italian prisoners of war, the British Government decided to send as many of them as possible overseas, mainly to British dominions. Stefano had been upset to read that the Duke of Devonshire, at that time, had justified deportation by stressing the advantages of using resources wisely by "getting rid of useless mouths and so forth". Those "useless mouths" had been Stefano's people.

Less than a month after Italy joined Germany in the war, the former luxury cruise ship *Arandora Star* set sail from Liverpool, bound for St John's Newfoundland. On board were over 1500 internees, many of them Italian. The ship did not display the sign of the Red Cross, which would have shown that she was carrying civilian prisoners. On 2nd July 1940, off the northwest coast of Ireland, the *Arandora Star* was sunk by a German torpedo. Over 800 lives were lost in total, and many of the drowned were carried by the sea and washed up on various beaches on the coasts of Ireland and Scotland.

Stefano had made a note of where other memorials were but felt he also needed to see a copy of the *Arandora Star* embarkation list, which would mean a trip to the National Archives in London. He knew from experience that when dealing with disasters involving many casualties, the published numbers were very rarely accurate, so he would go through all the lists and data with an open mind.

He rubbed his forearms vigorously. The cool chapel air had given him goosebumps, and he needed to move. With a final backward glance into the chapel from the doorway, he stepped out into brilliant sunshine, still feeling upset, then made his way back through the cemetery and down the steps to find Michele leaning up against the car, waiting patiently.

The long drive to Milan on the A1 through beautiful countryside took just under three hours. Michele was quite happy to chat about food, football and family. Not wanting to stop on the way and knowing that Stefano had a plane to catch at four fifteen, he had brought along large slices of homemade pizza, *biscotti*, small, sweet pastries and an endless supply of bottled water in a cool box. He told Stefano that he was familiar with the route to the airport as many families from the Bardi area found it far more convenient to hire a taxi than to catch a bus to Parma, then travel by train to the airport.

Stefano relaxed in the comfort of the passenger seat. A crucifix dangled from the rear-view mirror, and there was a sticker of the Virgin Mary under the radio. Michele was a good, steady driver, and during the silence between snippets of conversation, Stefano went over again in his mind what he had learned about Bardi, the reasons why so many of his countrymen had emigrated to find a better life and the tragedy of the *Arandora Star*. He planned out his next move.

He had to put in a request to the National Archives in London for the documents he needed as soon as possible. He had the web address for the shipping line which should be able to give him the figures for the Italian casualties. There were also other websites relating to the *Arandora Star* missing persons. He just needed time to study and compare all the information he had gathered to be absolutely sure he had not missed any reference to, or any clue to, the fate of Giorgio da Calvi. He had to admit to himself that if he was being totally honest and realistic, he did not hold out much hope for a positive outcome. Most likely, no one knew what had happened to Giorgio all those years ago.

Malpensa Airport was very busy. Michele dropped Stefano off as near to departures as possible, and with a cheery "ciao", drove away immediately, obviously delighted with the generous tip he'd been given in addition to his fare.

Cardiff was wet. It had drizzled incessantly since his arrival. His room was large but anonymous. He could have been anywhere in the world, but at least the bed was firm and comfortable, promising a good night's sleep. The drive from the airport to the city centre had taken more than an hour with so many hold-ups in the heavy after-work traffic. To his delight, he found early on in the journey that his driver was a rugby man, so although they moved at a snail's pace, the conversation never lapsed. They managed to communicate, overcoming the language barrier and strong accented English with plenty of laughter.

Booking into the hotel was easy, and there was even a bottle of bubbly waiting for him in his room. After throwing his jacket onto the bed and kicking off his shoes, he stood for some time, both hands in his pockets, just gazing out of the floor-to-ceiling window which looked out over the bay. Through the misty curtain of drizzle, he could just make out the form of a very small church, white with a black roof, its shape blurred by the raindrops on the glass. The whole scene in front of him was grim, to say the least, not helped by the murky, grey sea in the bay. Warm, welcoming Bardi felt a world away.

Not bothering to change out of his travel clothes, he put his shoes back on, found the light-blue cashmere sweater he had packed anticipating a drop in temperature then made his way down to the dining room. It was already very busy, and there was a lively atmosphere in the bar area. He chose a table where he could have a clear view of everyone else in the room. The service was excellent, so he decided to take a chance and order something he had never tried before. To his surprise, the beef cheek served with fondant potato and crisp vegetables was delicious, as was the more familiar crème caramel he chose for dessert. After such an excellent meal, he could almost forgive the insipid espresso that was served to finish off.

With a final perusal of his fellow diners, he headed back to his room, surprised to find that it was already past ten o'clock.

After a hot shower, he climbed into bed, not sure whether he would be warm enough during the night. At home, he slept naked, but when travelling, he relented and wore a pair of pyjama bottoms. He checked his emails, went over again in his mind his timeline for the following day, then flicked through some of the tourist information booklets provided by the hotel. When he realised that none of the information he was reading was actually registering, he switched off the lights, slid down under the thin duvet, and closed his eyes.

He slept surprisingly well—warm and comfortable. The large hotel was silent when he woke up at six thirty to pale sunlight. The brochure he had given up reading the night before lay open on the bedside table, so instead of getting up straight away as he usually did, he looked again at the picture in the brochure of the small white church he'd had difficulty seeing from his window the night before. The description was brief and told him very little, so he got out of bed, walked over to the window and took a longer clearer look at the little building across the water. In total contrast to the rain the day before, the sky was a clear blue, and the surface of the water in the bay rippled gently. The sun itself had not yet made an appearance, but the morning was bright, with the promise of a fine day ahead.

Stefano picked up his tablet and got back into bed. He googled "Norwegian Church Cardiff" and was instantly rewarded with all the information he wanted. The little church had been built in 1868, initially, to serve the religious needs of Norwegian sailors and expatriates but eventually opened to all sailors, offering food and shelter. The mission closed in 1972, but with the redevelopment of Cardiff Bay in the 1980s, funding was made available, and after lying derelict and vandalised, the church had been reconsecrated in 1992. The name Roald Dahl jumped out at him from the page. Years before, Stefano had read and enjoyed so many of his books: Danny, Il Campione del Mondo, Gli Sporcelli and Il Grande Ascensore di Cristallo amongst others. However, his favourite had been La Fabbrica di Cioccolato. He had no idea that the author had been born in Cardiff and that the Roald Dahl Plass was just a stone's throw away from the hotel.

Stefano sighed deeply and closed his tablet. So often on his fact-finding travels he came across places and buildings he wanted to visit and explore, just to satisfy his own curiosity and thirst for knowledge, but he was being paid to work, and although he told himself he would return in his own time, he knew he probably never would.

It was gone seven-thirty when he walked through the restaurant and out into the bright, warm conservatory of the hotel overlooking the bay, which he now knew had a fascinating history. There was so much food to choose from for breakfast, both hot and cold. Everything looked fresh and enticing. A young waiter showed him to his table, perfectly positioned to take full advantage of the view on such a beautiful morning. He was told where he could find cereals, fresh fruit and yoghurts. All the hot food was available down the right-hand side of the dining room, while the continental meats and cheeses were on the left. Breads and pastries were on the long table down the centre of the room. He could help himself to cold and hot drinks and, if there was anything else he needed, he only had to ask one of the staff on duty.

'Enjoy your breakfast, sir,' the young waiter nodded as he walked away.

Stefano sat down and smiled to himself. On previous visits to England, he could not remember such pleasant service, and he wondered if there really was a difference between English and Welsh hospitality, or if maybe, he had just struck lucky this time.

It was nearly nine o'clock when he eventually left the hotel. Although the cooked breakfasts looked inviting, he had stuck to his usual yoghurt, sweet croissant, and two cups of strong, black coffee. Back in his room, he had gone over yet again the da Calvi information and the advice he had been given in Bardi. He checked up on the location of his next port of call in Cardiff, then went down to settle his bill. There was no problem leaving his small case to be collected later.

It really was a beautiful day, and for a few quiet moments he just stood outside the glass doors of the hotel and lifted his face up to the sunshine. It would be an hour later at home, and this same sun would be beating down on the *piazza* outside his apartment. But, for once, he did not feel homesick. In fact, he felt quite energised and full of enthusiasm for the next part of his quest.

Stefano was not a fan of city walking. He was not a fan of cities—full stop. His route from the hotel to the Metropolitan Cathedral of St David took him through parts of the city's urban sprawl. After booking out of his room, he found it easy to leave most of his belongings safely locked away in a small storeroom behind the reception area. His laptop and tablet he kept with him in his shoulder bag.

Less than five minutes from the hotel, he stopped, took off his jacket, stashed his tie into one of the pockets then carried on walking, his jacket over his arm. He could feel the heat rising from the pavement. It was so unexpected. The streets were busy. The traffic constant. On Roald Dahl Plass, Stefano passed the statue of Ivor Novello, a famous Welsh songwriter he had never heard of and decided to walk along Bute Street, which, after ten minutes, seemed to be never-ending.

To the left were houses with neat gardens, many of them displaying early blossoming roses. There were numerous small supermarkets, mainly Asian and Polish. He passed more than one Halal butcher and another selling kosher meat next to the Roman Catholic Church of St Mary advertising Sunday Mass at eleven. He passed women in burkhas, women in vividly coloured saris and youngsters dressed in a variety of summer clothes, but mainly the "uniform" of blue denim jeans and T-shirt.

Across the very busy street ran the local railway line mostly hidden by a high stone wall and a row of trees. Although the route recommended on his tablet said it would take him nineteen minutes to get to the cathedral, he wanted to take the long way around to see a little bit more of the city. Eventually he came to the Hayes, a small commercial centre, bemused at the number of Italian restaurants dotted around the square, all of them busy with customers sitting outside in the sunshine. Walking on, he turned right into Hills Street, then made his way through to Charles Street, where he turned left. If he had not used Google Street View the night before, he would have passed the nondescript building that housed the Metropolitan Cathedral. Although the porch was open, he hesitated for a moment. The doors to the cathedral itself were firmly closed. The place looked deserted. He walked up the few steps into the porch where notices informed him that the Sacred Liturgy did not start until ten-thirty. He knew that he would wait. He had come this far, and there was a fair chance he would get the opportunity to speak to one of the clergy, someone in the congregation, or maybe even the priest himself. Just on the off-chance, he tried the door. Surprisingly, it opened easily, so he walked into the cool interior of the cathedral.

He spotted immediately what he had come to see. It only took a few seconds for his eyes to adjust to the gloom inside after the bright sunshine outside.

The *Arandora Star* memorial plaque was up on the wall to his right. He had found out that the design had been a joint effort by skilled artisans Susanna Ciccotti and Ieuan Rees, with the terracotta Virgin resting on a slab of beautiful Welsh slate, cradling the sinking ship in her arms. The plaque was accompanied by a list of victims. Stefano saw at a glance that the da Calvi name was missing, but checked more closely anyway, moving from the Ds of d'Ambrosio, d'Inverno and da Prato, to the Cs of Callegari and Camillo. There was no da Calvi in either list.

He turned away from the wall and looked around at the rest of the cathedral. As a former altar boy, he was more than familiar with the smell—a blend of candle grease, incense, furniture polish, dust and damp. He welcomed the peace and quiet, and although his journey had been a wasted one in terms of results, he was grateful for the calm and coolness inside the building. He sat down on the nearest chair for a few moments, closed his eyes and took some deep breaths before moving on. The street outside the cathedral was very quiet, so he took a few minutes to stand on the pavement considering what to do next.

'Excuse me.' An elderly man stood in the doorway of the cathedral, arm in arm with a smartly dressed lady of a similar age. Stefano recognised them as a couple who had been sitting halfway down the nave, heads bent in quiet contemplation.

'We saw you looking at our memorial and thought you might like to know more,' the man went on. He had a slight but unmistakable Italian accent which, for some reason, made Stefano's spirits rise.

'I am Leonardo Colla, Leo to my friends, and this is my wife, Paola. We have lived in the city for more than fifty years.'

Stefano shook hands and introduced himself before explaining briefly why he was there. To his surprise, Leo Colla clapped his hands and, with a wide smile, told Stefano that he and Paola had been good friends with Giuseppe da Calvi. The small *ristorante* owned by Giuseppe had been a regular meeting place for the small Italian community that lived in that part of the city.

'Do you have time to join us for a coffee?' Leo asked tentatively. 'We usually have one this time of the morning. There's a decent café not too far away from here. We can tell you more about our friend Giuseppe and of course, his wife, Maria.'

Stefano couldn't believe his luck. He accepted the invitation without hesitating and soon found himself in the most delightful Italian café, which made him feel very much at home. He paid for three coffees and a selection of pastries before sitting down to hear what Leo and Paola had to tell him.

'We came here a few years after the war, so we missed all the internment problems faced by Italians years earlier,' Leo began, leaving his espresso untouched. 'I had a job in the steelworks, and Paola did some cleaning in the local primary school.'

'We had to learn the language very quickly,' Paola took up their story. 'I had been a teacher in Italy, but Leo had found it impossible to find work, so we came here.'

'The situation was different for Giuseppe. He had farm work at home, and Maria had a decent job in the bank, but Giuseppe was desperate to find his brother. He searched everywhere and met up with so many other Italians who might have come across Giorgio but without luck. Anything could have happened to him.' Leo paused, gulping down his espresso in two mouthfuls.

'Giuseppe had it in his head that Giorgio had been interned and had been on the fateful voyage of the *Arandora Star*, and although Giuseppe and Maria settled here in the city, they always felt that somehow, they had failed. But they never gave up looking.' Leo shook his head. 'They even went up to the islands in the north of Scotland to see if Giorgio's body had been washed ashore and buried up there in one of the remote village cemeteries, but yet again, they came back more disappointed than ever.'

'The sad thing is,' Paola took up the story, 'that in those days there was no internet, no mobile phones and no social media. Google didn't exist, so a few years back, just to satisfy our own curiosity, we asked our son Riccardo to do some research for us, and within minutes, he had a result. We couldn't believe it!'

'On the screen in front of us,' Leo said excitedly, 'there was the passenger list. We couldn't believe it,' he repeated. 'And there it was. The name jumped off the page, I remember it well—*da Calvi Giorgio—Internee*. The name was slotted between d'Inverno Francesco and da Prato Silvio. Our Giuseppe had been right, but to our knowledge, his body has never been found.'

Silence fell over the table. Stefano sipped his cooled espresso while Paola just fiddled with her cup and saucer. Leo stared straight ahead.

'We think Giuseppe and Maria would have returned to Italy much sooner if it hadn't been for Maria Cristina,' Leo said quietly.

Stefano sat up straighter in his chair. This was a new name to him and could be the link he was looking for.

'Who was Maria Cristina?' he asked.

'Their beautiful daughter,' Paola replied with a broad smile. 'They only had the one child, and she was the light of their life. Not only beautiful but a lovely, clever girl. They were so proud of her.'

'What happened to her?' Stefano asked casually, not wanting to show how excited he was about this new discovery. A fact to him, a living person to his companions.

'She married a Welsh farmer,' Leo laughed. 'Not exactly the boy from a nice Italian family Giuseppe and Maria had hoped for. But it was clear to everybody from the start that David and Maria Cristina were perfect for each other. Giuseppe and Maria were very happy.'

Stefano rubbed the small sugar sachet between his thumb and forefinger and had to try hard not to pressurise the old couple into giving him more details.

'So, Giuseppe no longer lives here in Cardiff?' he enquired, sitting back in his chair.

'Oh, no! About a year after Maria Cristina died, they sold up and went back to Italy for good. They had already taken her back some months before.'

'But she must have been very young,' Stefano said, after doing a swift calculation in his head.

'Still in her twenties,' Paola said sadly. 'She had cancer. It was so very sad for everyone. The little one not much more than a baby.'

'The little one?' Stefano asked incredulously.

'Oh, yes. Giuseppe and Maria had a little granddaughter, but after a lot of soul-searching and family discussions, it was agreed that it would be best for her to be brought up by her father on the farm.'

'You don't happen to know where, by any chance? This could be really important in my search.'

Leo and Paola looked at each other, but Stefano could see doubt in their eyes. After all, he was a complete stranger.

'We know the father's name,' Leo finally conceded, 'but that's all.'

'No, it isn't,' Paola corrected him. I still have the wedding invitation at home in my collection. I'm sure there will be more details, maybe even an address on it.'

'I know how to scan and use email,' Leo said proudly. 'My son taught me. I could send a copy of the invitation through to you if you think it would help.'

'I have no doubt it will be invaluable, Leo. *Grazie mille.* I can't thank you enough.'

'It will be my first job when I get home,' Leo said.

Stefano wrote out his own email address on a clean *serviette* and asked Leo for his contact details, just to be on the safe side.

'I hope we have helped you. Giuseppe was a decent man. I'm sorry I can't tell you more about what happened to him after he returned to Italy. I recall that he did not intend to return to the family home. Too many painful memories, he said. Perhaps, they went back to Maria's family, but I really can't say.'

As they shook hands outside the café, Stefano thanked them profusely once again and said he looked forward to receiving the email which he hoped would move his investigation forward. He also promised to let them know the outcome of his search.

Stefano watched the old couple slowly walk away from him, arms entwined, before he turned in the opposite direction to retrace his steps to the hotel. He couldn't believe his extraordinary luck to be in the right place at precisely the same time as Leo and Paola and that, of all the people in Cardiff, they just happened to have known Giuseppe da Calvi. The meeting certainly made him reassess his belief in the existence of serendipity.

As soon as Stefano was back in his room, he called Seb and brought him up to date.

'Do you want me to stay and follow up on the information from Leo when it comes through? I'm sure it will arrive later today.'

'No, I don't think so, Stef. We should be able to get the details online. Check out and come home. We can talk things through in the office tomorrow. Good work again. What would we do without you?'

'If you've got thirty seconds to spare, I'll tell you!'

'*A domani,* Stef.'

'Yes. See you tomorrow, Seb. Late morning.'

Although his chance encounter brought him great satisfaction, for some reason, Stefano felt disappointed. He had hoped to see more of the city and even have lunch in one of its many Italian restaurants. Failing that, he felt he was being taken away from a job that was just coming to its natural conclusion. But Seb was the boss, so he checked out just before midday and took a taxi back to the airport.

His flight landed on time at Milan Malpensa, and after a very easy train journey south fortified by numerous cups of espresso, he arrived at his apartment, still feeling subdued and deflated. The rooms felt airless and stuffy, so he opened all the windows and shutters to let in what was left of the evening light. After unpacking his things and taking a shower, he settled in to put all his findings on the da Calvi case into chronological order, then saved everything into one, comprehensive document. Like Seb, he felt that there was just one more piece of the jigsaw to put into place, and that depended on the information in Leo's email.

That information arrived two days later. The old couple's son in Wales had found the person who he believed to be Giuseppe da Calvi's granddaughter. Further research into electoral rolls had proved him to be correct. Stefano let Seb know immediately, and a letter to the lady in question had been drafted and posted within the hour. This was an issue, Seb told him, that required a more traditional rather than hi-tech communication method. All they had to do was wait for the lady's response.

Chapter 11
Seb

Seb knew absolutely nothing about Cristina Jenkins. Just a name on a page. It had taken months of painstaking research to track her down and, even then, he had only come up with a possible address. He hadn't recognised the name of the place, so he had checked it out on the internet. The village she came from was on the west coast of Wales. The shoreline and cliffs looked natural and unspoilt—a beautiful place. Immediately, and inexplicably, he imagined Miss Jenkins to be a middle-aged lady who probably walked her dog along the beach near her home twice a day. Later, the reality would come as quite a shock!

Her response to his letter had been brief and to the point. She had no real idea what he wanted to speak to her about, but as his letter had aroused her curiosity, she could arrange to travel to Italy and be at his office at eleven o'clock on 4th August. If this was not convenient, would he be kind enough to let her know as soon as possible?

The evening before his appointment with Miss Jenkins, he went through once again the documents his grandfather had given him to make sure he had all the necessary information at his fingertips. For some unknown reason, he felt even then that he needed to make a good first impression. The information itself was sparse, but he found it intriguing, quite different from his usual work.

Ennio da Calvi, the old man who had lived alone in his hillside farmhouse, had passed away more than a year earlier. His body had been found, by chance, by an electrical engineer from ENEL, who had called at the farmhouse to check on the power cables after an electric storm had swept through the area during the night. Ennio had left a will, a very comprehensive, precise will, drawn up and signed by none other than Sebastiano Luce, his grandfather, and witnessed even more surprisingly by Marina, his grandfather's housekeeper. Two months after that meeting, Ennio had died and was buried in the cemetery at the far end of the village.

Most of the locals had turned out to witness what they all believed to be the funeral of the last of the da Calvi family. It appeared, however, that from the conversation his grandfather had had with Ennio before his death, the old da Calvi believed that there was another member of the family out there somewhere, so Sebastiano had decided to take it upon himself to mount a search for a possible descendant before finally declaring the case closed. The thought of the state benefitting from Ennio's will only added to his determination to leave no stone unturned.

The difficult task of tracking down Ennio's sole beneficiary, to his surprise, had landed on *his* desk, his grandfather claiming that he was the perfect person for the job. No explanation why, just the old man's belief that his grandson would not give up until every avenue had been explored. As usual, his grandfather was right.

He started with his grandfather but decided to keep his latest findings to himself for the time being just in case Miss Jenkins turned out to be a false lead. Was there more information Sebastiano could tell him about the da Calvi family?

'I could tell you so many stories,' Sebastiano said to Seb one evening in late spring. It had been a beautiful sunny day, perfect for sitting out on the terrace with a good book and an even better glass of *Conero Rosso*. The sudden early evening chill had eventually driven Sebastiano inside, and now, while he waited for Marina to serve the evening meal, he sat opposite his grandson, back straight, his palms resting on his thighs.

'But anecdotes take so long,' he went on, 'so I'll just give you the bare bones for now to get you started.' The old man leant forward and took a sip of wine, replacing the glass slowly onto the small, wooden, round table beside his chair.

'The da Calvi family,' he began. 'There was something a bit special about them. I can't quite put my finger on it, but there was an aura around each and every one of them. Ernesto, the head of the family, was big and strong, a fine role model for his four sons. Their house was always full of people, or at least that was how it seemed to me. There was always a welcome, and I know that apart from playing in the fields and in the woods down by the stream, one of the main reasons for us boys to go to the da Calvi house was to see Elena, the mother. Don't look so surprised. I was a teenage boy, and she was incredible. Even now, I can see her beautiful face, her huge, soft brown eyes, the mass of wavy hair and her fabulous figure in a simple, floral cotton dress. If I close my eyes, I can hear her voice, softly Italian but with a peculiar accent.'

He stopped speaking, his mind seemingly back in his youth reliving the moment, recalling how much in love he had been with a woman more than twice his age.

'It wasn't until much later,' he suddenly went on, opening his eyes and reaching again for his glass, 'that I learned she was, in fact, Greek, and not Italian at all. She treated us all in the same way she treated her own boys, and now, looking back, she must have found us so amusing, with our puppy-eyed gazes and enthusiastic offers of help to fetch and carry for her. Anyway, as I said, there were four sons. You know a little about Ennio, the only one who stayed on the farm, but to find your beneficiary, you'll have to track the movements of the others. I can tell you about Andrea, the eldest, but you will have to deal with Giorgio and Giuseppe yourself.'

'I know that Andrea went north to join Mussolini's forces, and I shall tell you more about him some other time. Giorgio followed him, but I understand that at some point on the journey he changed his mind and went to England. Much later, Giuseppe went to search for him to give Elena some peace of mind, but I don't think it worked out as they had all hoped. Giuseppe stayed in England for quite some time, but what he did there, I have no idea. I know that the da Calvi sons are all dead now, but you will have to find out if, somewhere along the way, any of them had a family.'

'In the will, Ennio just cites his brother's family. He couldn't remember which brother. He got more and more confused and angry with himself in our meeting about the will. He became so distressed that I promised to sort it all out for him when the time came. He was happy with that. He trusted me to do the right thing, and now I'm trusting you. Just one other detail which might help your search. I do know that Giuseppe married a girl who lived in the village, although I have a vague memory that she wasn't a local girl. She worked in the post office, or it might have been the bank, just after the war. If I remember correctly, her name was Maria Leone, but you'll have to check that yourself. Come back to me at any time if you think I might be able to help. I'd take great pleasure in knowing that someone, somewhere, can claim a link to the da Calvis. It is the least I can do for Elena.'

Armed with the scant information provided by his grandfather, Seb had set to work. He started by researching the birth, marriage and death certificates stored in the offices of the *Comune* in the regional capital. He found the marriage certificate for Ernesto and Elena and arranged for Stefano to travel to Greece to pick up family connections there based on the signatures of the witnesses to the marriage. To his surprise, he found that Ernesto and Elena had actually had six children, but also found the death certificates of the two boys, twins—Guido and Claudio—who had lived for less than three weeks. They had been the firstborn, so the arrival of Andrea exactly a year later must have been a time of great celebration and went some way to explain why he had been so adored.

Seb eventually found the death certificates for Giuseppe and Maria da Calvi, but nothing for their daughter, or Andrea, or Giorgio. Within two weeks, he received a full report from Greece. There was no one left in Elena's family. A distant great-nephew had been killed in a motorcycle accident more than twenty years earlier. He had no wife or children, so the Leftakis family had come to the end of the line.

Part Three
(West Wales, Present Day)

Chapter 12
Cristi

'I love you, Miss Jenkins.'

'What a lovely thing to say, Katie. Look! Mummy's at the gate. Go and show her your beautiful painting.'

Cristi Jenkins stood and watched as the last few stragglers made their way to the school gates. Most of them were waving their trophy artwork, eager to show what they'd done during the afternoon. Others just struggled with their book bags, happy to be going home at the end of a long day.

As the last of the little ones left the bottom playground, and the high-pitched sound of children's voices faded away, Cristi closed the wrought iron gates behind them and turned back towards the school. She looked up at the old building. The whole place was so familiar. She had been a pupil here herself twenty-five years before, and very little had changed, at least on the outside of the building. She wandered slowly back up the slope of the yard towards the steps.

Glancing up again, she could see the three arched entrances. All those years ago, the infants would line up together, and the boys and girls of the junior school would form separate lines at the bottom of the steps. When the teacher on duty decided the children were calm enough and ready to go into the building, at her signal, they would walk up the steps, then filter off from their line. The infants went in through the doorway that had *Babanod*—babies—carved in stone above the entrance. The junior boys went in through the door marked *Bechgyn*, and the junior girls entered beneath the carved *Merched*. These days, the children lined up with their class, boys and girls together.

When Cristi had attended the school, the boys had played in one playground and the girls in another. Now, everyone played together in one large area, the dividing wall demolished years ago. She loved the school. Situated high up on the hillside about a mile above the village, you could look down towards the calm waters of the bay. Built in 1904, it had served all the local children for well over a hundred years. Inside, the hall and classrooms were cool, with high windows which needed long poles with a hook on the end to open them. On her way to the staffroom, Cristi glanced into the cloakroom to check that no belongings had been left behind. The children still hung their coats on the original, heavy iron S-shaped hooks, and the cloakroom walls still bore dark green Victorian tiles.

The washbasins at the far end of the cloakroom were low and small, and although these days the children brought in their own plastic water bottles, Cristi remembered her father telling her that, in his day at break time, the children drank warm milk from small bottles and water from tin mugs, which were left at the basins for everyone to share. *No health and safety worries in those days,* Cristi thought, a wry smile on her lips as she thought of the detailed risk assessment forms she'd had to fill in that morning.

The staffroom was at the opposite end of the hall, which was flanked by three good-sized classrooms on either side. Cristi always found the school quite magical when it was empty and quiet, and in her mind's eye she could see and hear all the children who had worked and played in the building over the years, children in Victorian clothes sitting at heavy wooden desks, writing on slates with chalk, children being educated through two world wars when times were hard, then her own school days, coming to terms with the death of her young mother and coping with a father, so deep in grief, he had little time for his small daughter.

Cristi shook her head to clear the memories that threatened to upset her yet again. She walked purposefully through the hall, sunlight from the high windows casting beams across the beautiful, highly polished wooden floor. Dust motes danced in front of her as she made her way to the open door of the staffroom.

'All clear, then?' Julie Thomas asked, not bothering to look up from making a cup of tea.

'Just about.' Cristi replied. 'Only a week to go to freedom, and after these last few days, I can't wait.'

'I bet you the two of them will be back, probably next Wednesday, just in time to make sure they get paid for the holidays and don't have to answer too many questions about end of term illnesses.'

Cristi knew exactly who Julie was talking about.

'Do you really think they're skiving?' Cristi asked, shifting some ring binders to one side so that she could sit down. The staffroom looked as though a bomb had hit it. They had all agreed in the last staff meeting to have a really good clean out and tidy up. Six members of staff had started the work, now they were down to three, and one of those was heavily pregnant.

Julie brought over two mugs, gave one to Cristi, then sank down into the chair on the other side of the cluttered coffee table.

'For God's sake, look at this place. Papers, folders, brochures, documents everywhere. How the hell are we, and by we, I mean you and little ol' me—how are we going to clear everything? I suggest that every single little thing belonging to those two idle gits just gets put into a black bin liner and left for them to sort out.'

'Something tells me you're a bit cheesed off. Don't beat about the bush, just come straight out with it,' Cristi chipped in, smiling.

'Aw, c'mon, Cris. They must think we're two mugs. No way have they both got flu at this time of the year, and I'm more than cheesed off, I'm bloody furious!'

For once, Cristi kept quiet. Usually, it was quite easy to jolly Julie along. She was a super teacher, a hard worker with a great sense of humour, and nothing was ever too much trouble for her, especially where the children were concerned. She spoke Welsh fluently, played the guitar and could sing beautifully. Needless to say, she was a great hit with the children, and the feeling was mutual, and it showed. The "absence" of two of the other teachers, however, at such a busy time of the year, had really got to her and she needed to let off steam.

'If they weren't carrying on with each other, it might be more believable. I reckon they've gone off for a couple of days, even though we don't break up 'til next Friday, a cheap deal to somewhere warm and relaxing.'

'They wouldn't, would they?' Cristi gasped incredulously. Such an idea had never entered her head.

'Why not? What would you rather be doing, having a bit of nooky in the sun or cleaning up the mess in this staffroom?' Julie raised her hands to shoulder level, palms upwards like weighing scales. 'Sex or staffroom? Staffroom or sex? Mm…now, which one will it be?' She looked from one hand to the other, weighing up each option. 'Is your tea OK?' she asked, changing the subject abruptly. 'Any plans for the holidays?'

Cristi shook her head resignedly. 'It's Dad's and Gillian's silver wedding anniversary a week on Saturday. They're going on a cruise, leaving on Monday, so family and friends are gathering for a bit of a "do" on Sunday, unfortunately.'

'Don't tell me jolly Gillian is catering?' Julie asked with over-exaggerated surprise.

'Don't be silly! We're all going to the Whitebay. Dad's splashing out on one of their special carveries for everyone. At least, I'll be able to keep a low profile for the afternoon.'

'The Whitebay carvery is good, especially the puds. I'd take a doggy bag if I were you. You could stock up for the following few days.'

'You would,' Cristi laughed. 'Not really me. I'm a good girl, I am.'

'Exactly, so why doesn't Gillian like you?' Julie asked, not for the first time.

'I've told you before. She looks at me and sees my mother. It can't be pleasant for her having a constant reminder of her husband's first wife.'

'But your mum's been dead for over twenty years. Surely that's long enough for her to feel some security with your father, not to mention your two brothers.'

'Half-brothers,' Cristi corrected. My mother was special, different, a foreigner. Even though they've been together a long time, I think Gillian still believes she comes second best. Sad really, because she's devoted to my dad.'

'I wouldn't mind going on a cruise, or anywhere for that matter,' Julie said, wistfully, rolling her mug between her palms.

'I thought you'd booked to go to Majorca for a week?'

'So did I, until Dave confessed he'd left it too late to book his time off work. All the others have got children, so they get in early to book their leave for the school hols.'

'Mm...,' Cristi muttered doubtfully. Julie's sometime-to-be husband wasn't really Cristi's cup of tea. She'd known Dave Rhodes at school and was always suspicious of his motives. He worked for a local firm of electricians, but Cristi wouldn't want him in her house. He'd moved in with Julie the Christmas before last, and since then he'd let her down too many times. Just little things. Not able to collect her from school when her car was being serviced—an emergency job had come up. Not coming to the staff Christmas meal—sore throat, needed to stay in bed. Forgetting her birthday—so busy doing overtime so they could afford a holiday. Cristi liked Julie. They worked well together. Julie had talent, whereas Cristi had a certain something the children adored. She didn't know exactly what it was. Even the well-known little "naughties" behaved well for Miss Jenkins, horrified if they upset her in any way.

'Look, I'm not going away anywhere. I know it's not much compensation for Majorca, but we could have a couple of days out. What d'you reckon?'

Julie seemed to brighten up immediately.

'You're on. You'd be better company than Dave, anyway. All he wants to do is lie in the sun, flashing his tattoos. To be honest, Cris, I reckon I'd be better off living on my own again, like you. No one to answer to, no disappointments and no compromising.'

Julie got up swiftly and walked over to the sink to rinse her mug.

'I can't be bothered clearing any of this stuff up tonight. Come on, give me your cup. Let's go.'

'I don't even know what to wear to this "do" on Sunday.'

'Have you bought them a presie?' Julie asked.

'Yes, but I bet Gillian won't like it. I asked Cleo Rees to do four small watercolours of the farmhouse in the different seasons. They're really beautiful. I could do with keeping them for myself.'

'Her paintings don't come cheap. Anyway, your father will love them; that's the important thing to remember.'

'You're right as usual,' Cristi said, picking up her briefcase from the floor and slinging her bag over her shoulder. 'Switch off the computer Julie, while I do mine in the classroom.'

Cristi walked to her room to the accompaniment of the hum of the buffing machine raising the shine on the hall floor. Her classroom was peaceful and tidy. All the little chairs had been put upside down on the tables ready for the cleaners to sweep the floor. The monitors for the week had tidied up the books on the library shelves and had cleaned the whiteboard. *This time next week*, she thought, *I'll be free until September*, but the thought was followed swiftly by another— *freedom on my own isn't exactly going to be a whole lot of fun and no different from previous years.*

She said goodbye to Julie just outside the main gate and watched as her friend made her way down the hill towards the village before turning away to follow the narrow footpath, which ran between some old garages and the bottom wall of the school field. Cow parsley, foxgloves, cornflowers and late buttercups in the verges basked in the sunshine. The end of the stony pathway opened out onto the main arterial road running through the council housing estate, which stretched further up the hill to her right, but Cristi turned left and walked past the corner shop towards a row of four small cottages set back from the main road.

The children who went to the primary school lived mainly in one of three areas of the village. There were the two-up, two-down houses which had been built at the beginning of the twentieth century for the families of the men who worked in the harbour. There was another group of larger houses nearer the centre of the village, built for the railway workers and their families, and then there were the council houses.

Most of the children walked to school from the 1940s council estate, separated from the school by a large playing field. All the houses were clean and tidy, with well-kept gardens. Old-fashioned pride in the home and neighbourly kindnesses were still very much alive. Cristi had been brought up on the northern edge of the estate. Her parents' farm was tucked away behind a large copse about half a mile away from the last row of houses. When she moved out to live on her own, she bought an end-of-terrace cottage right on the south side of the estate with a view of the sea from her bedroom window. It took her fifteen minutes to walk to the farm and five minutes to walk to school. Dad and Gillian had to drive past her little cottage to get to the village or to the shops in the neighbouring town. Her father popped in briefly at least once a week. Gillian had been over her threshold only once in eight years.

Cristi's cottage was small and cosy. The garden, at first sight, looked overgrown, but to the discerning eye it was a gardener's paradise. She had planted a variety of wild flowers which self-seeded and intermingled naturally with cottage garden varieties. The stone path was lined on each side with lavender which brushed against her legs as she walked past. The blues and pinks of the lupins blended well with the richer blues of the delphiniums. A profusion of oriental poppies, cornflowers and lilyturf gave way to the densely flowered, yellow rambling rose that made its way up the wall beside the front door and crept along the low eaves above the bedroom window. If she was lucky and the weather was kind to her, the different flowers would all bloom at the same time and would last for most of the summer. A frisson of delight ran through Cristi each and every time she turned into her cottage, closed the gate behind her and walked up to her front door. Carved in Welsh into the old oak door itself was the one word, *Cartref*—home.

On the five-minute walk home from school, she had gone over her conversation with Julie again and again in her mind. A small part of her envied Julie having someone to go home to, and yet Julie seemed envious of *her* independence. Surely, there had to be something in between. And then there was Dad and Gillian. The relationship with her stepmother hadn't failed exactly, because from the outset, there had been no relationship. Gillian had never said anything, but by her looks and actions, she had made it clear that her priority was Cristi's father; the accompanying child was just part of the deal. Cristi had been fed, clothed and taken care of when she was ill, but any affection was sparse, coming from her father when he was not too tired from a long day on the farm, or when Gillian was out of the house. The arrival of two half-brothers only added to her father's new family commitments.

The cottage looked vibrant and welcoming, and in spite of her introspective thoughts, her heart lifted and she smiled contentedly as she pushed open the old, wrought iron gate, and walked up to her own front door. The slight, almost imperceptible scent of lavender reached her nostrils, and she noticed that, at last, the honeysuckle was starting to bloom. She unlocked and opened the door, pushing numerous envelopes and pieces of unsolicited mail further into the hallway. She left the door open behind her and walked into the sitting room, dropping her bag and briefcase on the old armchair as she passed through into the small kitchen. She helped herself to a tall glass of cold water from the tap before unlocking and opening wide the back door. Once the cottage was open to the fresh air, she finished her water, rinsed the glass then walked back to pick up her post.

Usual rubbish, she muttered out loud to herself. *Bin, bin, bin and bin.* Only three envelopes out of the pile appeared worth looking at. She put them on the stairs on her way up to take a shower and change out of her work clothes.

Everything about her home was small, which meant she either had to put things away and keep everything in order or be overwhelmed by clothes, papers and magazines. Her bedroom reflected her taste. She had painted the walls white with the merest hint of pink, which kept the room light beneath the heavy timbers of the original oak beams. Her bed linen was also white covered by a traditional Welsh woollen tapestry bedspread in white, pink and pale lilac bought from the local mill.

After showering, she put on a pair of khaki shorts and a white T-shirt, pulled her long, thick hair away from her neck, then twisted and fixed it into a knot on top of her head. Ahead of her lay the whole evening. She needed to put a wash on, wrap up the anniversary paintings and write the card to go with them. The weather forecast was good for the weekend, so she could leave the jobs that needed doing in the garden until the following day. More and more as she got older, she felt she was becoming entrenched in her ways, nearly thirty-one, unmarried, not even a relationship on the horizon and five whole weeks to fill. She already knew that on most days there would be nobody to speak to unless she made the effort to walk down to the village and, very soon, she would be so set in her ways that she definitely wouldn't want to share her life with anyone.

Too much time on your own, that's your trouble, she told herself as she put her clothes away, *and talking to yourself is not exactly an encouraging sign either.*

She picked up the envelopes from the bottom of the stairs and wandered out into the small back garden. She had bought a wooden bench in the garden centre end-of-season sale the year before, found a couple of squashy old cushions to soften the seat, and now spent a great deal of time sitting with her feet up, reading, during the long, summer evenings. She had managed to sit out only four times this year so far, the wood burner in her living room providing warmth rather than the rays of the absent evening sun.

As she sat down at one end of the bench, she glanced again at the envelopes in her hand. The first, she could tell, contained nothing more than her bank statement. Even after paying the mortgage and utility bills, she still managed to save a decent amount every month. Her initial pleasure in having substantial savings always gave way to despondency. *Let's face it*, she thought, staring at the balance in bold at the bottom of the sheet of paper in her hand, *I don't go anywhere, and I don't do anything, so the cash is bound to build up.*

She had already put away the maximum amount allowed in the Premium Bonds and also had an Investment Savings Account. The idea of travelling was always appealing, but she never did anything about it. She wasn't extravagant with clothes or shoes, yet Julie always maintained that even dressed in a sack, Cristi would look gorgeous. Glancing again at her bank balance, she told herself that the time had come to break out of the old routine and actually do something different. Just a few days more, and she will have completed eight years teaching at the same school. Life was easy—too easy. She had become complacent and staid without realising it. She hated the concept but knew that her body clock was ticking. At times like this, she could have done with having her mother nearby, her beautiful, vivacious *mamma* she hadn't had time to get to know.

Don't go down that road now, she told herself out loud, putting her statement to one side, and slitting open the second envelope. She pulled out a garishly patterned card, an invitation for "you and your partner" to attend the opening of a new Indian restaurant in the next small town four miles along the coast. God, not another one! There were already two other Indian restaurants, one Chinese, one Cantonese and two Italian, not to mention the fish and chip shops and all the pubs doing meals for a population of under five thousand. The opening night was at the end of September and, remembering her new resolve, decided there and then to make an effort and find someone to go with her. *Easier said than done,* a little thought whispered across her mind, but at least it would be a night out.

The third envelope looked and felt more official. She turned it over in her hands, noting the curious handwriting. Such envelopes usually had printed labels, but her name and address had been hand written. The Italian stamp made her pause, but she was unable to make out the lettering on the pale postmark. As far as she knew, she didn't know anyone in Italy, especially someone who would write to her officially. For some inexplicable reason, Cristi was reluctant to open the envelope, so she delayed the inevitable, went inside, and started to make herself something to eat.

She had her meal of salad and prawns sitting at the round, pine table that just fitted into the corner of her small kitchen. Recently, salad in many different guises had become her staple diet. Most evenings after school, she couldn't be bothered to cook for herself, so she had to decide between ready meals for one from the supermarket or her own "throw-together-in-two-minutes" salads. She told herself that for health reasons she'd opted for the latter, yet slowly but surely, the attraction and feelings of self-righteousness of perpetually eating fresh lettuce and salad vegetables were starting to wane, no matter how much variety she put on the plate.

From her seat at the table, she could still see the unopened envelope lying expectantly on top of the other papers on the bench. She decided to leave it there until later, until the sun had gone down, and she had settled in for the last part of the evening. She'd be able to concentrate better then.

She finished her uninspiring meal, failing to eat the last few green leaves lying abandoned on the sauce she'd rustled up from mayonnaise and tomato ketchup. Prawns weren't exactly her favourite, but they made a change from cold meat. She scraped the leftover bits into the bin, washed her plate, water glass, knife and fork and put away the salt, pepper and place mats. She liked to have the table clear apart from a small jar of sweet peas one of the children had given her at the end of the previous week.

She hummed along to the music on Radio Two while she pottered about, and then checked the "to do" list stuck onto the fridge door by a magnet which reminded her that *A balanced diet is a chocolate in each hand*. She enjoyed ticking things off, and even her ticks were small, neat and precise. How could you ask children to take pride in their work if their teacher produced careless scribble? She often gave children the kind of work they could mark themselves, encouraging them to take care. She usually made her job list while eating breakfast before leaving for school and happily ticked off each job as she went through the day. Seeing most, if not all, the jobs ticked off, gave her a feeling of achievement before she went to bed.

Two hours later, not only had she dealt with the anniversary present and card but had pruned the roses, dead headed all the early flowering geraniums in the pots and window boxes and watered the baskets hanging from each upright fence post along the length of her back garden. She fed the tame blackbirds and solitary robin that appeared from nowhere as soon as she opened her back door. She avoided the letter astutely, even when she sat down again on the bench late into the evening. Two years earlier, she had planted some jasmine on either side of the back door, and in the warmth of the twilight, the musky perfume from the flowers threatened to overwhelm her, it was so intoxicating. Not a breath of wind disturbed the foliage around her, and the scent of summer flowers lingered on the night air. She sat perfectly still, her hands lightly clasped in her lap, closed her eyes, breathed in deeply and relaxed. Only birdsong disturbed the peace, the sweet notes of the blackbirds washing over her, feeling very much alone, but not lonely.

Eventually, when the backs of her bare arms started to feel chilly, she gathered up her papers and the two magazines she'd read from cover to cover and went indoors, reluctantly giving up on the evening. She locked the door behind her, and instead of putting on the main light, decided to switch on the table lamps which gave her small living room a warm, welcoming glow. The bookshelves in the two alcoves beside the fireplace housed her mini music centre as well as the many books which overflowed into low piles on the floor beside her armchair. She had read them all but never considered giving any of them away. She didn't even like lending her books to other people, so shied away from ever borrowing, preferring to use the local library or buy from the charity shop in town.

With all jobs for the day ticked off her list, she decided not to wait until breakfast, found a pencil and started to write out another one for the following day, quickly dismissing the thought that she was becoming list-obsessed. Finally, she left the rest of the post on the seat of her armchair, heated a mug of coffee in the microwave and settled back into the plump, comfortable cushions of the settee, tucking her legs under her, the mysterious letter in her hand.

She didn't tear open the envelope as she usually did but got up and found the silver letter opener Julie had given her for her last birthday. The letter inside was written in English, on the best quality paper. Cristi unfolded the single sheet, pressed it out flat on her thigh and began to read.

Chapter 13
David

Everyone in the village knew and admired David Jenkins, Cristi's father. He was a quiet, unassuming man, who got along with all the locals he had grown up with. He had broad shoulders and the healthy complexion of someone who spent a great deal of time out of doors. His fine, straight hair was the colour of wheat, much lighter now with many white strands. He had always loved working on the land and enjoyed the comfort of his own home. Left to his own devices, he would have preferred a small gathering of close family and friends with the minimum amount of fuss for their anniversary. Gillian, on the other hand, was far more conscious and concerned about how it would look to other people in the village if they didn't celebrate properly.

'Everyone knows it's our twenty-fifth this year, and they'll be expecting us to put on some sort of a "do",' she'd argued in the petulant voice that always irritated him.

'Shouldn't it be them putting on something for us?' David had replied, not for the first time feeling more and more anti his wife's suggestions. They had finished the usual Sunday roast and their two boys, still living at home, had gone out over the fields on their quad bikes.

'Those two should be off our hands and married by now,' he went on. 'You look after them too well. Why find a wife when your mam feeds you and does your washing and ironing?'

'Don't change the subject. I don't want us to look mean. Everyone we know has made some sort of effort for their anniversary. Staying married for twenty-five years these days is quite an achievement. Come on, David, don't be such a cheapskate. You go and book the Whitebay, and I'll take care of everything else.'

He didn't like the sound of "everything else", and as he watched his wife load the dishwasher, he realised that she was starting to look her age. Her straight, light brown hair was cut into a short bob, and as usual she wore a short-sleeved flowery blouse, navy slacks and a pair of sensible, flat leather sandals. Her style, if it could be called a style, hadn't changed in all the years he had known her, and that was considerably more than twenty-five. Gillian had pale brown eyes and a neat nose, made to look smaller by her wide mouth and full lips. She had always been slim, and her angular features only served to make her look older than she really was. He often felt pleased that both boys looked more like him, then felt guilty for his unkind thoughts. He liked Gillian. He liked Gillian a lot, but no more than that. No matter how hard he tried or how ashamed he felt, he could never find or summon up a stronger passion for the woman who had taken such good care of him for such a long time.

'I'll deal with it first thing after milking in the morning,' he suddenly acquiesced. It was the least he could do for the woman who was the mother of his two sons—*but not the mother of my daughter*, a little voice whispered in his head.

'It'll be fine, you know it will. You'll enjoy it when you get there. You always moan when we go out then you usually enjoy yourself more than me,' Gillian went on with more enthusiasm now that she'd got her own way. She closed the dishwasher door firmly and switched it on.

'This machine is still one of the best presents you ever gave me, same as the tumble dryer. Most women wouldn't see it like that, I suppose, but I do. Anything to save time.'

'It'll be a tool set next then,' David Jenkins quipped. 'You can start to save me a bit of time by fixing the steps of the barn.'

'Very funny,' Gillian said, her face flushed from the effort of bending down and stacking the dishes. Her eyes sparkled with excitement as she sat down again at the kitchen table opposite her husband. She had always had the knack of dismissing from her mind any difficulties or objections to her plans as soon as the opposition had given in.

'Now make sure you ask for the carving buffet, not the finger one, and tell them there'll be between forty and fifty guests. We'll confirm numbers nearer the date. Try hard for the twenty-second. That's the Saturday nearest the actual date.'

'Are you sure you wouldn't rather do it yourself? I'm bound to get something wrong,' David asked with more than a hint of hope in his voice.

'Don't be silly. You're the man of the house. I want people to see this as a joint effort, not just me organising everything and you just tagging along. You know how they talk around here, so you can do it, and I'll make a start on the invitations.'

He watched her get up from the table to fetch her notepad and a biro from the top drawer of the old Welsh dresser that dominated their kitchen. She returned to her chair, flicking open the small pad to the first clean page.

'I'll make a list, then you can have a look at it and make any changes you want, OK?'

He took a deep, silent breath and smiled inwardly. *Fat chance of that*, he thought.

'Just don't go mad on numbers,' he prompted. 'I'm going for a stroll up to the top field, see what those boys are doing.'

He didn't expect a response. As he left the kitchen, Gillian was intent on compiling her list of the locals she intended to impress in a few weeks' time.

Chapter 14
Gillian

She loved clean paper. How many times had she been told off in class for not filling a page right to the bottom line? She hated starting a new piece of work halfway down the page, and whenever possible, avoided writing on the left-hand page altogether. She loved the smell of paper, not just writing paper, but magazine pages and new books. Just as some people sniffed their food before eating, she would open a book or magazine and inhale deeply, eyes closed.

She knew her affinity with paper came from her early childhood as the only child of the local newsagent. Her arrival had been a great shock to Jack and Blanche James. They had always wanted children, but by the time they both reached their mid-forties, they'd all but accepted the fact that it wasn't meant to be. So, Blanche's pregnancy had been greeted with a mixture of joy, genuine fear and a certain amount of embarrassment. What would the locals think? Sex at their age didn't exactly fit in with their image and definitely not with the chapel mentality of the village!

In the end, it didn't really matter. Gillian arrived safely, and they doted on their new daughter. She had been precious, a little miracle, showered with love and attention, not only by her parents but by everyone who came into the shop where she spent every minute of the day. The shop itself was a focal point in the village. At the front was the usual outlet for newspapers, magazines, sweets and cigarettes. There was even a low shelf along one wall where children could buy sherbet flying saucers, liquorice laces, coconut mushrooms and an assortment of old-fashioned sweets you could pick and mix for a couple of pennies. At the back of the shop was the barber's salon, with a wide bay window which overlooked the railway line below and gave a magnificent view of the sheer cliffs of the coastline in the distance. The older men would gather here to chat and put the world to rights, even when they didn't want or need a haircut.

Gillian did well at school and had been encouraged to follow her aptitude and talent for art and design. She was the best in her class in maths and amazingly had been allowed to join the previously all-male technical drawing class when she had chosen her options for the GCE O level exams. Yet, as the year went on, she slowly came to realise that her future was going to be totally different from the one she envisaged, and quite different from that of her friends.

While they all made plans to go away to university or college, she found herself taking on more and more responsibility for the business. Although they were only in their early 60s, her mother was having difficulty standing on her feet all day, and her father had slowed down considerably without her even realising it. The business however, was, if anything, more successful than ever. With no other family, it would all be hers one day.

'Don't forget,' her father would say almost daily, 'all this is yours, Gill. You'll be a wealthy young woman when your mother and I are no longer here. Yes. A little goldmine we have here.'

There was no way she could turn her back on her parents' lifetime's work, so she put all her own hopes and dreams of becoming an architect out of her mind and concentrated all her energy into making the business an even greater success.

The page on the pad in front of her was pale cream, speckled with tiny, light-blue spots, and was still totally blank. She hadn't even put a title, although she'd had a pen in her hand for at least ten minutes. Gillian smoothed her hand across the pad. GUEST LIST she wrote at last in clear, bold letters at the top, desecrating the purity of the page. She paused again, resting her chin in her hand, her elbow on the table. *He hadn't been able to get out of here fast enough,* she thought.

As soon as the anniversary celebration had been mentioned, she'd watched his discomfort and withdrawal. Of course, he thought she didn't know, but she'd lived with the knowledge that she was second best for twenty-five years. She tolerated it and accepted it. She didn't have much choice in the matter. She had considered David Jenkins to be her ticket out of the solitary life that lay in store for her as the spinster lady who ran the paper shop. She'd been under no illusions whatsoever when she married him. He'd wanted someone to look after his daughter, and she'd wanted someone to be there to look after her once her parents died. Having the boys was a bonus, and she knew for certain that her predecessor, beautiful as she had undoubtedly been, had not had the time to get to know or win over the locals. Gillian James was David Jenkins's wife. The foreign girl all but forgotten. Well, almost.

When she eventually told her parents her plans to marry the local farmer, there had been no spontaneous words of congratulation, no smiles of delight, just a heavy silence.

'Of course, I'll still run the shop,' she'd reassured them, 'but I'll be living up at the farm.'

Her father had just nodded, but even now, at the back of her mind, she could still hear her mother saying flatly, 'Change your name but not the letter, change for ill and not for better,' before turning away and walking out of the room.

Gillian couldn't describe her marriage as "ill" exactly, but neither had it ever been fully "fit". David truly believed she was happy and always had been. He actually thought that having a nice home, two decent children, no money worries and the freedom to do as she pleased was all she could ever want. Not for one moment did he consider that all she actually needed, even craved for, was his affection and attention—spontaneous—not when she demanded them. Oh, he was kind, gentle and more than generous, but reserved and untouchable at the same time. Not cold exactly, but so very distant even when there was just the two of them in the same room.

Perhaps the forthcoming cruise would lighten the spirit and produce a little romance. The two of them far away from the farm, the village and…'*I won't hold my breath,*' she told herself out loud as she wrote the first name on her list. Cristi.

Chapter 15
David

David could feel the warmth of the wood under his forearms as he leaned his full weight on the old gate, his large hands clasped in front of him, fingers interlocked. The sun had been shining down ferociously since early morning. There wasn't a hint of cloud, just a warm gentle breeze which ruffled his greying, fair hair.

The heavy, five-barred gate was a favourite. He remembered how proud he felt helping his father and grandfather put it up over forty years ago. He knew it had been expensive even then, recalling his grandmother's voice as she told the men standing in her kitchen, 'You get what you pay for, and that field needs a good-quality gate.' As always, they had listened to her and bought the best. The old gate had outlived both his grandparents and his parents, and feeling the strength of it now under his arms and against his foot resting on the first bar, he reckoned it would definitely outlive him as well. Maybe even his boys.

He could see them both in the distance riding around on their quad bikes. Unlike him, they'd had the sense to put hats on to protect them from the heat of the sun, but he'd left the kitchen without thinking, just wanting to get out. Now, instead of enjoying the peace enveloping him, he felt annoyed with himself for being so hasty and stupid, but he also felt guilty for wanting to escape from Gillian with just a brief "see you later" as he left the kitchen.

He shook his head and tightened his lips, thinking again that he did indeed like Gillian. He was grateful to her. She'd looked after him, given him two fine sons and still kept an excellent home. She was a good cook, intelligent and was respected by everyone in the village who knew her. As far as he could tell, most people liked his wife, even if she was a bit overbearing at times. He knew all this, but it didn't make any difference. No matter how much he tried, he did not and could not love her. He would go through the motions of the silver wedding celebrations for her sake. She deserved it, but at times like this afternoon, he just had to get away, finding the company of his wife so overpowering he felt like screaming. Thank God for the open space of his fields and the infinite sea beyond.

His boys were no longer in sight. Neither of them had been brilliant at school, but both of them had done well enough and could have gone on to higher education. In some ways, he wished they had broken away from the village and spread their wings a bit more, but if he was truthful with himself, he had to admit to being overjoyed and proud when they decided to stay and work beside him on the farm, just as he had done with his father.

He'd enjoyed school, not because he was any good in lessons, but because he'd been a talented rugby player. Oh, yes! Mr Popular he'd been at school with the other boys and with the girls. He shook his head again and smiled at the memory. He hadn't bothered in the slightest with any of the girls. All he'd wanted to do was train twice a week after school then play a match on Saturday morning. Although he wasn't particularly tall, he was incredibly fit and strong from working on the farm. He could also sprint faster than all the other boys his age, so by the time he was fourteen, he was regularly selected to play for the first fifteen, and a year later, won his first county cap at scrum half.

Life had been good. He loved his life on the farm, kept up with his schoolwork and enjoyed his rugby more than anything. Only later did he realise how much his talent on the field had reflected on his father and grandfather, who both revelled in his success.

He glanced down. An orange ladybird was making her way along his arm, crawling slowly through the thick, sun-bleached hair towards his elbow. He didn't bother to flick her off, leaving her to find her own way. Instead, he pulled up the collar of his shirt to protect the nape of his neck from the sun. Just another ten minutes, then he'd wend his way back down to the house.

The year he was due to sit his A Levels, everything changed. He loved being in the sixth form at school. He was a prefect and House Captain, but had asked not to captain the rugby team. He knew he was probably the best player in the team but also knew he was no leader. He needed the freedom to play his own game without responsibilities. He'd gone back to school in high spirits for his final year after the long summer break. Very little had changed.

There they were, all the new little first formers of course, and a few new members of staff. Among them was the new Deputy Head. Everyone knew that they never appointed senior staff from within the school itself, so the new arrival was a stranger to everyone. Edwin Thomas. David smiled at the very thought of the stern but wonderful Mr Thomas. He came from the Rhondda Valley, taught maths, but most importantly of all, he was a rugby fanatic who had actually met members of the Welsh international team.

Looking back, David suspected that Mr Thomas quickly got to know all the members of the school teams better than the rest of the staff who'd been there for years. He came to all the training sessions, never shouted instructions, just had a quiet word on the touchline with any player he thought could do with the benefit of a bit of extra advice. David had got on with Mr Thomas like a house on fire, and the hero worship increased when every member of the first fifteen and the reserves was given a letter to take home to parents a few weeks before the rugby international matches were due to start.

Although he was a regular member of the team and had been for almost four seasons, he had never had to stay away from home overnight. Even when he played for the county, he always returned home, arriving back at the farm at two or three o'clock in the morning. He hadn't been on any tours despite being invited to go with the local club every Easter, usually down to Devon and Cornwall, but also to France and Ireland. He always gave his work on the farm as an excuse, but if he was really honest, he just didn't want to leave home.

Although he loved playing, he wasn't too keen on the drinking culture that went with the local club scene. He even felt quite nervous when he saw some of his team-mates doing stupid, dangerous things after having one too many in town on a Saturday night. So, when he handed the letter over to his father to read, he wasn't surprised to see raised eyebrows and the inevitable question.

'You really want to go on this?' his father asked, waving the sheet of paper in front of him.

'Yes, I do this time, Dad. Edwin Thomas is in charge, and it's a school thing, so I reckon it'll be a good couple of days. Can I go?'

'Good God, boy, you're nearly eighteen years old. You don't have to ask permission.'

'Yes, I do, Dad,' he persisted. 'You have to sign the slip for me to take in tomorrow.'

He could still hear his father's lilting Welsh voice and see him in his mind's eye, sitting in the old, well-worn armchair in his usual checked shirt under a grey pullover, his work trousers showing signs of wear and tear. Dad always wore thick, grey woollen socks, not bothering to put on his slippers in his own house.

'So, let's get this straight,' his father went on, holding the letter at arm's length, still too proud to admit he needed glasses. 'You're going to play a team from the Valleys, is that right?'

'Mr Thomas came to us from a big "comp" in the Rhondda, so he's arranged for us to play the first fifteen from his last school. We travel up on Friday afternoon and have a meal and some sort of disco thing at the school in the evening. We stay with our opposite number overnight then play against them on Saturday morning. The school will give us lunch, then we go in to Cardiff for the international. Mr Thomas has already got the tickets…'

'How'd he manage that? They're like gold!' his father interrupted, amazed.

'He knows people at the RFU, so we've all got tickets, even some of the girls who are going. Anyway, after the match, we find something to eat in Cardiff then the bus leaves about half six. It's only one night away, so I thought I'd give it a go. You and Grandad will be OK for one night, won't you?' he teased, a look of mock concern on his face.

'We managed before you were born, and we'll manage without you again. About bloody time you did something away from the farm and the village!' his father had surprised him by saying, at the same time getting up and walking over to scrabble around in the top drawer of the Welsh dresser to find a pen. 'Go and enjoy yourself and at the same time show those valley boys how a scrum-half should play.'

The ladybird seemed to have fallen asleep midway between his wrist and elbow. The boys were still out of sight, and the sun was higher in the sky even though his watch told him it was getting on for three o'clock.

His memory of that weekend so long ago, was as clear as if it had been yesterday. Mr Thomas had booked a 53-seater coach. Ticket priority had been given to the first fifteen, then to the second fifteen. Any girlfriends who wanted to go could have any tickets that were left. Spare seats were filled by other staff who just fancied a day out in Cardiff.

Thinking back, he'd had a wonderful time. He'd got on well with John Payne, his host from the other school. He had been welcomed into the Payne household and fed to within an inch of his life. The disco had been a bit of a social challenge. The local girls expected to be asked to dance but, as usual, he felt shy and awkward. He couldn't dance, but after a while he realised that all he had to do was change from one foot to the other in time to the music and wave his arms about. He chuckled to himself and shook his head at the image he had in his mind of his efforts on the dance floor. He couldn't have been that bad though as he had a partner for every dance!

Walking back to the Payne's house at the end of the evening, he knew that although he'd really enjoyed himself, he needed a good night's sleep if he was to play his best game in the morning. His rugby came first, even if the match was just a "friendly". He hoped the other members of the team had the same thoughts. As it turned out, he needn't have worried. After what Mrs Payne called "the full Welsh", the biggest breakfast he'd ever seen, he'd made his way back to the school with John to get ready for the match.

The valley team was strong, especially their pack, but the visitors had a turn of speed that couldn't be matched in open play, and they ran out easy winners by fifteen points. Lunch was the standard post-match fayre of spam, mash and baked beans, followed by jam tart and custard. Opposing captains made their speeches, thanking everyone involved and expressing the hope that the trip would become an annual event. Richie Jones, the visiting captain also extended an invitation to the opposition to travel west so that he and his team could return the wonderful hospitality they'd received.

David shook his head again and frowned, a sudden sadness coming over him. Poor old Richie had been killed a few years later on his way to work at the harbour, knocked down by a hit-and-run driver who was never found. His three children still lived in the village, all grown up now.

The ladybird was still asleep as he marvelled at how clear the images of that trip were in his mind, especially as it was well known in the family that he had a memory like a sieve. He recalled that everyone had left the beautiful, old school on the hillside above the valley with regret, but had soon been preoccupied with the buzz and excitement of experiencing match day in Cardiff city centre. Wales were playing France in the first match of the season, and hopes were high for a home win. The traffic had been heavy, and an hour later than scheduled, the coach dropped everyone off at the Civic Centre with a simple street plan of the centre of Cardiff—Queen Street, Cardiff Castle, St Mary's Street and, circled in red, the hallowed ground of the Arms Park. Since then, of course, a new stadium had been built, but he hadn't had the chance to see it and already its name had been changed again from the Millennium Stadium to the Principality Stadium.

For him, Cardiff Arms Park would always have a soft spot in his heart. He knew from the television that Cardiff had undergone major regeneration. The docklands were now home to much sought-after luxury apartments overlooking the bay, with the original Bute, Splott and Grangetown areas consigned to a place in folklore. Queen Street was now pedestrianised, and the new Welsh Assembly had more say in how Wales should be governed.

How things have changed, he thought. He preferred to remember the city as he saw it that day. Bright and colourful, the red and green flags of Wales being waved next to the red, white and blue Tricolore of France—the dragon challenging the cockerel. The atmosphere, like the match, was electrifying.

Funny, but at the final whistle, the actual score didn't seem to be all that important to the crowd. They'd seen a great match, the power of the Welsh against the flair of the French, but after all the excitement, all the fans wanted was some fun with plenty of food and drink in the pubs near the ground. He hadn't wanted to go drinking and was quite happy to go off on his own to soak up the atmosphere and find something to eat.

As it turned out, his team-mate, Kevin Lewis, one of the twins who played in the front row, didn't want to go with the others either, and like David, he didn't have a girl in tow, so they wandered back into the city centre together to find a reasonably priced meal before rejoining the others at the coach.

Without realising it, his hands had tightened over the top bar of the gate, and he could see the whites of his knuckles where the bronzed skin stretched tightly over the joints. He let his head fall forward, his chin on his chest. '*I've tried to love you Gillian, but I can't,*' he whispered, blinking back tears and consciously releasing his hands and flexing his fingers. '*I gave it all away. There was none left for you.*'

He felt even worse voicing this ever-present truth, but it was a fact he'd lived with for the last twenty-five years and would continue to live with always. *I should get back*, he thought, staring once again into the distance, although he doubted Gillian would notice how long he'd been away. Too absorbed in her lists. God forbid she'd do anything spontaneous for once! *That's unfair*, he scolded himself immediately. If it was left to him, they'd do nothing and go nowhere. No! Gillian was a great organiser, and boy, did she organise!

The ladybird was on the move again, disturbed by his fingers flexing. The breeze, though still warm and dry, had strengthened and the leaves rustled in the trees along the lane disturbing the all-enveloping silence. He looked up into the startlingly blue, clear sky and knew instinctively that they'd have a few more scorching days like today before the much-needed rain arrived.

He wasn't quite ready to go back to the house. He needed a few more minutes alone, his mind still full of the events of that weekend. At the far end of Queen Street, just before the railway bridge, Kevin had spotted a small café slotted between a very busy betting shop and a deserted employment office. The menu, but more importantly the prices, suited their limited budget, and the whole place looked clean and inviting. To two country boys, the red-and-white check tablecloths, and the unmistakable Italian atmosphere verged on the exotic. They even admired the plastic vines hanging from the ceiling, and the Roman urns standing on small alcove shelves cut into the walls. Most of the tables were occupied, always a good sign, but Kevin nudged him towards a table for two just inside the door. He could hear Kevin's voice in his head as though it were yesterday.

'There'll be a draught every time the door opens,' Kevin said resignedly, 'but I'm starving, and we're running out of time. Just sit down.'

They'd both looked at the menu and at each other, but in the end had gone for spaghetti with meatballs, not trusting themselves to choose something they didn't recognise. A short, dark-haired waiter, obviously Italian, took their order and asked what they would like to drink.

'Let's push the boat out,' David had said.

'Agreed,' came the reply, a broad grin creasing up Kevin's eyes.

'Two cokes please, without the ice,' David ordered, then as the waiter moved away, shook his head and commented, 'that old line is wearing a bit thin now, I think.'

'Yeah, but it still makes me smile. How much time have we got?'

'About half an hour,' David said, checking his watch. 'I hope they don't keep us waiting too long. I reckon we're about a ten-minute walk from the bus.'

Then *she* was there, standing at their table with cutlery and red serviettes in her hand. She smiled at both of them as she put their spoons and forks on top of the serviettes in front of them on the table. He remembered vividly being unable to breathe properly. Never had he felt so completely stunned. She was the most beautiful girl he'd seen in his life, with thick, dark wavy hair drawn back from her face and held in place by a large, wooden slide. Her eyes were the colour of rich caramel and her mouth curved into what David believed was the most perfect smile ever. Her smooth olive skin was accentuated by the crisp white blouse she wore with smart, tailored black trousers. He couldn't take his eyes off her and something inexplicable told him, or had it been just wishful thinking, that she was equally smitten?

'Not bad, eh?' commented Kevin as the waitress moved away.

'Mm…' he had managed, not trusting himself to speak. He had fiddled with his fork, keeping his head lowered until the waiter arrived with their drinks. He sipped the chilled liquid slowly, only lifting his head when he realised their food had arrived. Her nails were pale against long tanned fingers, and he remembered clearly the soft, downy hairs on her arms. He had felt awkward and very young. He had wanted to speak to her, say a few words at least, but all he could manage was a brief "thanks". Kevin was already twirling his spaghetti erratically, dripping sauce all over his plate, but David couldn't start to eat until she had moved away. He had felt her staring at him as she asked if they wanted parmesan or black pepper with their pasta.

'Just pepper, please,' he'd answered eventually, lifting his eyes to look at her directly. He'd never heard of the first thing she'd offered, so hadn't dare chance it. He saw her smile at him before walking to the other end of the café, pick up the largest pepper mill he'd ever seen, then walk straight back towards him, her beautiful smile still on her lips. He had smiled back, and for some unknown reason found himself relaxing, thanked her again, and without thinking said, 'I'm David. Here for the rugby.'

'I'm Maria Cristina. Did your team win?'

'Yes, but only just. Do you work here every day?' he'd asked, his meal and Kevin totally forgotten.

'I help my parents when I can but not all the time. Sorry, I must see to other customers. Enjoy your spaghetti. The sauce is made by my mother.'

He had forced himself to eat the pasta. The sauce was delicious, but he was constantly aware of Maria Cristina, where she was and what she was doing.

'That's the best mince I've ever had,' Kevin broke into his thoughts. 'I've splashed quite a bit down my front, but no one'll notice. No time for a pud. We've got just over ten minutes to get back to the bus. I need the bog. Here's a fiver. You pay.'

He'd found a matching five-pound note in his wallet then raised his hand shyly to call her over. The pasta and drinks had cost less than £6, but he told her to keep the change as a tip. Then, on impulse, and before Kevin came back to spoil things, he'd asked if he could borrow her pencil. On the back of his receipt, he wrote his name, address and telephone number.

'Will you call me?' he asked hesitantly.

'Would you like me to?' she asked back, smiling even more if that was at all possible.

He could only smile back and nod. She picked up a serviette from the table, scribbled down her name and number, folded it in half, then held it out to him.

'You call first,' she said. 'After seven in the evening would be best.' Then she walked away, checking on tables as she passed by.

'Come on, we'll have to run,' Kevin announced, walking briskly out of the café. 'Where's my change?'

David hadn't answered, too busy looking back at the girl who was watching him leave.

He'd married her five years later. Her parents had insisted that she finish her nursing course first so that wherever she went, she could get work. He hadn't minded waiting. They both knew they belonged together. She meant everything to him, and he never ceased to wonder that she could feel the same way about him. In the meantime, he left school with three decent A Levels, did a one-year course on farm management, then settled into a routine back home on the farm, which suited him perfectly. He still played rugby for the town side but left the first Saturday of every month free so that he could catch the early train to Cardiff to spend the weekend with Maria Cristina and her parents. He was even asked to do some waiting in the café if they were particularly busy, which meant he got to spend even more time with her. It took nearly a year before her parents allowed her to visit the farm. Her first few visits were just for the day, but the more they got to know and trust him, they allowed her to stay longer. Eventually, it was agreed that they would get married on her twenty-third birthday.

The ladybird had gone, disappeared under his arm, and crawled away along the top bar of the gate. He'd been standing in one position so long his back was starting to ache, but he was still reluctant to make a move.

He'd married her twice. The first wedding was in the large Roman Catholic church in Cardiff. A long, drawn-out, serious service with so many guests he'd never met before, most of them from the Italian community. By contrast, the reception had been a joyous, noisy affair with an endless supply of food, wine, music and dancing. The welcome given to the few members of his own family had been overwhelming and he'd tried his best to join in the celebrations.

Even now, he remembered feeling guilty. All he'd wanted that day was to be alone with Maria Cristina. He'd been selfish. He'd wanted her all to himself, even though he knew that her parents were going to be desolate when she left them to live on the farm with him.

He married her for the second time in the small, stone-built Norman church out on the headland just a few miles from the farm. Six people attended this service—Mam, Dad, Grandad, her parents and Kevin. Only after this simple ceremony did he feel that Maria Cristina da Calvi truly became Mrs David Jenkins, his wife.

Chapter 16
Cristi

The Whitebay Hotel nestled on the hillside surrounded by the finest woodland of tall pine trees and dense rhododendron bushes. Built at the very beginning of the twentieth century, the hotel first belonged to the Great Western Railway Company. The railroad from London terminated at the port just beyond the hotel, and there was no access for vehicles beyond the hotel itself. With fifty-four rooms, many with magnificent views of the bay and the rugged coastal cliffs, The Whitebay was the only local venue that could cater for more than seventy people.

For many years, the hotel had survived by attracting large coach parties rather than individual bookings, but after a million-pound refurbishment just before the millennium, the new management team had refined their marketing strategy, bringing The Whitebay into the technological age with website advertising. Described in its promotional material as having "modern facilities combined with elegant, traditional touches", the hotel no longer relied on its impressive exterior to attract guests.

There was only one access road to the hotel, and considering its importance in the community, parking facilities were poor, to say the least. The road ended at the main entrance, so a great deal of manoeuvring of vehicles was always called for. All the locals knew that the trick was to turn the car around where the road was at its widest, about fifty yards before the hotel came into sight amidst the trees. As usual, everyone had the same idea—arrive early, turn the car round, reverse nearer the entrance, then park facing the way they had come for a swift getaway at the end of the celebrations.

With all this in mind, Cristi decided to walk, even though the morning was very overcast. The sky was leaden without a hint of sunshine. The haze of a low sea mist obliterated the coastline, but she knew that this would probably lift by mid-morning and give way to a glorious afternoon.

The dawn chorus had disturbed her sleep just after four o'clock, yet even at that hour it was no longer dark. On a school day, she was up at six thirty, and breaking that habit was virtually impossible. She rolled over under the duvet, deciding to lie there and listen to the birdsong for a while.

Years before, when she had moved in, the first thing she treated herself to was a good-quality double bed. Back at the farm, her room had been the smallest with just enough space for a single bed and a free-standing single wardrobe with a drawer at its base. When she got into her teens, her father had put a full-length mirror up on the wall behind the door which had to be closed if she ever wanted to see herself, which was not very often.

Now, propping herself up on her elbow, she gazed around her bedroom with a frisson of pleasure. There was enough space for a double wardrobe, chest of drawers, dressing table and cheval mirror. On the wall facing her bed were two watercolours of the bay, painted by the same artist who had produced the anniversary gifts. On the left, the artist had captured the blue tranquillity of a full tide, the sea appearing to nestle comfortably between benign-looking cliffs. The other one, however, was her favourite.

The calm ripples of summer had transformed themselves into a seething rage of foam, swirling up the cliff face before recoiling in anger. The white-horse waves pounded the rocks relentlessly, determined to win the battle. Cristi found the mood swings of the sea absolutely fascinating, for the artist had illustrated the polar extremes perfectly. She felt pleased with herself for not leaving everything until the last minute. She had bought the gifts for the summer anniversary well in advance, taking advantage of the artist's stall in the farmers' market at Easter.

The words in the letter from Italy ran a parallel course in her thoughts as she lay admiring her bedroom. She needed to read them again to make sure she had not missed something, some obscure clue in their meaning.

No longer feeling relaxed, she got out of bed in one fluid movement, then gave her long thick hair a cursory brush and twist before securing it at the nape of her neck with one of her many scrunchies. She would give herself an hour to walk to the hotel later but, in the meantime, she slipped on her jeans and a yellow T-shirt and made her way down for the first coffee of the day.

The letter lay open on the dining table where she had left it the night before. She passed it by with no more than a fleeting glance, poured some cornflakes into a bowl, added a few raspberries and a dash of cold milk from the fridge. She always regarded herself as a coffee heathen, preferring instant to the real thing. The smell of percolating coffee was so enticing but she always found the taste a great disappointment. She spooned the coffee granules into her mug, added water from the kettle then topped it up with cold milk. The morning sun had not managed to break through the mist and reach her garden, but she opened the back door wide anyway before sitting down at the table to have her breakfast.

With some reluctance, she picked up the letter once again. It was clearly addressed to her, and someone had taken the trouble to handwrite the contents in very formal English. The message was vague. At the top of the single sheet of good-quality paper was the name of an Italian *avvocato* with all his contact details. Why on earth would a solicitor from some obscure place she had never heard of be writing to her? According to the brief note, he was in possession of a document which he believed was relevant to her. He was legally obliged to discuss the matter with her in person so would she be kind enough to contact his office as soon as possible, to arrange a mutually convenient appointment? The letter ended, however, not in English but in Italian with *Distinti saluti, Sebastiano Luce.* For some unknown reason, she rather liked that.

Cristi read the letter once more and came to the same conclusion, that she didn't have a clue what it was about except a vague notion that it probably had something to do with her mother. She would mention it to her father later if by some remote chance she had the opportunity to speak to him alone.

Even though most of the guests lived in the village less than a mile from the Whitebay, it appeared they had all come by car. Cristi couldn't understand why they didn't want to walk on what had turned out to be such a beautiful, warm day. There was no longer a cloud in the sky and hardly a breath of wind. The tide was full, and the sea looked like a sheet of azure glass. She was one of the last to arrive, and the red carpeted foyer of the hotel was empty apart from the receptionist Cristi knew well.

'Hi, Jan. How's it going?'

'Not bad, Cris, you OK?' Jan asked, in a soft, lilting Welsh voice.

'Much rather be down the beach than in here. Have most of them arrived?'

'You're about the last. I think they've all gone out into the gardens at the back to have some photos taken. Everyone looks as if they're dressed for chapel. All the men in suits, and Mrs Rees the Chemist even has a small hat on.'

Jan Williams was the same age as Cristi but had a policeman husband and two young children under school age. She had always been good for a laugh and knew everybody in the village from working in local shops, the pub on the square, and now as head receptionist at the Whitebay.

'Are you on all afternoon?' Cristi asked, silently admitting to herself that the longer she stayed chatting to Jan the less time she would have to spend with everyone else.

'I'm off at five. Your "do" will be petering out by then, I should think.'

'God, I hope so,' Cristi said with more feeling than she had intended. 'I suppose I'd better go in and show willing.'

'You look great,' Jan commented, as Cristi moved towards the door of the main lounge. 'That colour really suits you.'

'Do you think so? I had a devil of a job finding something decent. Thanks for the compliment. Can never have too many of those. See you later, no doubt.'

'Enjoy!' Jan called after her as she walked reluctantly through the double doors towards the dining room, her confidence boosted by Jan's comment. After much thought and changes of mind, she had finally decided to wear her white linen cropped trousers with a pale turquoise and white floral pure silk blouse nipped in at the waist. The dainty capped sleeves and scooped neckline showed off her smooth, olive skin. Finally, she had paid particular attention to her thick, wavy hair, drawing it away from her face before twisting it into a plait which hung loosely down her back. She had put on her gold watch and chosen her mother's plain gold stud earrings as her only concession to jewellery.

As she wandered into the main bar area, the first person she saw was Gillian, and as usual, for no apparent reason, her stomach sank. Her stepmother was chatting animatedly to an elderly couple Cristi knew well. Mrs Knightly had been her dance teacher for many years, and her distinguished-looking husband had been the harbour master before his retirement. They were what her grandfather had called "English incomers", but like many others not born locally, they had settled into the close-knit community without too much trouble.

At the very moment Cristi spotted her, Gillian broke off her conversation and came over.

'You look nice and summery,' Gillian said enthusiastically, air-kissing Cristi on both cheeks. 'Isn't it marvellous all these lovely people have managed to come?'

'Yes, brilliant,' Cristi replied, making every effort to match Gillian's enthusiasm, although it was very obvious to Cristi that Gillian was trying really hard to be the perfect hostess almost to the point of overdoing it. The unkind word that came to mind was *obsequious*. Her stepmother had evidently had her hair cut short and restyled, which made her look more youthful, and instead of her slacks and blouse uniform, she was wearing a very smart calf-length floral summer skirt in varying shades of blue with a short-sleeved, pale cream, collarless jacket. For the first time ever, Cristi thought she could see why her father had found this woman attractive all those years ago.

'I've brought a present for you and Dad,' Cristi went on, holding out what she thought was a beautifully wrapped gift, even though she had done it herself.

'Just plonk it over there on the table by the door, will you? We'll look at all the presents later,' Gillian responded, waving a careless hand towards a white cloth-covered table which was already laden with gifts of all shapes and sizes. 'In fact, we intend to leave everything until we get back from the cruise. Far too many last-minute things to be getting on with before tomorrow. Ah! There's John and Lillian. Help yourself to a drink, won't you? Your father's here somewhere.' And in a cloud of what Cristi recognised as Chanel No 5, Gillian left her side, arms open wide to greet the other couple.

'And does the most beautiful woman in the room have a hug and a kiss for her old dad then?'

Cristi had not seen her father approach and touch her gently on the elbow, a glass of wine in his other hand.

'Only if her "old dad" is wearing a suit and tie,' she laughed teasingly, taking a step back to look him up and down. 'Very smart indeed, I must say, and you've had your hair cut. I didn't realise how handsome and presentable you could be with just a bit of effort.' She stood on tiptoes and kissed him properly on both cheeks. 'No, seriously,' she went on, 'you both look good.'

'That may be so, but as soon as we start the food, this jacket is coming off. I feel like one of my trussed-up chickens,' he said, running his finger round between the collar of his shirt and his neck.

'I didn't think you had a decent suit, only that old grey thing you trot out for funerals.'

'Gillian insisted. Anything for a quiet life. Idris Lewis did me a deal, so I can't complain too much. Let me get you a drink. What do you fancy?'

'Just a white wine, please. It's still a bit early for me,' she said, watching him grab a glass of ready-poured wine from a tray on one of the many tables. He was back within seconds.

'Brought you some sparkling, perfect for a summer's day. Have you broken up yet?'

'Not until next Friday lunchtime.'

'You teachers don't know you're born, all those holidays,' he quipped.

'Don't start, Dad,' she answered, a warning smile on her lips.

Gillian had never understood the teasing banter Cristi and her father indulged in. It was just one more little thing that distanced the two women in his life. Gillian didn't do banter. Sometimes, Cristi wondered if Gillian actually had a sense of humour at all.

'Dad?' Cristi asked.

'What is it?' her father responded, a slight frown creasing his forehead as he looked at the beautiful young woman standing in front of him.

'I've had this letter from Italy,' she went on, noticing her father's frown deepen and a slight pursing of his lips.

'What sort of letter?' he asked, keeping his eyes on her face as he bent his head to take a sip from his glass.

'I don't know really. It's from a solicitor's office in a place I've never heard of. I googled it and found it's a small town out near the Adriatic coast. According to the letter, they have some papers, some legal documents, and my name is in them. They want to discuss things with me in person. I don't know what to do. Do you know what it might be about?'

'I don't, sweetheart,' her father replied, shaking his head slowly. 'Our only link to Italy was your *mamma*, and we've been without her now for over twenty-five years.'

Suddenly, Cristi realised that the sparkle of a moment ago had deserted her father. His eyes looked incredibly sad, and his shoulders slumped, even as he spoke.

'Oh, Dad,' she put her arm through his. 'I shouldn't have mentioned it. Not today. I'm sorry, really I am.' She squeezed his arm into her side.

'Today or any day, it wouldn't make any difference. She's with me always. I can't help it, so I stopped fighting it a long time ago and just got on with things.

All I can tell you is that your mother came over here with her mother at the age of two, so by the time I met her, she sounded more Welsh than me. Her father had already been working in Cardiff for a few years before they joined him. I got to know her parents well. Then your *mamma* got ill, and after she died, they decided to sell up and go back to live in Italy taking her with them. We all agreed it was the best thing to do at the time. The rest, as they say, is history. Isn't it awful?' he went on.

'I never thought to ask questions about where her family came from. I suppose I was just so happy that I'd met her and that she actually wanted to be with me. That's all that mattered. What went before didn't seem important. I'm no help to you at all, am I?'

'Somehow, I didn't think you would be,' Cristi answered, feeling awful for bringing up memories for him today of all days. There were still lots of unanswered questions. Why had she never asked where her mother had been buried? Had she been buried or cremated and, if so, where exactly in Italy? She doubted her father even knew, but she would definitely have to question him when he returned from the cruise, whether it upset him or not. She needed to know.

An old-fashioned gong put an end to their conversation.

'Ah, food at last. I hope this famous carving buffet lives up to Gillian's expectations. I wouldn't want to be in the manager's shoes if it doesn't,' her father exclaimed, with false jollity.

Cristi was glad to see that he had regained some of his earlier light-hearted good mood, but she still held on to his arm as they joined the others making their way into the dining room.

'You'd better go and find Gillian,' she encouraged, giving him a little nudge in the direction of his wife, who was now watching them closely.

'I'll speak to you later,' she said, turning her back on him and wandering over to the seating plan next to the double doors. She noticed that the family had been spread out among the tables. Her two half-brothers, who she had not noticed in the far corner, or spoken to for months, were already settled, chatting away to the other, mostly younger guests on their tables. She had been allocated a place on a table far from her father and Gillian, whether on purpose or not, Cristi couldn't tell. It was either that, or she was becoming paranoid! Anyway, she knew all her table companions well, so it was nothing to make a fuss about.

The hotel had done them proud. There was something for everyone. Two tall-hatted chefs were on duty to carve the succulent-looking joints of beef and pork. There were two large, dressed fresh salmon, bowls of new potatoes and a wide variety of crisp salad dishes with a choice of dressings. The desserts would not be put out until the main course had been eaten and the dishes cleared away. Cristi knew that Bryn, the Head Chef, another friend from school who specialised in pastries and desserts, was very particular about not revealing his offerings, especially the ones decorated with fresh cream, until he had everyone's attention. For someone whose reputation for bad behaviour had followed him right through school, it was amazing that he now had quite a different kind of reputation, that of being a leading *pâtissier*, with some of his creations considered works of culinary art.

As soon as all the guests were seated, the vicar, who had officiated at the marriage all those years before, stood up to say grace. Although an outdated practice in many circles, Gillian had been adamant about including it at the beginning of her celebration meal. The brief prayer of thanks over, one table at a time, was invited to serve themselves from the buffet.

'This sort of thing saves queuing,' Delia John, the district nurse, commented, speaking to no one in particular at the table. 'I bet you Billy Rees will put so much on his plate he won't have to eat another meal 'til Tuesday, then I'll be called out because he can't get his diabetes under control.'

'You know us too well, Delia,' Cristi laughed.

'He always was a greedy little so-and-so when we were children. I keep telling him he needs to lose weight, but look, look at his plate. And that's just his first visit!'

The conversation around the table did not lapse for a minute. There was plenty of good humour, some gossip and lots of compliments for her father and Gillian. The food was excellent, and Bryn had produced the most mouth-watering summer desserts anyone could ask for. Tall structures of meringues, strawberries, raspberries and blueberries held together with clotted cream dominated the serving table. Large chocolate, coffee and hazelnut roulades vied for space with bowls of traditional trifle and jugs of cream and fruit sauces.

The same chefs from the main course were on hand to serve the desserts, making sure everyone had the chance to sample as much as they liked. Cristi couldn't help but notice that Billy Rees only managed two trips this time, but he made sure he tried everything on offer with lashings of cream. *Delia would have her work cut out next week,* she thought to herself, smiling.

'Your father hasn't spared any expense on this champagne,' Delia commented, helping herself to a second glass to make sure she was ready for the toast.

Cristi felt so proud of her father after he made such a good speech at the end of the meal. Although brief, he praised and thanked Gillian for the life they had shared for twenty-five years, made the usual joke about who said it wouldn't last, then praised his three children who, he said, had brought deeper meaning to both their lives. Finally, he asked everyone to raise their glasses and toast his wife. As all the guests stood, raised their glasses and chanted, 'To David and Gillian,' Cristi noticed that her father raised his glass slightly higher, this time glancing heavenwards, the merest of smiles on his lips. Back in his seat once again, his eyes locked with hers on the far side of the room and, imperceptibly, she saw him nod his head. She smiled back at him in acknowledgement. Her mother had not been forgotten.

By early evening, most of the guests started to disperse. It had been a warm, sunny afternoon, a light sea breeze preventing it from being uncomfortably hot. Everyone had spilled out of the dining room onto the beautiful, manicured lawned area of the hotel which swept down towards the coastal path and the glittering, blue sea. The white sails of four yachts could be seen gliding very slowly towards the jetty. Not really a good day for sailing, Cristi thought as she wandered across the grass to thank her father and Gillian for a lovely afternoon, realising with some surprise that she had actually enjoyed herself.

'Thank you for coming,' Gillian said, as though Cristi's attendance had somehow been in doubt.

'Have a wonderful holiday,' Cristi said to both of them. 'Make the most of it, you deserve a good break.'

'I'll walk you out,' her father said, firmly folding her arm around his. 'Won't be a minute, Gill,' he said to his wife, already moving away, and walking towards the exit.

'I've been thinking about your letter, love,' he said as soon as they were out of earshot. 'There are a couple of old battered suitcases up in the loft at the farm you might be interested in. They're right at the back in the far corner. Nobody'd know they were there unless there was a major clear-out. I haven't had the heart to even look at them. I know one or two of them belonged to your *mamma*. She brought all her worldly goods in them when she came to live at the farm. I know she used to go through all the bits and pieces every so often. There might be some sort of clue for you. I'll tell the boys you'll be up in the week to collect more of your stuff from the loft. Take what you like.'

'I love you, Dad,' she said, her eyes filling up, a silly lump in her throat. 'You enjoy yourself on that cruise and take plenty of photos. Don't worry or even think about me. I'll get this letter thing sorted by the time you get back.' She hoped her voice sounded far more confident than she was feeling.

A couple of weeks later, Cristi scraped the cobwebs out of her hair. Balancing precariously on the top step of the loft ladder, she rubbed her fingers firmly together to get rid of the sticky strands clinging to her skin. It was a good job she didn't mind webs or spiders but really should have been prepared for the mass of fine filaments zigzagging across the gap which gave her access to the roof space at the top of the farmhouse.

Her father and Gillian were already almost halfway through their three-week cruise, and Cristi wanted to do her searching long before they returned. A postcard from her father that morning had stirred her into action. His message had been short and sweet: *'Here I am in Italy at last. You should be here with me. Love, Dad.'* He had chosen a beautiful scene of Venice in the early morning sea mist, with no sign of the hordes of tourists who flock to the city at all times during the year. She knew that Venice was often referred to as *La Serenissima,* and looking at the postcard she could understand why.

Cristi had been ready for her summer break. Too many staffing problems at the end of term had added to everyone's stress levels. The headteacher had been signed off for another three months, so it had fallen on Cristi's shoulders to bring the village school to a successful end of year. New children had arrived from the Infant Department, and her older pupils had to be prepared to move on to the secondary school in the nearby town.

Their farewell show had been a great success, thanks mainly to Julie and a band of loyal, enthusiastic parents. Being in charge of the whole school was a huge responsibility, but Cristi was determined to make it work like clockwork. At least one decision she made received full approval from her colleagues. In a staff meeting three days before the end of term, she announced, to what could only be described as a despondent and demoralised staff, 'If it's OK with you, I intend to close the school a day early for the children. This will give us all a chance to come in, clear up, or do whatever we need to do for September without interruption. If we get on with it, we should all manage to get away before lunchtime or earlier if possible.' From the prolonged applause, anyone would have thought she'd given them an extra week's holiday.

On the final day of term, she was the last to walk out of the school, nearer to three o'clock than lunchtime, but with a spring in her step. There had been no last-minute problems, and she had six weeks of freedom to look forward to. She would face the challenges of being the acting head when she returned in September, but felt she already had the support of the staff.

The first week of her holiday quickly disappeared. The time just flew by. She pottered around the house and garden, had her six-monthly check-up at the dentist and had her boiler checked and serviced. She listened to music and made a start on the first of numerous books she hadn't managed to find the time to read during the term.

She walked down to the beach every day and had a swim when the tide was in. A mile long breakwater stretched from the beach out into the open bay, and rather than meet all the children from school on the sands, she would launch herself into the cold water from the breakwater rocks a few hundred yards out from the beach. In recent years, she was so used to spending most of her time alone that she rarely noticed it.

Only once in a while, usually in the evening, she wished she had someone to talk to, to share her views and opinions with, even her grumbles. At these times, she would tell herself to snap out of it and not waste her emotional energy on impossibilities. Sometimes, she frightened herself with the force of her reactions. She knew she was brilliant at her job, but her personal life left a lot to be desired. Even her initial curiosity about the letter from Italy had waned as the days came and went. Then, the postcard from her father arrived bringing Italy and the existence of the letter back into focus once again.

For years, her Italian heritage had not really figured in her life, yet twice in as many weeks, Italy had come to call. Rummaging around in the farmhouse roof on a summer's day had not appealed to her in the slightest, but today she had woken up to find her cottage shrouded in a fine sea mist that had crept in during the early hours. The weather forecast promised an overcast yet humid day with the likelihood of showers.

She glanced up at the sky as she walked down the front path and out of the gate. The sun wasn't even trying to get through the blanket of cloud, so she made the snap decision to drive up to the farm. She had bought her car, reluctantly, five years earlier when she found it increasingly difficult to get to school meetings using the reduced local public transport system. The car was kept in a block of three garages opposite her cottage and hardly ever saw the light of day, but with the threat of rain and the possibility of having to carry a suitcase back with her, using the car felt like a sensible option. The drive to her old home took her through the housing estate, which seemed to be having a lie-in—even the dogs that usually roamed the pavements were conspicuous by their absence. Driving also meant she didn't have to stop to chat to parents. They were all very pleasant, but having to deal with them during term time was quite enough.

Just before eight o'clock, she found herself at the end of the track leading up to the farmyard with the large stone farmhouse a little way off to her right. She could see two large baskets full of petunias, trailing geraniums and lobelia hanging on each side of the entrance with fuchsia-filled pots and tubs standing under the large windows. Gillian certainly had green fingers and an eye for colour, Cristi mused, and although the door was wide open, she gave it a firm knock before tentatively walking down the hall and peering into the large farmhouse kitchen. Owen and Rhys Jenkins were just finishing off their breakfast. They would have already put in two hours work on the farm, she knew, and neither of them seemed in a hurry to dash out again.

'Come on in, stranger!' Owen said, waving her in with his hand as soon as he saw her in the doorway. Although they had little to do with one another, she got on well with her half-brothers, knowing that they found her a bit of a mystery.

'Good morning, you two,' she replied brightly. 'Any more tea in the pot?'

'I'll make some fresh,' Owen said. 'I could do with another mug, how about you?' he asked his brother, who was reading the sports pages of the newspaper.

'What do you think?' came the enigmatic reply. 'It's a bit grim out there this morning, Cristi,' Rhys went on, folding his paper neatly and setting it aside with one hand as he pulled out a stool for her with the other.

Rhys was the younger of the brothers. Everything he did was careful and precise. Cristi had always thought of him as the clever, studious one, and had been surprised when he started work on the farm as soon as he could leave school. She had imagined him going away to study modern agricultural methods and practices, then coming back and helping his brother bring the farm right up to date. She couldn't have been more wrong.

'What do I want to go away for?' he'd asked her years before when she had questioned him about his plans. 'I can read, and anything more I need to know I can get off the internet. Owen and I have plans, so don't you worry about us.'

She hadn't mentioned the subject again, feeling that she had, in some way, been told to mind her own business. She knew her father was delighted that both his boys wanted to stay at home, and between the three of them they had managed to turn the farm into a very lucrative business.

'Dad said you'd be up some time,' Owen said as he placed a mug of tea in front of her. 'I can't remember the last time anyone went up into the roof. What are you looking for anyway?'

'Oh, just some more of my things. I took most of them when I moved out, but I know there are more boxes of mine up there. I've got three big black bin liners with me. One for rubbish, one for the charity shop and one for the stuff I want to keep, which won't be much. Shouldn't take me too long. Does the light up there still work?'

'Wouldn't know,' Rhys muttered, not really interested.

'I'll check it out for you and get the folding ladder down,' Owen offered, 'but have your tea first. Do you want sugar?'

'No, thanks, but I wouldn't mind one of those scones.'

'Help yourself. Mam left loads in the freezer. Probably thought we'd starve if she didn't stock up.'

Cristi sat at the table and helped herself to one of Gillian's scones. It was still slightly warm, so she spread it thickly with butter, which immediately started to soak through. The strawberry jam was homemade, whole strawberries clinging to her knife. She smiled when she heard Owen refer to his mam. She had never thought of Gillian as anyone but Gillian, certainly never as "mam". Her own mother she remembered as *Mamma*, the beautiful lady who had always called her *Cara*, never Cristi.

'When we're ready, we're off up to the top field to check on the fences. Are you OK here on your own?' Owen asked, rinsing out his mug and putting it on the rack to dry. 'Come on, Rhys, let's get going.'

'Just a quick visit to the bathroom, and I'll be with you,' Rhys replied good-naturedly, scraping his chair back on the tiled floor. 'See you out by the gate.' He carefully pushed his chair back under the table, folded the newspaper, then took his own mug to the sink and rinsed it out quickly.

'I'll go and get the ladder down for you, Cristi, and check that light,' Owen said. 'Enjoy your morning. You'll probably be gone by the time we get back. Nice to see you.' And with that, he disappeared into the hallway and thudded up the stairs.

'He's right, you know,' Rhys said, folding his arms and leaning back against the work surface. 'You don't come up here half often enough. We are family, after all, and we like to see you.'

Cristi was amazed. This was the most she'd ever heard Rhys mutter and was doubly amazed at what he'd said.

'That's a really nice thing to say, Rhys. You've made my day. I mean it,' she told him, smiling broadly as she noticed his cheeks go red with embarrassment. But he hadn't finished.

'We know you're cleverer than us, and everyone always says what a great teacher you are and how lucky we are to have you as our sister, but we never see you, so you don't feel like a sister, and I just think it's a shame, that's all.' Saying this, he pushed himself away from the sink and started for the door.

'Wait a minute, Rhys,' Cristi spoke quickly, her scone totally forgotten. 'Me being supposedly clever and being a teacher has nothing whatsoever to do with me not coming up here to see you. Please. I'd hate to think that you felt I believed myself to be in any way superior. I most definitely don't. You two, Dad, and Gillian are a lovely family unit, whereas I...I'm a little bit of an outsider.'

'Is that because of your mother?' Rhys ventured to ask quietly, but Cristi was saved from having to give him an answer by Owen returning to the kitchen doorway.

'The ladder's down and the light's fine. Just pull the cord to put it off when you're done. Leave the ladder. I'll put it back up later. Come on, Rhys, or it'll be nearly time for lunch. Lovely to see you, Cristi. Hope you find whatever it is you're looking for. Come on Rhys, shift yourself.'

'See you, Cristi. Nice to talk to you,' Rhys muttered again, and with that, she found herself alone, nursing a rapidly cooling cup of tea.

Cristi felt uncomfortable. Here she was in Gillian's kitchen, sitting at Gillian's table, drinking out of Gillian's bone china mug, having eaten one of Gillian's delicious fruit scones. She was an interloper, and yet, she had a right to be here. After all, this was also her father's kitchen, and he knew she would be here at some time while he was away.

Slowly, she looked around her. Was there anything left in this room she could remember from her childhood? Or had she been too young to even notice her surroundings? Although she lived at the farm until she went away to college, she hadn't realised until years later how much time she had actually spent alone, up in her room. During all those schooldays, it always seemed to be the family of four, with her loitering somewhere on the periphery. The farmhouse had been extended and redecorated more than once since those days, so it came as no surprise that she could see nothing familiar from her time there. Maybe she'd have more luck up in the roof.

After washing up her mug and plate, and covering the remaining scones with a clean tea towel she found in one of the drawers, she left the kitchen and made her way to the stairs. The house had two large reception rooms downstairs, and Cristi didn't even try to avoid the temptation to have a good look into both.

The room on the left of the hallway was bright and spacious, even with two three-seater settees and a very large armchair perfectly positioned in front of an enormous plasma TV screen. The shelves in the alcoves on each side of the fireplace were full of books. Shades of pale green and apricot paint were delightful and brought a touch of summer into the house. She was just about to turn away when two things caught her eye at the same time.

To her surprise, in pride of place on the chimney breast were the water colour prints she had given Dad and Gillian as an anniversary gift, and on the wall, just to the right of the television, was a black-and-white photograph in a silver frame. It must have been taken when she was about six years old. Just the two of them. Her father looked incredibly handsome, casually dressed in jeans and a polo neck sweater, but his smile didn't reach his eyes, even though his small daughter was gazing up at him adoringly. *What a sad picture,* Cristi thought, and couldn't understand why her father would keep such a reminder of that difficult time in his life in full view every day. She stared at the photograph for a few moments longer, then turned away and left the room.

The other sitting room was obviously where her brothers hung out. The décor was all browns and creams with a variety of car, hill-trekking, farm vehicle and rugby magazines scattered over the settees and the floor. Another huge TV screen dominated the wall opposite the door, with a state-of-the-art music system on one side of the inglenook fireplace and more shelves full of books and maps on the other. There were two electric guitars leaning against the wall behind the door next to a saxophone and clarinet. She had no idea her brothers were interested in music or could play any type of instrument for that matter. She shook her head in wonder and admitted to herself that she really didn't know these people at all.

Except for a bright red woolly hat and scarf, Cristi's earliest memories of Gillian were not very clear. She could remember her father trying to explain to her that her mother would not be with them anymore, that she had gone to a better place where she would be happier and find peace. For a very long time, Cristi had struggled to understand why her mother, who had laughed and smiled a lot, hadn't been happy with them. Why had she needed more peace when she, Cristi, was such a good, quiet little girl, and why hadn't her mamma told her all this herself instead of just not being there?

There was a period of time at the farm when everything felt empty. Time dragged by, and there was no longer any fun and games in the yard or out in the fields. Her father always seemed to be too busy in the daytime and too tired in the evenings. She was met from school by a neighbour who had children of a similar age. She would walk Cristi to the end of the farm track, usually in silence, then say, 'Here we are, then. We'll watch until you're at the door. See you tomorrow,' and off she'd walk on her own, up the rough track to the farmhouse. Sometimes, she'd look back, but the neighbour would be nowhere in sight.

She spent her evenings colouring or reading, her father a silent figure at the large, wooden kitchen table strewn with papers and folders. Now and then, he'd look up and smile at her, but the joy of sitting on his lap being read to, or just being silly, had gone. She knew, even at her young age, that her mother's departure had also taken their closeness away.

One afternoon after school however, when she pushed open the farmhouse door, her father was standing in the kitchen obviously waiting for her to get home.

'Ah, there you are,' he'd said kindly. 'I wondered where you'd got to.'

She had been pleased to see him and yet at the same time felt very uncertain, so she just smiled at him. She saw a swift frown crease his forehead, but it just as quickly disappeared.

'How do you fancy going to the fair tonight?' he asked while helping her out of her coat, taking her bag and hanging them on the hook behind the door. 'It's fair night. It only comes round once a year. We could go on the rides, have a hot dog and try to win some prizes. You'd like that, wouldn't you?' he asked encouragingly. 'So, shall we go?'

Cristi had heard the other children in her class talk about the fair, but she had assumed it would be one place her father would definitely not enjoy, too noisy, too many bright lights, loud music and far too many people. If anything, he had become quieter and quieter in recent weeks. Recognising he was making some sort of effort to be kind to her, Cristi nodded and said quietly, 'Yes, please.'

He already had her hat, mittens and scarf warming on the range, even though the fair didn't start, she was sure, until it was dark and near her bedtime. The autumn night sky would be clear, the air crisp and cold. Before going out, he left her on her own in the house to have her tea of marmalade sandwiches, her favourite, while he finished off his evening chores on the farm.

It didn't take him long to shower and change, and he made sure she was wrapped up nice and warmly. He had even remembered to warm an extra pair of socks. He whistled tunelessly as he switched off the lights and locked the door behind them. She hadn't been in the old Land Rover for months, and she felt quite strange perched high up in the front seat. Whenever they had gone out as a family, she had always been strapped in the back seat, her mother sitting in the front. Now, she sat with her mittened hands clasped in her lap, wondering why her father was in such a light-hearted mood. He kept glancing her way and smiling. If she hadn't known better, she would have said he was nervous.

'Are you warm enough?' he wanted to know. 'Are you comfortable here in the front with me? You're really going to enjoy tonight, I just know it,' he told her as they parked in the large field opened up to the public just for fair night. Cristi remembered nodding each time he spoke, not really knowing what she was meant to say to him.

The field was almost full, even though they had arrived early. Her father lifted her down gently, her wellies sinking into the mud churned up by all the cars. She could already hear music in the distance and could see an orange glow in the sky further down the lane leading away from the main road. There were lots of people making their way towards the fairground, many of them stopping to buy hot dogs or toffee apples from the vans lining the route. Funny, the smell of frying onions still reminded her of that night. Her father held her hand tightly and walked slowly so that she could keep up.

Just before they came to the entrance gate, he slowed down even more then stopped, looking back at the crowds arriving. Cristi moved closer into her father's side, feeling very small and overwhelmed by the noisy, laughing groups surging towards the rides and amusements. She felt, then saw, her father raise his arm and wave to someone in the crowd. Suddenly, the lady from the paper shop in the village was standing right in front of them, smiling broadly at her father.

'You made it, then?' he asked, looking back at her.

'Only just. I caught the bus. Didn't fancy parking in the mud then queuing for ages to get out. Hello, Cristi,' the woman said glancing down, 'you look nice and warm,' then just as quickly returned her attention to her father.

'Come on, let's go on some rides,' her father said excitedly and for the rest of the evening, Cristi was led around the fairground, her father's attention fully occupied with the paper-shop lady.

Later, in the bedroom she had shared with a shocking pink, fluffy shark and a green inflatable frog, Cristi knew she had not enjoyed the fair and couldn't understand why her father had bothered to take her. They had given the paper-shop lady a lift home, and Cristi had waited for what seemed like forever for her father to say goodnight. The woman had complained about having to leave the fair early, her whisper loud enough for Cristi to hear, but she was smiling when she waved from her doorway as the Land Rover pulled away.

'Gillian's great, isn't she?' her father asked when they got back to the farmhouse. He hadn't waited for her answer, just picked up the phone in the hallway to say a final goodnight to the woman Cristi now knew was called Gillian.

In the following weeks, Cristi spent more and more evenings with her babysitter. She looked forward to her evenings with "Auntie" Mary, who always had interesting things organised for them to do together. Miss Mary Evans lived in Number 5, Plas Mawr, a large, Victorian house opposite the church, and to Cristi, had appeared to be an extremely tall and statuesque lady. She had worked in the port manager's office for many years, but now stayed at home most days. Cristi never asked why, but felt it had something to do with the mysterious, small cushion ring Auntie Mary always sat down on carefully when they had tea together. Number 5 was next door to the police house, so Cristi always felt extra safe there. It was during these long evenings that she learned to spell and recite her times tables off by heart.

'Come on, Cristi,' Auntie Mary would say, clapping her hands together, smiling excitedly. 'Get your notebook and pencil case and let's see what you can do.'

Learning was always fun, and often she would forget her father for a while and stop wondering where he was and who he was with.

'Let's have a look. What new words shall we try to spell tonight?' Auntie Mary would ask, opening the large dictionary on her lap. Cristi knew that the big, heavy book must be very special, because it was always left out on the small round table next to Auntie Mary's armchair, together with her spectacles and the daily newspaper. '*I* know,' she'd continue, not expecting Cristi to answer her question. 'We'll have a go at some of the words a lot of children find difficult. Are you happy to try?' Cristi would nod, balancing her notebook on the wide arm of the other chair in the room, identical to Auntie Mary's. She knew there would be a small reward for her if she did her best.

'Are you ready? Can you spell…er…*because, friend, receive, where, were, before…?*'

Cristi would try so hard to get all the words right, knowing that in her class, all the other children were still working on short, three letter words that she found really easy.

'You're a clever girl,' Auntie Mary would tell her, and the few mistakes she made were easily put right. She learned little rhymes and rules, and many years later she would have her own pupils chanting *Big Elephants Can Always Understand Small Elephants* and see their delight when they realised they could spell "because" without any difficulty.

Drawing, colouring, reading and being read to, all featured in her visits to Number 5, but she never stayed overnight. She would often fall asleep, curled up in the wide, flowery armchair, then wake up the following morning in her own bed. She never remembered getting from one place to the other and never asked her father about it.

The Gillian woman became a regular visitor at weekends. Very often, she was already in the kitchen when Cristi got up, smiling sweetly and offering to cook breakfast. She didn't like it when Cristi preferred cereal and would suggest, in a concerned voice, that the little one was much too thin and needed to eat more. Cristi remembered her father saying very little, neither agreeing with Gillian nor standing up for his daughter. David Jenkins was a master of sitting on the fence. All he ever wanted was a peaceful life.

Chapter 17
Cristi

Although she had resolved to be self-disciplined, Cristi still couldn't resist checking out what else had been secreted away up in the loft of her old home. Dad had said she'd probably find what she was looking for in an old leather suitcase in the far corner of the roof space, but to get to that corner she had to pass so many other boxes and small cases just crying out to be looked at. In her imagination, she saw herself opening each and every container, and by doing so, releasing, if only for a second, the trapped souls of every forgotten item that had been stored away and imprisoned for so many years. The notion amused her, and if anything, justified her reluctance to restrict herself to only the one suitcase.

In a large, tall, cardboard box, which had once held a double duvet, she found a mass of soft toys: fluffy frogs, teddy bears, wriggly snakes and numerous velvety rabbits. Sadly, none of them looked familiar, and she realised that all the toys belonged to the boys. After stroking the heads of the rabbits, she put them back, closed the flaps and moved on. There were boxes of mismatched crockery, old pots and pans all in reasonable condition, and a pyramid of old suitcases and canvas holdalls.

Christmas decorations and ornaments filled the boxes that the television and satellite recorder had come in, and she had to squeeze her way between the plastic storage boxes which housed the hundreds of books collected by the Jenkins family over the years. Once a book entered the household, it never left. Her father loved books, and would never even consider lending one from his collection, let alone giving one away. So, here they all lay.

Cristi took off the lid of the top box and glanced at some of the titles. This was obviously the biography box: books about Aneurin Bevan, Matt Busby, Barry John and Gareth Edwards shared their space with and Martina Navratilova. Strange bedfellows Cristi mused, reading the synopsis on the back cover of

Humphrey Bogart. In the box below, she found her father's collection of travel books and her thoughts flew immediately to the cruise ship and wondered how he was getting on.

Under her fingers lay descriptions and dramatic glossy colour photographs of faraway places: Antarctica, Everest and a copy of Michael Palin's *Full Circle* about all the countries that surround the Pacific Ocean. Yet, her father, as far as she knew, had never been out of Wales, at least not until this anniversary trip Gillian had set her heart on. For the first time, Cristi admitted to herself that she didn't really know her father very well. She loved him and knew without doubt that he loved her very much, but she didn't *know* him, know what made him tick. 'And that's my fault,' she said out loud to the empty loft. 'I have never taken the time or made the effort to really talk to you, Dad, ask questions, take an interest, but that'll change when you get home.' With that decision made, she replaced the books about the Galapagos and Kinabalu, put the lid back on the box, then looked around for the case she had come to find.

She was feeling uncomfortably warm and just a little bit claustrophobic by the time she eventually came across the dark brown leather suitcase with old-fashioned locks that you had to move sideways to release the clasp. Both locks were tarnished and obviously hadn't been touched for a very long time. The case lay on its side, a leather belt firmly buckled around its middle.

Cristi stood perfectly still and stared at the case. Her original fanciful thought about releasing trapped souls came back to her with such force that, for just a moment, she felt herself holding her breath. The case lay alone. There was no other debris on top of it, just one or two old, abandoned wispy cobwebs spanning the gaps between the handle and the locks. Cristi felt as though it had been lying there, just waiting for someone to come and rescue it, and that someone was her. Slowly, she crouched down beside the case and ran her fingers along its edge. Her finger trail in the dust revealed a much richer, chestnut shade of brown leather of the highest quality. She knew instinctively that this was the case she had been looking for. It was unlike any of the others. Someone had paid a lot of money for this one.

She wiped the beads of sweat from along her hairline with the back of her hand. She had been in the loft for over an hour and had had enough of the airless space. She took hold of the handle and gently lifted the suitcase away from its resting place, surprised at how light it was. However, she didn't hear or feel anything move inside. She felt instinctively she wanted to take great care and time with the contents of this case, and she wanted to be alone without fear of interruption when she opened it. She needed to get home to her cottage and shut herself away to concentrate on her task. *I'll bring it back, Dad,* she promised in a whisper, as she made her way back down the loft ladder, the case held securely in her arms.

When she emerged from the farmhouse, she was amazed to find a cloudless, blue sky with no sign of the early morning haze which had prompted her to drive the short distance from her cottage. Now, with the suitcase in her hand, she was, for once, grateful for her little car. After securing the kitchen door behind her, she opened the car door to release the heat that had built up inside while she'd been in the house.

She placed the case carefully on the rear seat, then checked that there was no sign of Rhys or Owen, because the last thing she wanted to do was drive off without saying goodbye if they were anywhere near the house. Satisfied that they were still up in the top field, she closed the passenger door, got into the driver's seat, drove slowly down the farm track, and eased out onto the road. The street through the housing estate was still quiet. She knew that instead of playing out on the pavement or riding their bikes up and down, most of the children would be down on the beach for the day making the most of the unexpected sunshine.

Her telephone started to ring just as she opened the front door of her cottage. Leaving the case and her shoulder bag in the hallway, she snatched up the receiver.

'What's the point of having a mobile if you don't switch it on?' Julie demanded without a greeting.

'And good morning to you, too,' Cristi responded. 'I haven't given my mobile a thought since we broke up. I don't even know where it is.'

'You're hopeless. Where've you been, anyway? I've been trying to get you since nine.'

'Had to go up to the farm. How are the hols going?'

'Much too quickly for my liking. The farmers' market is on in town tomorrow. Do you fancy going, then having lunch? I'm dying to hear about the "do" at the hotel and why you had to go up to the farm. You never do that. If you're up for it, meet me outside the bank on the square at half ten.'

'I enjoyed wandering around the market at Easter,' Cristi said. 'It was really good, so I'll see you in the morning. I'll probably be on the coast bus leaving here at ten, so wait for me in case it's a bit late.'

'OK. Take care. See you in the morning.'

Cristi replaced the receiver. *I'll tell you all about the "do"*, she thought, *but not my reasons for going up to the farm.* Although Julie was a good friend, in fact, her only close friend, she still had an in-built reluctance, verging on fear, to share confidences. At least, she had the market and lunch to look forward to now.

The sun had moved round, and the small backyard was now bathed in bright light. She opened the back door wide to let the summer into her little kitchen. She put the kettle on and spooned instant coffee into her cat mug. As she waited for the water to boil, she filled her bright red watering can and started to spray the tubs and containers overflowing with petunias, begonias, lobelia and trailing geraniums. *One of the best things about living alone,* she thought, *was that there was no one around to tell you what or what not to do.* Cristi smiled. She knew she shouldn't be watering plants in the bright sunshine, but so what? She felt like doing it so water them she would!

Before sitting down on the bench to drink her coffee, she brought the suitcase and her bag from the hallway into the kitchen and put them both on the table, laying the case down on its side. She rummaged through her bag and eventually found her mobile, an old Nokia that had seen better days. She didn't need an all-singing, all-dancing contraption that took pictures and only just stopped short of making a cup of tea. As long as she could make and receive calls, send and receive texts and set some reminders, she was happy. The battery was low, so she set the phone on charge, then poured the hot water into the mug adding a drop of milk, making a mental note to buy some more. She had a choice of biscuits: bourbons, lemon puffs or milk chocolate digestives. She stood for a moment gazing down into her biscuit tin, both hands gripping the work top in front of her. 'What are you doing, Cristi Jenkins?' she asked herself aloud, silently acknowledging that she was talking to herself more and more. 'I know what you're doing,' she answered her own question. 'Just choose a damn biscuit, take your coffee and open the case. You can't avoid it any longer.'

With one of each biscuit in one hand and the mug of coffee in the other, Cristi wandered back outside to the bench and sat down. Idly, she noticed that the compost around the plants had already dried out in the sunshine, and as she sipped her coffee and enjoyed each biscuit, she glanced back through the open door and stared at the case on the table waiting patiently for her attention. In her mind's eye, the pathetic, neglected-looking article had taken on almost human characteristics, and she had been chosen as its guardian.

The sun was high in the sky, and Cristi could feel her cheeks starting to burn. She had prevaricated long enough. Slowly she made her way back into the kitchen, rinsed her mug, then turned round to face the case. Why was she so nervous? Silly. Then taking a deep breath, she lifted her hands and with both thumbs slid back the two locks at the same time.

The smell from inside the case was musky rather than musty. It was not unpleasant, and Cristi immediately felt enveloped in a welcoming warmth. She lifted the lid slowly with unbidden respect and gently laid it back onto the table, exposing the contents to some long-deserved fresh air. At first, she just stared at the silky, brown-and-cream-striped lining inside the lid. There were no smaller pockets, and everything appeared to be in good condition. She ran her fingers along the edges where the lining met leather. No damage or wear and tear. The suitcase had barely been used, and its fine quality was obvious. Cristi withdrew her hand and hesitated for a moment. She felt guilty, like someone opening someone else's letters or reading another person's diary, and yet, she told herself, her father himself had pointed her in the direction of the suitcase.

'You might find something,' he had said, 'or then again, it could contain a load of old junk—bits and pieces of no use to anyone. Have a look, love. Keep anything you fancy then throw the rest away. Too much rubbish in that loft, most of it forgotten, not touched for years.'

Now, face-to-face with what were obviously her mother's possessions, Cristi understood why her father had been so dismissive about what she would find. David Jenkins had neither the stomach nor the heart to throw away what had belonged to his first wife, so in a sense, by going through the case, she was doing her father a favour. Feeling justified, she gently picked up the first item, laid it flat on the table, then carefully opened the folds of white tissue paper.

Lying inside were dainty, pale blue rosary beads, cool and smooth to the touch. There were three more tissue-wrapped packages. The largest and heaviest held a white covered prayer book, a gold cross embossed on the front cover its only adornment, and each page was gold-edged. She gently turned to the first page. In beautiful script, someone had written a dedication in Italian. Surprisingly, she could understand what had been written—*First Communion 1972 Maria Cristina, Chiesa di San Francesco, Loro Piceno*. The little book had hardly been used. She let the delicate pages run through her fingers like gold dust before replacing the book in its wrapping.

The next little package revealed a gold cross and chain with a matching pair of earrings. Dulled from lack of use, they were exquisitely beautiful as far as Cristi was concerned, absolutely priceless. They spoke to her about her mother— small, delicate and precious. Lightly stroking each piece, she vowed to take care of them forever.

With an overwhelming sadness and a lump in her throat, she was determined to unwrap one more item at least. Not only were its contents wrapped in more layers of tissue paper, but also in a strong, unmarked envelope. Inside its protective layers, Cristi found a photograph, no bigger than her credit card. Two dark-haired men, obviously brothers, and a striking looking young woman with thick, shoulder-length wavy hair, her right hand resting lightly on the taller man's shoulder, stared out at her. In the taller man's arms was a pretty little girl in a white dress and matching sandals. They were all laughing at whoever was behind the camera, their sheer delight making Cristi smile.

She turned the photograph over. The writing on the back had faded badly, so she took the picture out into the back yard to get some natural light. *Gi...pe, Maria, En...o, Maria, Cr...tina, luglio 1966.*' The names were so indistinct, but Cristi knew immediately that the little girl was her mother, and a quick calculation told her that Maria Cristina must have been five or six years old when the photograph was taken. But who was the man holding the little girl? Who exactly *were* these people?

Cristi took the photo back into the kitchen, rewrapped it and put it to one side with the other packages. She felt emotionally drained already, so she decided to leave the rest of the contents for another time. Instead of making more sense of her family, she now felt even more confused. So many questions to ask, but who could she ask? Her father was the obvious choice, but he always looked so haunted and sad at the mention of her mother, and Cristi was not convinced that he knew a great deal about the family in Italy. But didn't she deserve to know about her background, and in some detail? Perhaps she had paid too much attention to her father's feelings and his reluctance to talk to her, to the detriment of her own understandable need to find out exactly who she was.

The telephone ringing loudly in the hall rudely interrupted her thoughts.

'Hi Cristi, it's me again. Didn't bother with your mobile this time. Can we make it eleven tomorrow? I've managed to get an appointment to get my hair cut at the Design Studio. It's the last chance I'm giving them after the hash they made of it last time. I've asked for Kim, not Tracy, and I've got a picture to give them some idea of what I want, so is a bit later OK for you?'

''Course it is. No problem.'

'You're lucky; you've got fantastic hair, not dry, not greasy…just thick and wavy.'

'My hair's a nightmare,' Cristi interrupted. 'It takes forever to dry, and it's so heavy.'

'I'd swap mine for yours any day. Have you heard from your dad?'

'Last I heard, they were in Venice, having a really good time. I can't quite imagine Dad on a gondola, though.'

'If Gillian says gondola, then gondola it'll be!'

'Julie, you're incorrigible. Couldn't you at least pretend to like Gillian?'

'No way. I remember her in the sweet shop years ago. A real misery. If it hadn't been the only sweet shop in the village, we wouldn't have gone in there.'

'My father seems happy enough,' Cristi said, at the same time wondering why on earth she was defending Gillian.

'Well, everyone knows what a nice man your dad is. She'd be mad not to thank her lucky stars she's got him for a husband. I don't think many men would put up with her hoity-toity ways. Good job your brothers take after your dad.'

'I'm glad at least three members of my family meet with your approval,' Cristi laughed. 'I'm sure they all love you.'

'Look, I'll see you in the morning at eleven. Come prepared to make a day of it. I might need cheering up after the hair fiasco.'

'See you outside the bank, and I'm sure your hair will be fine.'

'Take care. 'Bye!' And with that, Julie hung up.

Cristi put the phone down and instantly felt deflated. She needed to do something with her life—something different and interesting. She glanced at the tissue paper on the table and the gaping suitcase, which seemed to be mocking her, while at the same time inviting her to venture further into its depths.

'Later. I'll look at you later,' she said to it. 'I'm going for a walk. Wait there 'til I get back.' She turned away from the kitchen table and went up to the bedroom to change into her walking clothes.

Wherever she went, she always had to face the steep hill winding its way up the side of the valley. The local bus ran once an hour from the neighbouring town, but she couldn't bring herself to catch it when she was perfectly capable of walking. Only on cold, rainy days, would she make an exception. During the summer season, the bus service increased by fifty per cent with the addition of the Coastline Shuttle put on especially for the tourists wanting to visit the Coast National Park with its meandering pathways and breathtaking views. Today, however, needing plenty of fresh air and exercise, she took the easy path down to the village then power-walked out to the end of the breakwater.

She touched the weathered, blue-painted door of the lighthouse at the end, then took a breather for a few minutes. Only one or two other people were doing the same walk. Most families stayed on the beach, but Cristi loved the lapping, gurgling sounds the light sea ripples made against the seaweed-strewn rocks. In the early evening, grey seals regularly came into the warm waters of the bay to feed and to watch the walkers on the breakwater, their heads bobbing up and down like lost beach balls. Sometimes, she believed the seals also smiled at her, but it was too early in the day for them. Only noisy, squawking seagulls kept her company.

After a few minutes' rest, leaning on the railings looking across the bay at the Whitebay Hotel nestled on the hillside in the sunshine, she set off again at a good pace. She had taken up power-walking the previous summer after deciding that jogging was too much of an effort. She didn't enjoy running and neither did her knees. She had found herself concentrating on how she hated and resented having to do the sweaty exercise rather than relaxing and clearing her head which, as far as she was concerned, was the whole point of doing it in the first place. For once, she had bought the proper kit: flexible, supportive walking shoes and padded socks. She had even invested in a pedometer and a hydration sac for longer walks. The shoes had had plenty of wear, but as yet, she had not motivated herself enough to do longer distances.

Although there were so many people about on such a beautiful afternoon, she cut a solitary figure striding out. Once, some months before on a particularly lonely evening, she had looked up the meaning of *lonely* and *solitary* in the dictionary, just to see if there was a difference. She found that a lonely person was considered sad, having no companions or friends, but if you were solitary, it was because you had chosen to be. So, in an attempt at being positive, solitary was what she considered herself to be.

As she passed the steps down to the beach itself, she recognised some of the children from her school, all much too busy playing in the sand to notice her. She passed the new Marine Centre and the children's playground before slackening her pace. Her arms, which she used to propel herself along, ached more than her legs, so she shook them out loosely as she approached the ice-cream van.

Only two people stood in the queue, and both of them had caught too much sun across the back of their neck and shoulders. Cristi could imagine what sort of night they were going to spend trying to soothe and cool down the burning skin. Shaking her head, she couldn't understand why people didn't take heed of all the warnings about sun damage. She was lucky to have smooth, olive skin that did not burn easily, but she had plastered herself in factor thirty before leaving the house and had stuffed her hair into a floppy white sun hat all the same. Eventually, the two customers moved away, each carrying three cones piled high with soft ice-cream, sauce and all the other bits and pieces sprinkled on top.

'Hi, Cristi, how's it goin'?'

'Great, Tony, how's business?'

'Could be better but mustn't grumble.'

'Just a "99" for me today, please. How many vans have you got now?' she asked.

'Five ice-cream, two fish and chips, and the diner out on the A40. Do you want sprinkles?'

'No thanks, just the flake.'

Cristi watched as Tony swirled the ice-cream expertly into her cone. They had been in the same class at school, but whereas she had gone away to college, Tony had joined the family catering business. Just below the colourful ice-cream menu, she noticed his purveyor's licence and instantly felt the need to get home. *Tony Gambrini*—the Italian connection yet again. Why had she never thought about it before?

'Here you go Cristi. Extra flake, no charge for you today. How's your dad enjoying that cruise, lucky devil?'

'Having a great time, last time I heard. Probably won't want to come home. Thanks, Tony. See you soon,' she called back over her shoulder, moving briskly away from the van before Tony could ask any more questions about her father. When she saw he had another customer pointing to his selection board, she felt less guilty about walking away so quickly.

She pushed the two flakes further down into the ice-cream, then licked her way around them. She knew it was stupid, but she felt she had been away from the suitcase for far too long. She imagined getting home to find her dining table empty, the case and its contents nowhere to be seen. A mild form of panic gripped her, and she increased her pace. Eating while walking slowed her down, so she threw what was left of her ice-cream into the bin outside the newsagent's. The walk back up the hill would take at least half an hour. The bus took less than ten minutes and was due at any time. She decided to wait and, for once, take the easy option. She was in luck. The *Coastline Shuttle* arrived on time, surprisingly crowded so late in the afternoon. She knew all the drivers on the local service but the lady behind the wheel was a stranger.

'The first Pen-y-Lan stop, please.'

'That'll be 90p.'

No "please" or "thank you", Cristi noticed as she handed over a pound coin, took her ticket and sat down on the first free seat she came to. The shuttle did not hang about, pulling away almost immediately from the stop on the main square to start the steady climb up the hill. The short trip seemed to take forever, with the driver never moving out of second gear. Fortunately, no one was waiting at the stop halfway up, and eventually, the little bus pulled into the lay-by just beyond her cottage. She thanked the driver as she got off but had no reply. The doors of the bus slid closed almost before her feet hit the gravel of the lay-by.

She slipped the rucksack off her back and retrieved her door key from its ring in the top pocket. She opened the front door and walked straight into the kitchen. It was still there, just as she had left it. She dropped her bag on the floor, walked back to shut the front door then burst into tears.

Stupid, stupid, stupid, she chided herself as she flopped down into her armchair, her eyes fixed on the open case. There was no way she could explain the emotional pull she felt towards the inanimate object. It was totally irrational. She felt safe once again, back with the case and ready to look at whatever else it had to offer.

She needed to put the light on. Glancing at the clock, she couldn't believe her evening had slipped away. It was almost twenty to nine. The late sunshine had moved away completely from the back of the cottage leaving her little yard and kitchen in a twilight gloom.

After her tears of relief at seeing the old suitcase on her return at the end of the afternoon, she made herself drink some fresh orange juice and put together a ham salad sandwich. Once started on its remaining contents, she knew she wouldn't want to take a break for food. Even so, sitting on the bench outside the back door, she felt unable to take her eyes away from it. Although still in good condition, in spite of its age, she noticed that some of the stitching at one corner was starting to come away. There were scuff marks around the broad handle and the locks were far more tarnished than she'd first thought. But the rich, chestnut-coloured leather still shone in places, and Cristi thought once again that the suitcase must have cost a pretty penny when it was first bought.

She'd focused so hard on the case that she couldn't remember eating her sandwich. Not until there were only crumbs left on her plate did she realise she'd been on auto-pilot, just eating and drinking for the sake of it, not tasting anything. She rinsed out her plate and glass, put them to dry on the rack, wiped her hands, then returned to her task.

She picked up what looked like a simple sheet of plain paper which had been folded in half then folded again and again. Taking great care, she began to unfold each part. Inside the final fold, she found what had once been sprigs of lavender. Now, instead of the vibrant, perfumed purple flowers, all that remained were brown, dried-up dusty husks. How sad. Cristi stared at the dead flowers, deeply affected by the thought that they must have meant something important to her mother once upon a time. Again, with great care, she refolded the paper perfectly and set it to one side.

Larger items, all in tissue paper, had been placed carefully beneath the collection of small treasures. A little girl's dress, once white, now creamed with age, had been folded neatly and put away. Cristi unfolded the fine cotton garment, admiring the delicate lacework around the sleeves and neckline. The dress was too big for a young child, so it must have belonged to a girl in her early teens. Perhaps it had been her mother's first communion dress, Cristi mused, before refolding it exactly as she'd found it, smoothing out the fabric gently with her open palm. There was a small tray cloth with beautifully hand embroidered around the edges, and a set of three cotton handkerchiefs with the same, deep purple lavender motif sewn into one corner. There was a pair of short, white lace gloves and a length of white ribbon, again folded neatly. Not for the first time did the orderliness of the items strike Cristi. These were all treasured possessions, and she felt desperate to find out the story behind each one. She knew for certain that there *would* be stories and that they would all be part and parcel of her own history.

Finally, right at the bottom of the case rested a collection of cards and notes, tied together by yet another white ribbon. On the top of the bundle lay a picture-postcard of a cruise ship, the *Arandora Star*. There was no date or message on the back. She turned the card over in her hand a number of times but couldn't find any clues to why it should be in the case. She put the card down then picked up two identical train tickets, one dated 1948, the other 1949. The Italian print had faded, and she couldn't make out the rest of the date or the names of the stations—very frustrating.

It was totally dark outside, but Cristi knew she had to finish searching through her mother's belongings before she could even think of going to bed. There were two more documents to look at. The first was an immigration visa for Great Britain. She couldn't tell if it was the original or a copy. She couldn't make out the name, but it had been granted to someone from the district of *Macerata* in the region of *Le Marche*. The official stamp showed it had been issued in Milan in 1947.

The second paper was a medical certificate of some kind, but Cristi couldn't understand the neat, Italian script. Clipped to the certificate was what looked like a work permit. The address of the heavy steelworks in South Wales was quite clear and easy to read. These documents must have belonged to the grandfather she'd never met, or at least she never remembered meeting. Had she ever heard her mother's maiden name? Maria Cristina Jenkins was the only name that came to mind. 'Mamma,' she whispered, 'Dad loved you very much.'

Cristi's vision blurred, and for the second time in just a few hours, she let the tears come. Holding the old papers to her chest, she sat on the settee and cried. Only later in her own bed would she try and work out why she had been so upset.

For the second time in two days, Cristi found herself on the local bus. She knew that most of the passengers would either get off at the square in the village, or at the stop nearest the beach. The rest would carry on into the next town for the market. In spite of feeling a bit down herself, she had to admit that the happy holiday atmosphere on the bus was infectious.

She'd spent a wakeful night, only falling asleep an hour or two before she had to get up. Her habitual cup of coffee had done nothing to relieve her thick head and heavy eyes. It had been very late when she'd eventually put everything back into the suitcase and carefully closed the lid, leaving it unlocked. The musky smell had remained with her even after she had cleaned her face and brushed her teeth. Photographs and questions had vied for position in her mind. Images and uncertainties had kept her brain alert long into the night and she had woken up feeling miserable.

'Hello, Miss Jenkins,' the bravest of the children waiting at the bus stop greeted her as she was about to board the bus.

'Hello, Jordan, off to the beach?' she replied, forcing herself to sound enthusiastic.

'Can't waste this lovely weather,' interrupted Jordan Jones's mother, who had three other children in tow. 'Much easier than having them all at home. How's the cruise going with your dad? Wouldn't mind trying one myself.'

'They're about halfway through now and really enjoying it.'

'That's nice,' Jordan's mum went on.

'Well, have a lovely day,' Cristi said, moving towards the back of the bus making room for others to get on behind her. She found a seat two rows from the back and sat down next to the window. She loved teaching, but always breathed a sigh of relief when the weekends and holidays arrived. "TGIF" was Julie's mantra, and the same thought had started to enter Cristi's mind more and more. *Mrs Jones must be in demand every day four times over*, Cristi thought, but she didn't seem to mind. Her children were boisterous but did as they were told.

Kath Jones had been in the same class as Cristi and Tony at school and had chosen to stay in the village and get married. She now had four children and so many tattoos between her shoulders and elbows that at first sight, they looked like sleeves. The family all got off the bus at the beach, each little one carrying a bag, bucket and spade and a fishing net. Kath turned at the top of the bus steps and announced to no one in particular, 'Here we go again then. 'Bye, everyone!'

''Bye, Kath,' most of the other passengers answered, before the doors swished shut again.

The journey from the beach into town was much quieter. Cristi gazed out of the window at the rays of the sun striking the still water of the high tide. She could hear her father's gentle voice in her head. *'Sea's like a mill pond today.'* And so it was. The tide usually turned at two o'clock, and by three thirty, the rocks of the breakwater would be exposed halfway out into the bay, but at half past ten in the morning, the high tide was ideal for diving off the steps into the deep, calm sea at the beach end of the breakwater. If the steps were too much of a challenge, then it was safe and easy just to wade into the water from the beach itself.

The calmness of the sea and the hushed murmurs of the people still left on the bus only emphasised the turmoil in Cristi's mind. She was on holiday. She should be having a relaxing time and enjoying herself. Instead, she felt in limbo, cut off and insecure.

The routine of her job gave her stability, but she had to face another month without it. Knowing her father was just up the road made her feel safe, but even he wasn't there. She felt all at sea. *Get a grip, Cristi,* she told herself. *Do something positive and sort yourself out.* Somehow, she had to find answers to all the questions swimming around in her brain. As the number of passengers dwindled at each stop and the bus started its climb into the town, she made up her mind. She would go to Italy and put together as many pieces of the jigsaw she possibly could. Only then would she have a true picture of who she really was.

Chapter 18
Cristi and Julie

Cristi spotted Julie first. As the bus pulled into the bay outside the Town Hall, Cristi saw Julie emerge from the small arcade attached to the only hotel in the town centre. Her hair looked fine, a bit shorter than usual, but the style suited her with one side framing her face to chin length with the other side cut much shorter above the ear. Cristi liked it, thankfully, because she knew without doubt that Julie wouldn't be happy with it.

For a few moments, Cristi stood at the kerb and looked at the crowd wandering through the market stalls which had been set up on the square but had not seen a genuine market for more than half a century. The weekly market was a featureless indoor affair at the back of the town hall, but the current trend for outdoor farmers' markets had at last reached the little coastal town and been a huge hit, especially with the locals. So popular had the markets become earlier in the year that in the months of July and August only, the council agreed to divert traffic around the town, closing the square and two side streets to accommodate stalls of all kinds. The farmers' market was always on a Thursday when Cristi and Julie were at school, so this was their first chance to visit all the stalls since the Easter holidays.

'Don't say a word,' was Julie's greeting, shaking her head from side to side. 'God knows what she thought she was doing with those scissors.'

'I think it looks really good; stylish and a bit different from the usual bob, which seems to be the only style hairdressers seem to be confident with these days. The cut suits your face. Honestly, I really like it,' Cristi enthused. Julie's hair looked even better close up.

'Well, not much I can do about it now. Come on, I've been looking forward to this for days.'

Cristi smiled. Once Julie had had her little rant, she forgot all about her hair and was intent on enjoying herself and spending money.

People came from miles away to sell their produce and crafts. Even without definite travel plans for Italy, Cristi was determined not to buy any of the fresh meats, fruit and cheeses. They'd only go to waste, so she showed more interest in the craftwork. So many talented people, she mused, as her eyes were drawn to small water colour prints of the coastline, similar in some ways yet quite different from the ones she'd bought for her father and Gillian.

'What do you think of these?' she asked Julie, who was far more interested in the handmade chocolates on the next stall.

'Very nice,' came the disinterested reply, 'but a bit pricey.' she added, lowering her voice. 'Come and have a look at these chocs,' Julie went on with more enthusiasm.

'In a minute. I like these prints,' Cristi said. 'Go and choose your chocolates. I won't be long.'

Julie wandered off to the next stall, leaving Cristi to take a closer look at the artwork. There were other original paintings of the West Wales countryside done in a combination of ink wash and what looked like scattered blots from a flicked fountain pen. The effect was surprisingly eye-catching, and Cristi knew she wanted to buy one or maybe even two. The artist, George Hamer, sensing an interested customer, rose from his folding chair behind the stall and looked at Cristi expectantly.

'What a unique style,' she said. 'I really like it, especially on the isolated landscapes.'

'Thank you. They're my favourites as well, to look at and to paint. You have a good eye and excellent taste.'

Cristi couldn't decide if he was being sincere or whether flattery was all part of a sophisticated sales pitch. She hoped not. He was well into his sixties, she guessed, and obviously an experienced artist.

'I definitely want this one,' Cristi pointed to a very familiar scene from local postcards, 'but I need to think about a second one. Are you here every week?'

'I do five markets a week during the summer,' George replied, 'so I couldn't guarantee the same paintings will be here next week.'

Cristi looked along the row of stalls while George wrapped her painting. Julie was just handing over a ten-pound note to pay for her chocolates, so Cristi had to make up her mind pretty quickly.

'Give me the one with the threatening clouds over the hills as well, please. You've really caught the mood with that one.'

'About twenty minutes after packing up my materials, there was a tremendous thunderstorm. I only just made it back to the car, so those clouds are as authentic as you can get. There you go,' he said, handing Cristi both her prints, carefully wrapped and put inside a strong, paper carrier bag.

'I hope you enjoy looking at your paintings as much as I enjoyed working on them,' George commented, as Cristi moved away from the stall.

'He was a bit of a smoothy,' Julie said, her arm now linked through Cristi's, 'but then I suppose he's a happy bunny this morning with you forking out for two of his pictures.'

'I really like them,' Cristi said. 'Anyway, those chocs cost an arm and a leg, and by tomorrow night they'll all be gone.'

'What d'you mean, tomorrow night? These little beauties won't see tomorrow. I have plans for them for tonight.'

Cristi shook her head. Her spark of irritation with Julie and her negative comments about her buying the paintings disappeared in a flash. She could never stay annoyed with Julie for long, even though their tastes and temperaments were poles apart.

'Too many bodies here for me,' Julie announced. 'I want some cheese and some of that homemade red pepper relish, then I've done enough for one morning. Do you want anything else?'

'No. I've spent enough for one day. Get what you want, then we'll go and have lunch.'

'I booked us in at the Old Ship,' Julie said. 'I reckoned the town would be full today, so didn't risk not being able to get in anywhere.'

It hadn't crossed Cristi's mind that all the decent eateries would be full on market day. Sometimes, she couldn't believe how "not on the ball" she could be. At least, Julie had had her forward planning hat on.

There was the inevitable queue at the cheese stall.

'You go and get the red pepper stuff from over there,' Julie directed, pointing to a stall with a fresh-looking green and white striped awning protecting a variety of chutneys, pickles, relishes and jams from the sunshine. 'I'll catch you up in a minute.'

Two local ladies, both wearing colourful aprons, stood behind a stall displaying numerous jars and bottles. Cristi recognised the women as members of the WI and friends of Gillian.

'We don't often see you here, Cristi,' Dilys Evans said, before thinking.

'I'm usually at school, Mrs Evans,' Cristi smiled.

''Course you are. What a daft thing for me to say. How's the cruise going?'

'Fine, as far as I know. My last postcard came from Venice, and I'm not exactly sure where they are now. I didn't know you produced all these fabulous things, Mrs Evans.'

'Not on my own, dear. Do you know Nan Carter?' Mrs Evans asked, turning to the smartly dressed lady standing next to her. 'Jonathan Carter's mam.'

'Of course, I do. Hello, Mrs Carter. Is Jonathan still in Cardiff?'

'Just finished his degree, Cristi, and he's decided to follow in your footsteps. He starts his PGCE in September. Don't be surprised if he turns up at school, asking to get in some practice.'

'No problem,' Cristi enthused. 'I'm sure he'll make a super teacher.'

'Was there something you wanted?' Mrs Evans interrupted, obviously not liking being out of the conversation.

'Just a jar of your sweet red pepper relish, please.'

'That'll be three pounds forty. Do you want a bag?'

'No, thanks. It'll fit in my shoulder bag,' Cristi said, handing over a five-pound note. 'Nice to see you both. Give my regards to Jonathan when you see him.'

'I certainly will. 'Bye, Cristi.'

'Good timing,' Julie said, reaching Cristi just as she was turning away from the chutney stall. 'Lunch, I think. With a bit of luck, we won't have to queue. You can tell me what you've been doing with yourself for the last week. Far more than me, I bet.'

The last thing Cristi wanted to do was to tell Julie anything about her holiday so far, but the short walk from the square to the Old Ship Inn gave her the chance to make up one or two fictional, yet plausible, activities to satisfy Julie's curiosity.

As anticipated, the pub was full.

'Much nicer in here without the smoke,' Julie commented over her shoulder as she pushed her way through the customers milling around the bar. There was no need to answer, but no matter how clear the atmosphere was, Cristi preferred to be outside. As if on cue, the barman looked up from pulling a pint and called to them.

'I've put you out in the garden, Julie, third table down.'

'Thanks, John,' Julie shouted back.

'You remember him?' Julie asked as they found their table and started to look at the bar menu. 'He wasn't with us long. John Simmons. His mother married a cook off one of the Irish ferries, and he wanted John to go to the catholic school.'

'You're amazing, Julie. That must have been years ago,' Cristi replied, feeling guilty for not having recognised the young man behind the bar.

'Come to think of it, he'd probably left before you came. He has to be more than eighteen to work here. What're you having?'

The choice wasn't extensive, and the food, when it arrived, was basic but very tasty. The Greek salad was crisp and fresh, and the shared bowl of chunky chips soon disappeared.

'We don't get to do this very often, so let's treat ourselves and have a pud,' Julie said enthusiastically. 'Their lemon brioche bread and butter pudding is fabulous, or so I'm told,' she laughed.

'OK,' Cristi agreed. 'If I have a decent lunch, I won't have to cook tonight.'

Considering the number of customers in the Old Ship Inn, the service was very good, so they were soon enjoying their brioche. Yet again, Julie had come up trumps, and Cristi ate slowly, not wanting to finish her dessert.

'So,' Julie began between mouthfuls, 'did you enjoy the anniversary celebrations? Was Gillian the life and soul of the party?'

Cristi had prepared suitably vague answers to the inevitable questions she knew Julie would ask, until finally, Julie chipped in with, 'Sounds like it was a success, so what have you got on for the rest of the hols?'

Another question Cristi had dreaded. She hated having to lie, especially to Julie, but she really didn't want to share her plans.

'Nothing much. I like pottering in the garden and getting in plenty of walking. What about you?'

'Same, really. I'd like to go away, but after missing out on the Majorca trip, Dave seems to have dropped the whole idea of a holiday in the sun. "We can't afford everything", he whines ad infinitum. To be absolutely honest, I'm fed up with him. Until recently, I hadn't realised what a little twerp he really is. So, some serious future planning is called for. D'you want to know what I'd really love to do?'

'No, go on, surprise me.'

'I'd like to do a teacher exchange to the States, or Canada, maybe. What d'you think?'

'Brilliant! I think it's a brilliant idea for you, but not for our little school. Go for it, Julie. You've nothing to lose. Do something different. Break out a bit.'

With an indrawn breath, Cristi clapped her hand over her mouth. Julie's wide eyes across the table from her were enough indication that her spontaneous vehemence had shocked both of them. The usually calm, collected Cristi had sounded so emphatic even to her own ears.

'Let's do it together, then,' Julie seized the moment.

'Both of us couldn't leave the school in the lurch, especially without a Head. Maybe we could take it in turns, but I still think it's a brilliant idea.'

'I'd need a good reference,' Julie went on, sounding more determined than ever.

'No problem there, then,' Cristi said. 'Any school would be lucky to have you. You might not want to come back.'

'Apart from my job, I don't have a great deal to come back to, except you, of course,' Julie added as an afterthought. 'To tell you the truth,' she went on, looking directly at Cristi over the rim of the coffee cup she was holding between her hands, 'I've already got the forms. I just haven't filled them in yet.'

'When did you decide all this, then?' Cristi asked her, quite taken aback by the positive steps Julie had already taken to leave her job and the village.

'Gradually during the year, I guess. Everything just piled up. A useless Head who creates more and more work for us on a daily basis. The two prats who think we're blind as well as daft. They don't care about us, but what gets to me is they don't care about the children, either; not like you and me, anyhow. And then, of course,' she went on, putting her cup back on its saucer, 'there's Dave, the arse face, who only thinks of himself. No! It's time for me to shift myself and move on. Another five years, and I'll be forty. My God! What a thought. I need to get those forms sent off.'

'Do the exchanges fit in with our term times?' Cristi asked, not absolutely sure how the exchange system worked.

'I can start in January if I'm accepted, so don't panic. I'll be with you in September to start the same old routine yet again. Have you finished your coffee?'

Cristi took the last mouthful of the pale beige liquid in her cup. Coffee it was not, but she'd enjoyed her lunch which was more than could be said for her lunchtime conversation. Julie had already left the table and was waiting for the barman to return with her credit card and receipt.

'Lunch is on me today. You can do the honours next time,' she said, putting her purse away in her shoulder bag.

Cristi didn't argue. Previous experience of eating out with Julie had taught her that protesting was pointless. They pushed their way back through the bar and emerged into the bright sunshine once again.

'I'm going back to the market; what about you?' Julie asked, standing on the edge of the pavement.

'I've spent enough on these,' Cristi replied, holding up the bag containing her paintings. 'You go and wander without having to bother about me.'

'OK, then. I'll give you a ring about my forms. The Head should give me a reference, but as she's a regular absentee, I'd prefer to use you. Think about it, Cris. We could both escape.'

'I might just do that,' Cristi said unconvincingly, as she started to move away in the opposite direction from the market. 'Thanks for lunch. Don't spend too much.'

'I will,' Julie answered, and with a brief wave was swallowed up by the queue waiting to be served waffles and crêpes.

As she passed the small ornamental fountain and the manicured flowerbeds just around the corner from the noise and hubbub of the market, Cristi gave thanks for the peace and quiet she could find so easily in her little hometown. One morning in a busy, crowded market and lunch in a popular pub was quite enough activity to keep her going for weeks.

She decided to walk home, or at least back to the village where she would decide whether or not she had the energy to manage the hill. She needed to get her mind in some sort of order, especially after Julie's bombshell. Somewhere deep in her mind, she had an overwhelming premonition that her well-ordered, settled life was about to change, and when it did, she had to be prepared for it.

Too often these days, she found herself with a great deal to do. When she first started teaching, she prepared her lessons, taught them, marked the children's work and generally joined in and enjoyed the life of the school. Now, all those activities seemed to be a by-product of this policy and that policy, league tables, quality for money, Ofsted inspections and statutory attendance at certain courses during the year.

At times, her diary overflowed, and the only way she could keep her head above water was to write clear, concise lists. From her lists, she could prioritise which tasks were urgent, which were important, or which could wait. From bitter experience, she knew that if she tried to do everything she was expected to do, she would become less efficient and make mistakes. She had high standards, and nothing frustrated her more than poor-quality work. She always took time to encourage her children to take pride in their work to be the best they could be, and after time in her class, slowly but surely, the standard of their work and behaviour improved.

As she walked along the promenade, a light, warm breeze ruffled her hair, which she'd caught back in the leather barrette her father had given her when she was a teenager. She knew she needed a list. She had to clear her mind of all the conflicting thoughts and images which were tangled together, threatening to swamp one another. Before she reached the village square, she knew she was going to catch the bus. She needed to put her thoughts down in writing. It was still quite early in the afternoon, but she was impatient now to get on with it.

It didn't take long. Half an hour after getting home and two cups of coffee later, she surveyed her list, written in clear, neat handwriting. She had pondered over how to set out her thoughts, but in the end, just started writing. As it turned out, her thoughts sorted themselves once they left her head. She liked to use bullet points and decided to begin by detailing her current situation:

    age—thirty-one, nearly thirty-two
    single
    homeowner
    good job
    more responsibility next term
    Julie leaving
    future staffing problems
    Dad and Gillian happy

boys settled
hobbies – walking (solitary pursuit)

Before continuing, she highlighted her age, marital status, Julie leaving, school problems and her walking. In capital letters she wrote LONER, and threw down her pencil. What was the point? Being clear-minded was making her feel depressed. Seeing her situation in black and white pulled her up short and gave her food for even more thought.

Not finished yet, she told herself, glancing at the clock, surprised to see it was still only twenty-past five. She'd been quite oblivious to the sunshine outside but was determined to finish before going out into the garden to do some dead-heading, weeding and watering. Casually, she added "super garden" to her list.

The old suitcase still lay on the table in front of her. Cristi stood up, leant across the table and carefully opened the lid. Once again, the evocative smell she now associated with her mother wafted up towards her. Before sitting back down, she retrieved the letter she'd received from Italy well over a week ago. 'And you're another problem,' she said to the letter as she laid it on top of all the other items in the case. She couldn't explain why, but she felt they all belonged together somehow. 'What am I going to do about you lot?'

Cristi picked up her pencil and started to write again. She had begun to feel unsettled as soon as she'd opened the letter from that unknown person in that unknown place. Since then, uncertainty about herself and her future had increased. So, she started the next part of her list with,

legal letter
Italy
Sebastiano Luce
suitcase
photos
jewellery
bead
tickets and documents
prayer book
ribbon and lace
dead lavender

Then, in capital letters, she wrote MY MOTHER.

Cristi stared at the two parts of her list for a long time. The answer was there, right in front of her, and by the time she put her pencil down next to the paper full of writing, she knew exactly what she had to do.

Part Four
(Italy, Present Day)

Chapter 19
Cristi

She was still amazed that she had managed to get herself to the little town without too much trouble. She hadn't wanted anyone at home to know what she was going to do, because she didn't want to have to answer all the questions she knew would follow. It was going to be her own little adventure, and any problems that cropped up, she would just have to deal with on her own.

The first hurdle arrived much sooner than she had anticipated. How to leave her cottage and get out of the village without arousing suspicion? After a great deal of thought, she booked her train tickets online and just took a chance on catching the early morning train to London from the local station. She had her fingers crossed that she would be able to avoid any locals on the train, and because she was travelling on a Thursday, she had been in luck. She found it surprisingly easy to cross London to catch the shuttle out to the airport, and her two-and-a-quarter-hour flight had been on time. The spontaneous applause of her fellow passengers for the pilot after a safe landing only increased her excitement, and she had been impatient to get off the plane and face the next part of her journey.

She had flown into Ancona Airport, landing just after one o'clock. The intense heat struck up at her from the tarmac as she stepped out onto the not-so-stable aircraft steps. 'Welcome to Italy,' she whispered, stepping to one side at the bottom of the steps to take off her short linen jacket. The early morning temperature back in Stansted had been chilly, and she had been grateful for the extra layer. But now, even her short-sleeved, white T-shirt felt too thick and heavy for the stifling heat.

Not really knowing where to go or what to do, she just followed the rest of the passengers into the arrivals building, showed her passport to an unsmiling official, then waited patiently for her suitcase to glide slowly towards her on the belt of the carousel. She had treated herself to some matching luggage before leaving home, and an inexplicable ripple of excitement tugged at her stomach as she reached forward to grab her case before it sailed past and did another round on it. Pulling up the handle, she heaved the case, which matched her shoulder bag, towards her, walked out of baggage reclaim and followed the sign for the trains.

So far so good, she thought as she waited on the near-deserted platform for the express train that would whisk her down the coast to San Loreto. The canopy over the platform gave welcome relief from the sun which had reached its highest point overhead in a cloudless, azure sky.

She checked her watch, forgetting for a moment that she had added an hour after being reminded on board the aircraft, so it was not long before her train arrived. Within minutes, she was mesmerised by the startling, turquoise calm of the Adriatic Sea. At home, the colour of the water could change dramatically from dark, slate grey to sky blue very quickly, but never to such amazing shades of aquamarine.

More passengers boarded the train at Osimo and Potenza. They were noisy and happy, all looking forward to holidays further south. Most were families with young children, and, for a while, Cristi felt the odd one out, the only person in the carriage on their own. But no sooner had she settled into her seat than she had to get off and change to a smaller, regional train that would take her inland to her final stop.

Since leaving home, she realised that apart from thanking the cabin crew as she got off the aircraft and shyly saying *grazie* at the airport and the station, she had not really spoken to a single soul for hours. How on earth was she going to break through and have a conversation with anyone when she did not speak their language? There was a moment's panic, then common sense took over. *Phrase book, dictionary, hand signals and smile—everything I could possibly need*, her well-developed inner voice reasserted itself.

She had been relieved to find that the last leg of her journey was a short one. The local train turned out to be uncomfortable and slow, stopping at every small rural station. Far more like a bus than a train. Cristi was sure that if you stood near the track and stuck out your arm, the little train would grind to a halt and pick you up. No one, it seemed, was bothered about checking tickets. Perhaps it was just too hot.

When at last she disembarked, she found herself in the middle of nowhere. Total silence. Even the leaves on the trees were still. *Sleeping like everyone else, except me. What am I doing here?*

'*Signorina?*'

A very short, very dark, middle-aged man spoke quietly beside her. She hadn't heard or seen him approach, and she jerked her head away from him, her heart thumping in surprise.

'Taxi?' he queried, pointing to his car parked in the shade at the end of the station buildings.

'Hotel Centrale?' she muttered, managing an uncertain smile in his direction.

'*Certo, signorina,*' the taxi driver nodded, at the same time relieving her of her suitcase and striding off towards his car. *Go with the flow. Go with the flow. If he's an opportunist abductor, then he's in luck. Don't be so stupid. Get a grip of yourself.* Her inner voice was working overtime. The place was deserted. No one would see her get into the car. In fact, no one even knew where she was. Perhaps her idea of going it alone was not such a clever one after all.

'*Grazie,*' she managed again as she climbed into the back of his old Peugeot, surprised he was not driving an Italian car.

'*Mi chiamo Pino,*' he pointed to his chest as he pulled away from the car park and cruised along the quiet road towards the centre of the small town. Cristi took his lead, hoping she had understood him correctly. If not, she would feel very stupid indeed.

'*Mi chiamo Cristi,*' she tried, crossing her fingers, hoping he would not launch into a conversation which could only be one-sided. Fortunately, Pino just smiled and nodded, his eyes fixed on the road which had narrowed as it wound its way through high medieval stone buildings. Cristi believed she could reach out and touch the walls of the houses from where she was sitting. It was blessedly cool out of the sunshine, but her relief was soon shattered when the taxi emerged from the gloom of the cobbled street into the deserted town square. There were a number of cars parked around the monument in the middle of the piazza, but nothing moved.

'*Albergo Centrale,*' Pino announced, pulling up outside an attractive three-storey building in the far corner of the square. There were no signs or notices to indicate that it was, indeed, a hotel—just three, unoccupied tables enclosed by pots of photinias and pink and white oleanders giving a clue that food and drink were on offer at some point during the day. Cristi got out of the taxi, fumbled in her purse, and managed to overpay the driver quite easily with a ten euro note. No change was offered, and she had no idea how much the ten-minute trip had actually cost.

Once Pino and his taxi had been swallowed up by another dark street opposite the hotel, Cristi stood still and looked around her. Along one side of the piazza, she could make out the bank, a florist's, a small newsagent's and several other, more official-looking buildings that had a variety of plaques attached to the walls beside the doors. At the far end was an attractive church, its bell tower dominating the square. On the same side as the *Albergo Centrale*, she noticed the *Bar Centrale* and the *Ristorante Centrale*.

Smiling, she bent down and picked up her suitcase, then walked into the cool foyer of the hotel. Total silence. She stood in front of the reception desk, willing someone to appear. The last thing she wanted to do was press the button of the brass-based bell and shatter the peace enveloping her. So, she waited.

After what felt like an age but could only have been five minutes or so, the door behind her opened, and a short, rotund lady waddled through, a broad, friendly smile lighting up her face. She wore a calf-length black dress splashed with bright orange floral shapes. Her dyed black hair was fashioned into a tight bun at the nape of her neck and scraped back from what must have been at one time a very beautiful face.

'*Buongiorno, signorina,*' the lady greeted her, her tone light and welcoming, '*Signorina Jenkins?*' she asked.

'*Si*,' Cristi managed to say, instantly regretting not practising at least some very basic Italian words.

'*Prego,*' the lady went on, pushing a registration pad across the reception desk. Cristi looked uncertainly at the pad, then sighed with relief when she saw the English translation under each line.

'*E il suo passaporto, signorina,*' the woman demanded, holding out her hand.

Cristi opened her shoulder bag, took out her precious passport and handed it over. The woman fumbled under the desk, and Cristi realised that she was, in fact, making a photocopy. As she filled in her details carefully, she was well aware of the close scrutiny from behind the desk.

'*Sono Anna,*' the lady said, handing back the passport and a large room key. '*Camera numero sette,*' she said, pointing to the number seven printed on the heavy, cream, plastic key fob.

'*Grazie,*' ventured Cristi yet again as she followed Anna up the stairs. Outside the door to room number seven, she repeated what she had learned in the taxi.

'*Mi chiamo Cristi. Grazie, Anna,*' she said as she opened the door to her room.

'I speak a little English,' Anna surprised her, looking very pleased with herself as she turned and went back down the stairs.

The room was clean, plain and simple. The bed was old-fashioned and the mattress less than firm. Dark, heavy furniture filled up the space, and although the décor looked tired and had seen better days, Cristi immediately felt that she was in a place that was authentically Italian. If she had wanted contemporary surroundings, she could have booked herself into one of a number of international hotel chain establishments that seemed to be cropping up everywhere. No! This was what she had imagined, and that little thrill of excitement trembled once again in the pit of her stomach.

After a quick shower in the tiny but functional bathroom, she lay down on top of the bed cover in just her underwear and stared up at the ceiling, yellowed with age and cigarette smoke. *I'm here, actually here in my mother's country. Why has it taken me so long to come here?*

Her own cottage felt a million miles away. She had left home the day before on the boat train that carried passengers away from the port to many inland destinations. She couldn't believe she had considered going to all the trouble of catching a train away from her own station just because she wanted to keep her trip a secret. Why would she do that?

She was sure no one she knew would see her leave. The bed and breakfast she had booked into near Stansted Airport had been easy to find, and the Ryanair flight to Ancona had left only minutes later than scheduled. She had waited for something to go wrong, but now, relaxing in her cool hotel room, she admitted to herself that she had been silly to worry. If she didn't know any better, she would even go as far as to believe that she was meant to be here.

Cristi was woken up more than an hour later by raucous male laughter somewhere below her window. The *Piazza Centrale* had come to life. She swung her legs off the bed, put on a pair of navy linen trousers and a pale pink T-shirt, and looked out of the window. She couldn't see the men seated two floors below, but she could hear their animated chatter, a loud, good-natured discussion in the most rapid speech she had ever heard. Cars were on the move, and all the shops were open. She watched, fascinated, as people entered and left the bank opposite the hotel. She realised that each visitor had to press a red button beside the door, which would then slide open. Only one person at a time could step forward as the door slid closed behind them. The customer was temporarily trapped in a transparent cylinder before an internal door would open, allowing them access to the bank itself. *So much to see and learn, yet so little time.*

She moved away from the window and stood in front of the mirror on the wall facing the bed. Vines, grapes and large bows had been carved into its gilded frame. She brushed her hair, then gathered it back into her favourite barrette, letting the heavy waves fall down her back. She had bought new gladiator-style sandals and a small shoulder bag just big enough for her money, passport, mobile, sunglasses, book and phrasebook. With a final glance at herself in the mirror and a deep breath, she left the room and went back downstairs, suddenly realising that she felt ravenous. Although the lady at the B and B at Stansted had provided a really good breakfast, she had been too nervous to eat much and had not bothered about food during the journey.

At least six pairs of eyes that would not see seventy again swivelled in her direction as she stepped out into the square. She smiled and nodded at the group of old men who were putting the world to rights, which they probably did every day. She kept smiling and nodding at them as each one wished her, *'Buona sera.'*

'Buona sera,' she replied, increasing her pace away from the group just in case they expected her to say something else.

'Inglese...' she heard one of them say.

'Si, si, inglese,' they agreed as a group, before resuming their own conversation.

The air was still very warm, and all the tables outside the *Bar Centrale* were full of customers drinking coffee or eating ice-cream. Cristi knew from her guidebook that at this time of year, most Italians ate their evening meal much later, in the cool of the day. So, she decided to have an ice-cream to keep her going until the time was right to have a cooked meal. She could not believe the difference. At home, Tony Gambrini's ice-cream was considered to be the best in the county, but the pistachio cone she now licked at lovingly was in a league of its own. There had been so much choice.

In the caffè-bar, she had just stared for a long time at swirls of different-coloured ice-cream in large rectangular containers, dithering before pointing to the one she wanted. She could have had two or even three different scoops but stuck to just one to be on the safe side. Maybe next time, she would be a bit more adventurous, knowing there would definitely be a next time. She sat on a low wall outside the small library, unsurprisingly called the *Biblioteca Centrale.* That evening, she promised herself, she would relax and soak up the smells and the atmosphere around her. Plenty of time to deal with the official reason for her visit tomorrow morning at eleven o'clock.

The *piazza* started to fill up steadily. She had read about the Italian tradition of strolling in the evenings but could not remember the word for it. Everyone from the youngest baby to the old men and women of the village came out of their homes to walk slowly back and forth taking in the evening air. It was a time for conversation, debate and gossip. Teenagers, who did not want to parade, sat in groups on the steps of the *chiesa* or at tables outside the bar, eating ice-cream, drinking coke, laughing and joking. Alcohol, Cristi noticed, was conspicuous by its absence.

She realised very quickly that she felt quite at home in this place, and although she was alone, she did not feel lonely, but if she didn't walk across the square to the restaurant, she wouldn't get a table. Feeling a bit more confident, she found a table for two, separated from the *piazza* itself by a low, barrier of more, pink flowering oleander bushes. From her seat, she could still watch the world go by.

Playing it safe, she ordered *spaghetti al ragù* and a glass of red wine, relieved that the waitress could speak a little English. She picked at the slices of crusty bread which arrived in a small wicker basket at the same time as the cutlery and serviette, all neatly tucked inside a sachet with the name of the restaurant printed on the outside. She relaxed her shoulders which had unconsciously tensed up. *How could her grandparents have left all of this behind?* Once again, she could not come up with an answer.

Darkness arrived unnoticed, and with it a drop in temperature. Cristi rubbed the backs of her arms as she wandered inside to pay. To her surprise, her simple but delicious meal cost less than her taxi fare. She handed over her euros with a now automatic smile and just as Anna had done earlier, she added *"mille"* onto the end of her *"grazie"*. As she walked back through the tables on the terrace, she saw that her place had already been claimed by a young couple, totally engrossed in each other, oblivious to everyone around them.

She walked wearily back to the hotel, feeling emotionally drained. Although apprehensive about the following day, she knew she was tired enough to get a good night's sleep. As she approached, she could see Anna standing in the doorway, one shoulder leaning nonchalantly against the door frame.

'Ah, *signorina*, you have eaten, yes?' she asked, moving to stand upright in front of Cristi.

'Yes, thank you, I've had a lovely meal.'

'You must have a drink with me to help you sleep,' Anna went on. 'I have wine, beer, tea, coffee or hot chocolate—all very good.'

There was no way Cristi could refuse the offer without giving offence, so she plumped for hot chocolate. Too much wine would dull her senses, beer and coffee would keep her awake no matter how tired she felt, and she was not too confident about Italian tea. Anna pointed to an old wooden chair beside the door, so Cristi sat down and put her bag on the floor. The same old men were still there, nodding and smiling at her.

'Bella...' one said.

'Bellissima...' added another more forcefully, his mouth devoid of teeth and with more grey hair sprouting from his ears than from his head. Cristi beamed back at them all, trying to imagine what they must have looked like in their youth. They had obviously been the boys of the village in their day.

'Eccola, signorina,' Anna said, holding out a large cup of hot chocolate.

'Grazie, Anna,' Cristi replied, taking the cup and raising the steaming liquid to her mouth. Too late! She found it was not liquid at all but a concoction with the consistency of runny chocolate mousse. It had a strong and bitter flavour that no amount of sugar could counteract. Anna stood looking down at her with a satisfied grin as Cristi tried hard not to show how awful the drink really was.

Fortunately, the telephone on the reception desk rang as she was about to take her second tentative sip, so she stood up quickly, slung her bag over her shoulder, raised a hand to wave goodbye to the old men then followed Anna into the hotel. As she passed, she caught Anna's eye, pointed to the cup then pointed up the stairs, nodding. Anna nodded back and Cristi made her escape. Once in her room, she poured the chocolate gloop down the sink. It gathered rebelliously around the plug hole and refused to drain away until Cristi inserted her finger and rotated it until the brown water flowed clear. She rinsed the cup and added the incident to her ever-growing list of new experiences.

She slept well and woke up feeling excited but apprehensive at the same time. Although worried about her meeting later in the morning, she was, in all honesty, really looking forward to it. Something new. Something different. Just what she needed.

She had her breakfast of coffee and sweet almond croissant sitting outside, a few feet away from the regular clientele. Had they been there all night? With nothing much else to do, what better way to pass the time than to socialise with good friends? Anna came and refilled her cup, taking it for granted that she would want more coffee.

Before breakfast, she had reread the letter that had brought her to this village. Her meeting with the *avvocato* was scheduled for eleven o'clock in the neighbouring town. She couldn't decide whether to walk or take a taxi, so when on her way to breakfast she met Anna, she asked for her help.

'I have to go to Passo Santino this morning. Is it far from here?'

'*No, signorina, due chilometri,*' Anna replied, holding up two fingers. 'You walk. I show you the road by the *chiesa, si?*'

'*Grazie,* Anna,' Cristi replied. *At least, she was fluent in one word of Italian.*

The road behind the church turned out to be a narrow track that skirted around the hillside. It was stony and uneven, but the views across the valley were spectacular. Rolling green meadows flowed effortlessly from the skyline down to the main road that wound its way down the valley, often obscured from view by lines of cypress trees. Although it was already warm, the sun was still rising, and Cristi knew that very soon, it would be much too hot for her to be exposed on the pathway. Anna had been right. It took her just a little more than half an hour to pick her way carefully over the stones and emerge eventually near the small supermarket in Passo Santino.

At first glance, the place looked little bigger than where she had come from, but she knew from her map of the area that the town was deceptive. Its modern exterior with shops, offices and car parking gave no indication of what lay behind the old stone walls and the impressive archway. The town centre dated back to the early Middle Ages and deserved far more time for exploration than Cristi could give it this morning. But now that she knew how to get here, she would make the time to return and wander around at leisure, preferably in the cool of the day.

Intentionally early, she found that she had over half an hour to kill before her meeting. Already feeling uncomfortably hot, she made her way to the bar, ordered a cappuccino and settled herself away from the sunlight. The interior of the little bar in Passo Santino was gloomy. Cristi sat well inside, with her back to the rear wall and stared into the froth on the top of her cappuccino, annoyed with herself for not ordering something cold. After only two days, she should have known better. She liked her coffee piping hot, not lukewarm. She was slowly coming to realise that Italian coffee had all the taste she loved, but not the heat!

Her first drink disaster had been the hot chocolate she had asked for at the hotel. The smell of cocoa and the sight of the creamy foam on top had been so inviting when Anna had placed the cup in front of her. The thick contents underneath, unfortunately, had been undrinkable, having the consistency more akin to a gloopy, chocolate mousse.

Gazing around the bar, she noticed that most of the customers didn't sit down. They ordered their drinks then stayed at the bar chatting, reading a newspaper or generally staring into space. Everything seemed to be done at a slow and steady pace. There was nothing manic, rushed or aggressive going on, and for a moment, Cristi cast her mind back to all the jostling and elbowing in the pub at home just to get to the bar and to find a table for lunch with Julie on market day.

She shook her head. She didn't want to think about home, especially not this morning. She had to focus on her meeting and what information she was going to be given. Would she even understand what she was told? She took another sip of tepid coffee, breathed in deeply and slowly replaced the cup on its saucer.

The round table was just about big enough for two people. Its glass surface protected the image of a glamorous twenties film star. Prints of stars from early black-and-white films adorned the walls. She recognised Marlene Dietrich and Charlie Chaplin, Clarke Gable and even Rudolph Valentino, and suddenly felt at ease, although she could not have said why. She sat perfectly still for a few more moments, glanced around to see if anyone was looking at her, and then, when she was satisfied that she was not creating any undue interest, delved into her shoulder bag and took out the slim, white envelope.

The corners were dog-eared, and there was a small tear across the seal. She had lost count of the times she had read and reread its contents. Now, she was here. On impulse, she had come to this little town, and in a matter of minutes, she would cross the road to the offices of the *Comune,* find the *avvocato's* office and finally discover from the lawyer exactly what her letter meant.

The walk felt like one of the longest she had ever taken. Instinctively, she knew that whatever happened in the next half hour, her life would never be the same again—whether for better or for worse remained to be seen.

Chapter 20
Seb

Giulia closed the door gently behind her. She had gone through Signor Luce's diary with him and put a jug of chilled mineral water and two glasses on one side of his desk. He had a full day ahead of him, and she thought he already looked tired. She was in her mid-forties and had worked in the same office since leaving school. She'd been so lucky. The three generations of Luce men were all gentlemen and wonderful to work for, but this youngest one worried her. If anything, Seb worked too hard, and as far as she could tell he didn't have much of a life away from the office.

'You need to get away for a while,' she'd told him only yesterday. 'Your father can come and manage on his own for a couple of weeks.'

'I know, I know, and I promise to take some time off after I've dealt with the da Calvi mess.'

'I thought you'd made some progress with that estate. Who's the woman coming in at eleven? Isn't she your missing link?'

'Your guess is as good as mine. I couldn't tell anything from the brief note she sent, agreeing to come and see me. She could be anyone, for all I know, and the way I feel at the moment, I can do without any other mysteries.'

'Well, you've got about twenty minutes to go through those ground rental contracts for the Bassi brothers before your mystery woman arrives. I'll leave you to it. Oh, and don't forget, your grandfather is expecting you for lunch, so the da Calvi business needs to be sorted by midday at the latest.'

The land rental contracts were straightforward, bread and butter work, which, although simple, were repetitive and tedious. After he'd checked again that all the financial agreements matched the number of hectares to be rented, he would have to get the three Bassi brothers into the office to sign the twelve-page document in triplicate, which would take the best part of a morning.

The three men, all in their fifties, teased one another mercilessly, argued and complained in equal measure. Not well educated, they took ages signing each page, then insisted on taking him across the road to share some pizza and a glass of wine. He always made sure the Bassi appointment was on a Friday so that he could go straight home afterwards.

Seb loved his job. He had willingly followed in the footsteps of his father and his grandfather. The name Luce was highly respected in the area, and for the most part he was happy. In his role of lawyer, he oozed confidence and charm, but away from his comfort zone he was, he felt, socially inept, painfully shy and self-deprecating. His two sisters were married with children and had moved north to live near Urbino. He knew his father was proud of him but would be happier if his only son didn't live alone and spend what little spare time he had following solitary pursuits.

'You know I love walking in the mountains, and I love reading,' he would protest when his father brought up his situation for the hundredth time.

'It's not right. An Italian man should have a family. By your age, I already had three children,' his father would reply impatiently, not realising that Seb had already switched off, having heard the same old lecture too many times before.

But Giulia was right. He felt weary and jaded. He'd lost some weight, and the stifling heat didn't help. He needed to get into the mountains, and as soon as his current workload decreased, that's exactly what he'd do. The Apennine Mountains were so close, he had no excuse.

He poured himself a glass of iced water, noticing the time on his wristwatch as he held the glass. The woman had three minutes, then she'd be late. He had read through the relevant documents the night before just to refresh his memory. It was an interesting case, and it had taken his firm over eighteen months to track down any family members associated with old Ennio da Calvi, finally ending up with this woman who lived in some godforsaken place hundreds of miles away in a different country.

'Signor Luce,' Giulia's voice penetrated his thoughts. 'Signorina Jenkins,' she announced, standing aside to admit the woman who was spot on time for her appointment. Seb didn't know what he'd been expecting exactly, but whatever it was hadn't come close to the petite, striking young lady who walked towards him, her hand outstretched as she hesitantly ventured a quiet *'Buongiorno, Signor Luce.'* He saw Giulia raise her eyebrows and give a knowing smile, then suddenly realising that he was actually staring, pulled himself together and reached across his desk to shake the newcomer's slender hand.

'Please, take a seat,' he said, pointing to one of the two client chairs in front of his desk. He resumed his seat, a comfortable, high-backed soft leather chair that had been a welcome gift from his grandfather when he had joined the firm.

'I'm afraid I don't speak Italian,' the young woman apologised immediately.

'That's not a problem, *signorina*. I'm sure we'll manage,' he replied in perfect English.

I'm not really sure why I'm here,' she continued, pulling his letter out of the bag balanced across her knees. 'There were no details, just a request for this meeting.' Carefully, she extracted the letter from its envelope and opened it out.

'When I wrote to you, *signorina*, there was still information I had not yet received, so my letter to you, I admit, was most vague. The case in question is quite a complicated one, so I preferred to explain it in person rather than write it all down. Of course, I am sure you will want to ask many questions…but excuse me. I have forgotten my manners. May I offer you something to drink?'

'I've just had a coffee, thanks,' Cristi replied quietly, already looking a little more at ease in his company. He started to feel more relaxed and comfortable himself and found it easy to change the tone of his voice to conversational rather than official, making the meeting less formal. 'On second thought, I wouldn't mind a glass of water. It's taking me a while to get used to the heat,' she added, fanning her face with the empty envelope.

'Believe me, *signorina*, you never get completely used to it. You just learn to live with it.'

Seb walked around the desk to hand her the glass of water. Her hand and forearm, although slightly tanned, were much paler than his dark, olive skin, liberally sprinkled with fine black hairs. She looked up at him and smiled.

'*Grazie,*' she said automatically, then giggled.

'You find something amusing, s*ignorina*?'

'Oh, I'm sorry, but the only Italian word that seems to have come out of my mouth since my arrival is *grazie*, and please call me Cristi. *Signorina* is a little bit too formal. So why am I here?' she asked directly, not giving him the chance to ask her to call him by his first name.

'Yes, well…' he began, sitting down once again behind his desk and adopting a more business-like tone. 'Eighteen months ago, on February 2nd to be exact, Ennio da Calvi died here in Passo Santino.' He glanced at her across his desk to see if his words evoked any kind of response, but there was only a look of puzzlement and curiosity. 'All his legal documents had been left in our safekeeping some months before, including his will.' There was still no response, so he continued: 'Ennio was a simple farmer, a local man known and respected by everyone who knew him. His family had worked the land here for over a century.'

'But what does all this have to do with me?' she finally interrupted him.

'It would appear, *signorina*,' he went on, not yet comfortable with using her name, 'that you are his only living relative, at least the only one we have managed to find after searching for more than a year.'

'I don't understand. I'm not sure I've heard of Ennio da…'

'da Calvi,' he prompted her.

'da Calvi,' she repeated hesitantly. 'And I had never heard of Passo Santino either, until your letter arrived.'

'The situation is a complicated one, as I said earlier, but the truth of the matter is that you are the sole beneficiary of the last will and testament of Ennio da Calvi.'

'I still don't understand. Are you absolutely sure you have the right person? Couldn't there be some mistake? I'm not even Italian.'

'Perhaps you would be kind enough to answer a few questions.'

'Of course. Anything to clear this up.'

'Are you Cristina Elena Jenkins?'

'Yes, that's me.'

'Are you the only child of David and Maria Cristina Jenkins?'

'Yes,' she replied, even more hesitantly this time, finding it odd to hear her father's name mentioned in an Italian lawyer's office so far from home.

'In that case, you are the right person. Your mother was the only child of Giuseppe and Maria, and their family name, *signorina*, was da Calvi.'

His little speech was met with total silence and a slow shake of her head, a look of sheer disbelief in her eyes.

'I never knew my mother's maiden name,' she whispered. 'Isn't that dreadful? My beautiful mother, and I didn't even know her name!'

Without warning, she burst into tears, startling him into action. He moved swiftly from behind his desk.

'Here, *signorina*,' he said gently, holding out a clean, white cotton handkerchief.

'I'm sorry,' she said quietly, 'but I feel so guilty. Why didn't I ask? Why don't I know all about her and her family? I should have been more curious and asked lots of questions.'

'She died a long time ago, *signorina*.'

'That's no excuse. She was my mother. She was different. Special. I should have made my father talk about her instead of keeping her to himself.' Slowly, she got herself back under control, wiped her eyes, but still kept the handkerchief clutched in her hand.

'I am really sorry, but I feel so angry with my father for not telling me these things.'

She folded his handkerchief, but instead of giving it back to him, she put it in her handbag.

'I don't mean to sound insensitive, but what exactly is in the will? You said he was a simple farmer, so I'm sure there can't be much. Whatever there is, I certainly don't deserve it,' she finished off, positive that, by the end of the meeting, Sebastiano Luce would have fulfilled his legal obligations by executing the terms of the will, and she could then make the necessary arrangements to go home.

'In his will, Ennio left you his old farmhouse and some other land. He had a little money saved and had already made provision for his funeral arrangements and burial. For me to go through everything with you in detail, we shall need a second meeting. I hope you don't mind, *signorina*, but I think you have had enough surprises already for one day.'

For a moment, he just looked at her across his desk, understanding her confused expression, then surprised himself by saying, 'Perhaps you would be kind enough to join me for dinner this evening. You have come such a long way, and I would like to show off one of our finest restaurants.'

'That would be lovely,' she accepted immediately, not wanting to spend another long evening on her own far from home.

'Where are you staying?'

'At the *Albergo Centrale* in Montegrano.'

'Mm…basic but clean and friendly,' he commented, obviously unimpressed by her choice of accommodation.

'I shall pick you up at eight if that's convenient for you.'

'That will be fine. I shall look forward to it.'

'And shall we meet here again tomorrow morning, say, at ten-thirty, when I shall go through Ennio's will in detail with you?'

'You've been really kind, thank you. I now need to go away and do some thinking and try to get my thoughts in some sort of order.'

She took another couple of sips of water, put the glass down on the edge of his desk and got up to leave.

'Enjoy the rest of your day, *signorina*. Sorry, I mean Cristi.'

'I'm sure I will, and thanks once again. I'm sorry about the tears. I don't often get that emotional.'

'No problem. See you later,' he said, holding the door open for her, and with a final smile, she left his office. As she passed him in the doorway, she caught the briefest, lightly perfumed smell of the handsome lawyer and realised that she was indeed attracted to a man for the first time since she'd left college all those years ago.

Mere seconds later, Giulia appeared with more papers requiring his signature.

'Nice girl,' she commented, watching his face closely.

'Mm…very pleasant.'

'Did you ask her out? No, don't tell me. You let her slip away as usual.'

'I can't ask every young woman I meet to go out with me.'

'Hah!' she scoffed. 'You don't ask anyone out, ever.'

'Well, this time you're wrong, not that it's any of your business. I shall be taking Signorina Jenkins out for dinner this evening.'

'Somewhere decent, I hope. It's a shame she's not a nice Italian girl.'

'Isn't it just?' he mumbled to himself, as Giulia retreated to her office.

Chapter 21
Cristi

Although she listened intently, she couldn't hear a sound. The hotel was silent and nothing and no one stirred in the *piazza* below her window. She felt like the only person on Earth cocooned in total peace and quiet. She hadn't bothered with lunch, yet didn't feel at all hungry. Her palms resting flat on top of her stomach couldn't feel the turbulence going on inside. In the heavy silence, she went over again the morning's events in her mind.

She had timed her arrival at the *avvocato's* office perfectly, not too early and definitely not late. She had pressed the white button on the security panel set into the wall to the right of a very heavy, solid wooden door, and a second later, heard a disembodied female voice greet her with the now familiar "*buongiorno*".

'Cristi Jenkins to see Signor Luce,' she'd replied, sounding far more confident than she felt.

'*Si, signorina, avanti.*'

Hearing the clink of the door—release mechanism, she'd pushed the heavy door open and walked through to find herself in what looked like a monastery courtyard with cloisters all the way round. A smartly dressed woman in her forties stood on the threshold of an open doorway directly in front of her, lifting her hand in a slight, beckoning wave.

As Cristi walked towards her, she marvelled at how someone could look so stylish and chic in a simple, navy, high-waisted pencil-line skirt, a pink and white floral silk blouse and plain, low-heeled navy sandals.

'*Prego, signorina*,' the woman said, standing to one side to allow Cristi to precede her into a small, neat office kept cool by thick stone walls. One goldfish bowl-shaped vase full of "stargazer" oriental lilies prevented the room from looking too clinical.

'*Un momento, signorina,*' the woman had said softly, looking back over her shoulder with a smile as she gave a sharp knock on the door directly opposite the entrance. Without waiting for a reply, she opened the door and announced Cristi's arrival. Turning back, the woman Cristi now presumed was the *avvocato's* secretary, stood to one side, held out her arm and nodded Cristi in to meet, she assumed, the man who had sent her the letter.

As the door clicked shut behind her, Cristi had received her first shock of the day. The *avvocato* was not some stuffy ageing lawyer surrounded by dark antique furniture and bookcases full of legal tomes gathering dust, but a striking man, not much older than herself, sitting behind a desk, on which appeared to be every hi-tech gadget he could possibly need in his line of business. His thick hair was black but with sprinkles of grey, and when he stood and walked around his desk to greet her, she noticed he was taller than most of the locals she'd come across. *He had smooth, olive skin—natural,* she thought, *not from artificial tanning.*

Now, lying on her bed in the peaceful privacy of her room, she chuckled to herself out loud. She couldn't believe that even in those first nervous moments, she had been subconsciously ticking off her list of "Mr Right" requirements! So far, he had passed the hair and height test, and his amazing blue eyes and long, thick lashes were a bonus.

'Signorina Jenkins,' Seb had said quite formally but gently, holding out his hand to shake hers. Another tick, she'd noted. He had beautiful hands with long fingers and broad, strong nails. His handshake was firm, without being bone-crunchingly forceful. Finally, a swift glance down at his clean shoes in soft black leather filled another box on her list. Seb Luce was passing the test he was quite unaware of taking.

She'd been relieved when he told her he spoke English, and, she thought, *To such a high degree of fluency that he must have studied or worked in England for quite some time, as there was no hint of an American accent.* Her summing up of the *avvocato* took only a matter of seconds, and for once she was glad that she'd taken a bit more trouble over her own appearance, even if her tailored white linen trousers and taupe, sleeveless, cowl-necked top didn't quite have the same style as the woman in the outer office.

The next shock, of course, had been the news that the reason she'd been contacted was because of an inheritance, not that it would actually come to very much. On the way from the station to the hotel, she couldn't help but notice how neatly the fields were kept. All the maize, wheat and vines stood proudly in regimented rows, and yet, so many houses built in the local stone were unoccupied and, in many cases, left derelict. What would she do with one of those? Sebastiano had called Ennio a simple man, so goodness knows what she could expect.

Then, there had been the tears. How embarrassing. Where on earth had they come from? She'd never been a teary person. She couldn't remember the last time she'd cried, and yet she'd blubbered like a baby in front of a perfect stranger. Why hadn't she known the da Calvi name? Why had she never heard of her mother's family? *Because you never took the time to find out,* she answered her own questions. *And the tears came from your own disappointment with yourself.* On the very rare occasions her father had spoken about his first wife, she had been referred to as *Mamma*, and that had been enough. But now, she needed to know more. But not today. She would ask all her questions in the office tomorrow morning. Tonight, she would have a pleasant evening with only two more tick boxes to fill.

The *piazza* was deserted when Seb had dropped her off in front of her hotel just after midnight. The walls of the medieval village had glowed gently in the mellow light cast by discreetly placed floodlights. *The whole atmosphere was magical,* Cristi thought, as the taillights of his car disappeared into the darkness of the one-way system. She stood absolutely still, just for a few moments in the silence. So many of the buildings around her, she realised, had been there for hundreds of years and looked as if they would last forever. Not for the first time since her arrival in Italy did she get the strangest feeling that, somehow, she belonged, that she was meant to come, and dare she admit it, she was meant to stay.

Later in bed, covered only by a light cotton sheet, she wondered if her thoughts about staying had something to do with her dinner companion. *Don't be ridiculous,* she told herself in no uncertain terms. *You've only known the man for what, four, five hours? Flights of fancy don't suit you, so let it go!* But try as she might, she couldn't. Instead, she let her thoughts drift back over her evening with the lawyer.

Earlier that evening, after greeting her at her hotel with a broad smile, and a bright *"buona sera"*, he had concentrated on driving what Cristi considered to be a rather small, understated BMW through the locals, milling around the *piazza*. He had picked his way carefully through the seemingly impossible narrow side streets that wound their way, serpent-like, down between the tall stone buildings until they eventually passed through a wide "*porta*" in the wall which, in medieval times, had helped protect the settlement from invaders. Once out on the open road, Seb had turned his attention back to her.

'I hope you don't mind, but I have chosen a special restaurant for you a few miles away. Although the town has one or two good restaurants, the one we're going to I particularly like, and it's well worth the drive.'

'I'm happy to go wherever you like,' she'd replied enthusiastically, just excited to be going out for the evening with a man who looked as good as he did. Although he was wearing clothes similar to what he'd been wearing in the office that morning, somehow, he had managed to look exceptionally smart yet at the same time cool and casual. He obviously favoured pastel shades, considering his pale lemon, short-sleeved shirt which accentuated his olive skin. He held the steering wheel lightly but confidently, and she felt safe and secure in his company.

'Where are we going?' she asked as he skilfully merged with the heavy traffic on the dual carriageway.

'Out to the coast,' he replied, surprising her, but not elaborating further. 'Did you have a pleasant afternoon?'

'Mm…lots of thinking to do, so I went and sat in the park overlooking the valley.'

'Nice place,' he went on. 'Even when there are lots of people there, it's never noisy. I go there myself sometimes. The ice-cream from the kiosk is homemade and rather special.'

'I'll remember that. Walking through the narrow streets kept me cool, and I just soaked up the atmosphere.'

He nodded, a look of approval on his face. Glancing at his profile, Cristi was once again struck by the length and thickness of his lashes, and from a distance, you could have been forgiven for thinking he was wearing mascara and eyeliner. His nose was aquiline but stopped short of being Roman, and he appeared to have a soft smile permanently on his lips.

The drive took nearly half an hour. They didn't speak a great deal, yet the silences were comfortable. They reached the large town of Civitanova Marche on the Adriatic coast, and within minutes, he had found a parking space a couple of blocks from the beach and the promenade.

'We have to walk a little way. Not too far,' he spoke across the roof of the car as he pressed the central locking system on his key fob, walking around the front of the car to join her on the pavement. 'This way,' he pointed to his left. 'The restaurant is just around the corner.'

If she hadn't known it was there, Cristi would never have realised that the narrow, white-fronted building was a restaurant. A discreet sign above the doorway announced its existence—*Il Gatto Che Ride*—The Laughing Cat. There were only about eight tables, varying in size, all set beautifully with white linen, silver cutlery, and wine and water glasses. Each table had a waxy, deep red anthurium in a tall, narrow cut-glass vase as its centrepiece. Once again, Cristi recognised understated quality and elegance. She now expected nothing less from Sebastiano Luce.

They were shown to a table for two, not far from the bar. The waitress was in her mid-twenties, plump with straight, black hair scraped back into a ponytail. She obviously knew Seb, greeting him with a wide, friendly smile and the constant chatter of familiarity as she led them to their table. She waited for them both to sit down, then handed out two large menus bound in black leather. A cartoon-style grinning cat standing on a fish skeleton tooled into the soft leather gave Cristi a clue as to what kind of restaurant Seb had chosen, and for a second, her stomach sank.

'What would you like to drink?' Seb asked, his menu resting on his thighs.

'Sparkling mineral water, please, no ice.'

He gave their drinks order in rapid-fire Italian, and as the waitress moved away towards the bar, he opened the menu, glanced at it briefly, then raised his head and smiled at her bemused expression.

'This is the best fish restaurant in the region,' he said with more than a hint of pride in his voice. 'Along the coast, there are so many, most of them very good, but this is the best.'

She felt his enthusiasm and pleasure but had to take a deep breath in through her nose when she saw the mass of beautifully printed yet unintelligible items listed on the menu. Four large pages of dishes to choose from, but before she could admit that she was totally out of her depth, he had taken pity on her.

'I eat here quite regularly, so would you like me to recommend one or two things?'

'Oh, yes, please. I wouldn't know where to start,' she confessed, closing her menu and placing it carefully next to the cutlery.

'I don't know if you have already found that Italian meals are not exactly like those you are probably used to?' he said, his tone questioning. Without waiting for her reply, he went on, 'The meal starts with an *antipasto*, but on a menu, you'll see *antipasti*. This is the starter which can often be the size of a main dish, very filling if you have bread as well. Then, there is the *primo piatto*, the first course. This is nearly always some kind of pasta dish. The *secondo* comes next. This is when you have your meat or fish, and if you want vegetables, you order *contorni*.'

'*Contorni*,' Cristi repeated, to show that she was listening and not just gazing doe-eyed across the table, although she had indeed taken full advantage of the opportunity to sit and watch her companion. He was even more attractive when he was animated, and she couldn't believe, or at least hope, that he hadn't been snapped up by some lovely Italian girl who fitted perfectly into the kind of lifestyle his profession could afford. Apart from his expensive-looking watch, he didn't wear any other jewellery as far as she could tell, no wedding ring and there was no sign of paler skin where there should have been one.

'…if that's OK with you?' he asked, not realising she'd missed the last part of his explanation.

'Sorry. Will you say that last part again, please?'

'I only suggested that you might like to choose your own *dolce,* your own dessert. You will recognise most of the words as they now appear on many English menus.'

'Yes, of course,' she smiled. 'I love my puddings, so I must make sure I leave enough room for one. The other courses sound quite daunting.'

The waitress returned with their drinks—chilled sparkling mineral water for both of them. Noticing her glance at his glass, he said he preferred water, but he had taken the liberty of ordering a good white wine to have with the meal.

The food was delicious and expertly served. Seb had chosen tender mussels still in their shells, cooked in three different ways. A light starter but one that confirmed the excellence of the restaurant. The pasta course was cooked to perfection, fine ribbons of fresh, homemade linguini in a light, creamy sauce laden with small pieces of octopus, squid, lobster and prawns. Throughout the meal, Seb had chatted away, totally at ease.

'You're a teacher, aren't you?' he asked, then answered his own question. 'I had to go through all the paperwork when we were trying to track down the family. What age? Young ones or teenagers? I couldn't teach either.'

'I teach little ones just before they go on to secondary school, so most of them are ten or eleven years old.'

'Do you enjoy it?'

'Oh yes, very much,' she replied instantly, surprising herself with her automatic response.

'And what do you like to do away from school, that is, if you manage to find any free time? One of my sisters teaches maths and economics in Bologna, and she never has the time to breathe, let alone enjoy herself. But then, Claudia always did like playing the martyr. I love her, really,' he continued, laughing softly to himself, obviously thinking about his beautiful, clever sister. 'I have three sisters, by the way, all older than me, so I have been mothered to death since birth!'

'It doesn't seem to have done you any harm,' she commented lightly.

'No. I love them all to bits. We get along really well, although now and again, I have to remind them that I have grown up, not that it makes any difference! Anyway, back to you. What do you like to do in your spare time?'

'Rather boring, I'm afraid. I like to get my boots on, pack a small day sack and just walk. I live on the coast, so I can follow the path around the coastline going north or south. Sometimes I go inland, it depends on how I feel, but I prefer to be near the sea.'

'Do you walk alone?'

'Oh, yes. Always alone—just me and my thoughts. I sort out so many things in my mind when I'm tramping across the fields.'

'Amazing,' he said, leaning away from the table and just looking at her.

'Not that amazing, surely?' she quipped.

'It is when you consider that I do exactly the same thing. I have to drive to start my walks, but I spend hours, sometimes days, in the Sibillini, the mountains a few miles from here. It's easy to get to the trails up there, and you'd be amazed at how many of the world's problems I sort out along the way. Anything else?'

'Mm…I read anytime, anywhere.'

'What sort of books?'

'Psychological thrillers, crime fiction, espionage. Anything like that. You look surprised.'

'Nothing educational, then?'

'It depends on what you call educational, I suppose,' she went on mildly. 'I learn a lot about DNA, criminal procedures, forensics and deductive thought processes. So, it's not really mindless stuff. The last thing I need is a brain challenge after a day surrounded by lots of children demanding my attention.'

'I read books on the First and Second World Wars. Books, journals, diaries letters, poems. Anything I can lay my hands on. It never ceases to amaze me that just twenty-five years after the war to end all wars, Europe was at war again,' he said, shaking his head. 'So, it would appear we have at least two pastimes in common, Signorina Jenkins,' he said, smiling broadly as he raised his glass towards her before sipping more wine.

They eventually finished their meal, deciding to share the panna cotta dessert with cherries steeped in liqueur. She had declined a coffee, but Seb had opted for an espresso, which was served in the smallest cup Cristi had ever seen, apart from the plastic ones in the Wendy House in the Infants' Department back at school. She didn't see him pay the bill, so assumed he had some kind of standing arrangement with the management. Did he often eat here with female guests? He seemed to know the place well. She had tried hard not to let the thought bother her, but it did. She liked him, and even though she'd be leaving Italy in two days' time, she still wanted to believe that the evening was something special to him as well as to her.

'That was an excellent meal. I enjoyed every mouthful. Thank you,' she said truthfully, as he pulled his seat belt across his chest before switching on the ignition.

'I'm pleased,' he said, carefully pulling smoothly away from the kerb. 'Here, I picked these up for you.' He handed her two small paper coasters, round with a fluted edge. The same cat-with-fish-bones motif was printed in gold in the centre of each one. 'A little souvenir for you.'

'Thank you,' she said, popping them into her shoulder bag resting on her knees. 'Shall I let you into a secret?' she asked, turning slightly towards him.

'Yes, of course, if you want to,' he replied, sounding a bit more serious.

'I don't usually eat fish. I've never liked it.'

Before she could qualify her confession, Seb had pulled the car over to the side of the road and cut the engine. Turning in his seat so that he was directly facing her he asked, his voice little more than a whisper. 'Why didn't you say? Why didn't you tell me? We could easily have gone somewhere else.'

Cristi was mortified. He looked upset and embarrassed. She hadn't intended to offend him. He looked as though she had physically slapped him.

'I'm sorry. I feel terrible,' she said firmly. 'I told you the truth. Everything I ate tonight, and I *did* eat everything, was fantastic. It all tasted quite different from what we have at home. It didn't even smell fishy.'

'That's because it's so fresh.'

'I realise that, and from now on I shall order fish, but only in a proper fish restaurant like the one we've just been to. Just think,' she went on, not convinced he was totally appeased, 'that if I'd told you, I would have missed the experience of eating such a delicious meal.'

'In future, please tell me things, OK?' he said, putting the car in gear and pulling away. 'OK?' he repeated.

'OK, I definitely will,' she agreed, nodding her head emphatically, making sure he knew that she had understood his message. A little thrill of excitement had bubbled inside her at his words. She couldn't think beyond tomorrow, but he obviously could.

He had been a little more subdued, Cristi thought, *when he said goodnight.* He'd enjoyed the evening, thanked her for her company, confirmed the time of their meeting the following morning, and then with a swift wave of his hand, had driven off. Still staring up at the ceiling, she asked herself again why she'd opened her big mouth about the fish. Such a little thing, not worth mentioning, but she'd done it all the same. She could only hope that she hadn't alienated him even slightly.

That was the very last thing she wanted to do.

Cristi couldn't remember falling asleep, and only the slamming of a car door in the *piazza* woke her up. She checked the time and found that she had slept right through the night, and it was already eight-thirty. Although she had eaten far more than usual the night before, she felt ravenous.

She took a very quick shower, taking care not to wet her hair. She pulled clean underwear out from the bottom of her case, then stood in front of the heavy, ornately carved wardrobe, both doors wide open, and tried to decide what to wear. She'd brought a selection of different-coloured cut-off trousers and a selection of T-shirts, but until the business with the law firm was completed, she felt she needed to dress a bit more formally than smart casual. With this in mind, she decided to wear her navy linen trousers with a navy silk capped-sleeved blouse dotted with tiny pink flowers. She'd only brought one pair of sandals, so they'd have to do.

As she walked down the marble steps to the reception area, she felt a mixture of excitement and apprehension. Today, she'd learn the truth, the extent of her inheritance, and what it would all mean. But these thoughts were accompanied by the anticipation of seeing Sebastiano again.

The piazza was already very busy. Women of all ages were shopping, men were chatting in pairs or in small groups, delivery vans were weaving their way around one another and a queue was forming outside the bank, waiting patiently as each customer went through the time-consuming security process. The old men were there, of course, and if she hadn't seen the empty chairs at midnight the night before, she might have believed they had never been home. She acknowledged them with a smile, a nod and a wave, which were returned by each one of them. No sooner had she sat down than Anna was there with her coffee and almond croissant.

'*Grazie, Anna,*' she said determined to learn to say at least a few more words before going home. Although she took her time over her breakfast and lingered to do some more people-watching, she found she still had an hour and a half to spare before her meeting.

After cleaning her teeth and checking that she had her passport and Sebastiano's letter in her bag, she left the hotel to walk the short distance to Passo Santino. The narrow path soon gave way to a wider lane, which brought her out between a three-storey block of flats and the building that housed the *carabinieri*. Instead of turning right and making her way towards the offices of the *Comune*, she turned left and wandered to the far end of the town. She didn't pass many people, but vans, trucks and old cars passed by slowly in both directions.

The apartment blocks all looked neat and well-kept with an abundance of trailing geraniums cascading from window boxes, their pink and red petals standing out against the pale grey or yellow render. These buildings outside the town walls had features more in keeping with modern-day Italy. Cristi was happy to see that roses seemed to be a favourite plant. Up the side wall of the small supermarket, a magnificent climbing rose weighed down with masses of large, scarlet blooms, brightened up an otherwise dull building. She stopped to see if the rose had a perfume, but no, its striking colour was enough to attract the bees and other insects.

She glanced at the notice stuck on the window beside the multicoloured plastic strips which hung down over the doorway. In her head, she read out the days of the week, repeating them four or five times in a determined attempt to remember them. She guessed that *ore* meant hours and worked out that on Wednesdays, the shop was *chiuso,* closed, in the afternoon. She'd often heard people say that the best way to learn a foreign language was to live in the country and be immersed in it. Absolutely right, she told herself, and not only hearing and speaking but reading as well.

She walked past the small car park for the shop, shaking her head when she saw the haphazard parking. Obviously, the locals were quite used to driving in off the main road down the side of the supermarket and parking wherever there was a space. One or two cars had parked neatly at right angles to the wall, but she didn't fancy their chances of having a clean or easy getaway.

There was a large rectangular truck delivering fruit and vegetables parked up behind a white, electricity-company van, with "ENEL" printed clearly on the side. New brightly coloured cars, which, in her mind, belonged to ladies who did the shopping, had been left in the company of rusting little Fiats driven, she imagined, by little old men just like the ones outside the hotel. Right on the end, just off the walkway, stood a three-wheeled customised tuk-tuk, its black bodywork shining through the leaping orange and yellow flames painted up one side and over the roof.

As she stood admiring it, she heard the crackle of the plastic curtain and turned to see a boy no older than sixteen or seventeen jump into his pride and joy in front of her, throw his shopping onto the seat next to him, start up the noisy little engine, and drive away, looking both ways repeatedly before pulling out onto the main road.

She walked on a little way but soon realised that there was very little to see on the edge of the town, so she crossed the road in front of the ladies' hairdresser's, aptly named *Capelli,* and started to wander back on the opposite side of the road. She still had forty-five minutes before her meeting, so she took her time, sauntering rather than walking. The day was heating up, and she had already learned that if you needed to do something or go somewhere, you either got going very early so that you had finished by mid-morning, or you left everything until the evening. In this part of the world, at least in the summertime, anything that required physical activity between the hours of eleven o'clock and six o'clock could be very uncomfortable and ill-advised.

The *carabinieri* offices at the top of her path lay opposite an *Api* garage, which stood back away from the road with just enough room for cars to pull in for fuel. A little way farther along, set into a tall, red brick wall covered in

Virginia creeper, she noticed a plaque which told her, she guessed, that she was 438 metres above sea level. So different from home. She could smell the aroma of freshly baked bread, and tucked away between two taller buildings she discovered a small bakery. It was obviously very popular, with a constant stream of customers going in and coming out a few minutes later, carrying paper bags of various sizes. The baker must have been aware of their regular order, so they were served without delay. She made up her mind to come back and go inside once she had dealt with the main task of the morning.

Keeping a close eye on the time, she carried on along the main road towards the offices of the *Comune*. A few metres further on, there was a more modern *pasticceria*, which sold fancy fresh cream cakes and colourful fruit flans as well as biscuits and bread. Although they looked absolutely delicious, the enticing aroma of freshly baked dough was missing.

The *piazza* ahead of her was really busy. For a few moments, she just stood and watched. *If you enjoyed the dodgems at the fair,* she thought, *you'd love all the manoeuvrings to get a parking space.* There didn't seem to be any order or system, and yet, all the little cars seemed to manage to find a place. There were businesses on two storeys down one side of the *piazza*, and she could see a *pizzeria*, a bank and some offices on the first floor. At street level, there was another small supermarket, not as bright or as welcoming as the first one she'd seen, and next door was another dark shop selling stationery, toys and all kinds of inexpensive knick-knacks. The hardware store was squeezed between the florist's and the bar with the obligatory group of old men sitting outside watching the world go by.

The closer she got to the square, the more the butterflies in her stomach fluttered. Suppressed excitement warred with nerves as she made her way through the parked cars and walked under the cloisters to her meeting with Sebastiano. She made sure she wasn't too early and entered Giulia's office a couple of minutes before ten-thirty.

Giulia greeted her with what Cristi considered to be an excess of enthusiasm. She was shown into Seb's office immediately, but not before noticing that yesterday's lilies had been replaced by pale pink and white orchids. Giulia must love her job, Cristi thought idly, as the door closed behind her, and Seb came from behind his desk, a broad, welcoming smile on his face.

Seb looked just the same as he had the day before, but somehow, he felt so much more familiar. Without having to ask him outright, she had managed to tick off her final two boxes. He lived on his own, he had told her, not in a modern apartment but in one of the smaller houses on the hillside overlooking the valley below that had uninterrupted views of the Sibillini Hills to the west. He could walk to work, and, on most days, this was the only exercise he managed to fit in.

'Good morning,' he greeted her in English.

'*Buongiorno,*' she replied, raising her eyebrows. '*Come sta?*' she asked, showing that she had extended her vocabulary by at least three words.

'*Bene grazie, e Lei?*' he answered her without hesitation.

'*Molto bene,*' she said, then continued in English: 'Anna at the hotel told me what to say. I'm sure she thinks I need looking after, so she has taken charge of me.'

'Are you OK with that? I would have thought you'd want to do your own thing.'

'I don't mind. She's being kind and helpful, so it's not a problem.'

'Did you sleep well after eating so late?' he asked, still wondering, no doubt, if she had had to force herself to eat the fish.

'I slept so well. I actually overslept, and I never ever do that at home.'

'Good. Sometimes the *piazza* can be a bit noisy even after midnight. Can I offer you something to drink?'

'No, thank you. I think we had better get on and sort out the papers you have for me. You must have other work you need to be getting on with.'

'You're right, of course,' he said, his tone switching from familiar friendly to business formal.

Yet again, she felt she had offended him. She was more than happy to sit chatting and would have loved a cup of Giulia's coffee, but on the other hand, she didn't want to make him feel obliged to be kind to her. She was out of her depth. Her dealings with men in social situations were virtually non-existent, and the last thing she wanted to do was distance herself from the delightful man sitting across the desk from her.

'I have your file here,' he said, opening a green folder which, to her surprise, held quite a few documents, papers and letters.

'Don't worry too much about this lot. You'll learn that every document has to be signed in triplicate. Italian bureaucracy is renowned for its complicated and often unnecessary restrictions. We could get by on a quarter of this stuff. Did you bring your passport?'

'Here it is,' she said handing over the precious little navy-covered booklet. This was the first time she'd had to use a passport, and she had examined it closely with child-like pleasure when it had arrived by special delivery. Printed in gold on the front cover were a lion and a unicorn on each side of a crown. A Latin, a French and an English word joined the single word "PASSPORT" printed in capital letters, and beneath this, also in gold, was the symbol which meant the holder could pass through passport control electronically without showing it to an official.

He flicked to the details at the front of the booklet and made a note of her full name, date and place of birth and her nine-digit passport number. He wrote out each piece of information on three separate forms using a very expensive-looking fountain pen.

'I need you to sign at the bottom and date each sheet please,' he said, handing them to her across his desk. 'Here, use my pen,' he offered.

She took what turned out to be a Mont Blanc fountain pen, still warm from his fingers. She leant forward and wrote her signature on the top sheet. As she slipped it over to one side to allow the ink to dry, she glanced up to find him studying her passport photograph.

'Not a bad likeness, for once,' he commented, not at all embarrassed that she had caught him staring at her picture. 'When you've finished, Giulia will also sign the papers as a witness. Be prepared to sign lots more papers before we're done.'

As she completed the last sheet and put the top back on the pen, he left his seat, went to the door, and asked Giulia if she would kindly spare him a few moments. His elegant secretary glided into the room, smiled brightly at Cristi and then, without further instruction, put her name on each sheet using her own pen.

'Good, now that's done, we can move on,' he said in his most business-like tone. 'But before we get into all the legalities and serious stuff, I have a confession to make.'

Oh, oh…here it comes, she thought, instantly feeling deflated. The polite dismissal. She took in a deep breath and consciously made her shoulders relax. *I bet he has a nice, suitable Italian girlfriend and he's only been doing his job making the inexperienced little foreigner feel at home.*

'Are you OK?' he asked, concerned.

'Fine,' she replied with only a slight croak in her voice.

'Well, as I was saying, I have lunch with my grandfather twice a week. He's called Sebastiano as well, by the way. So, after our meeting yesterday, I went to see him as usual and mentioned your name. He was born here in Passo, so of course, he knew the da Calvi family, and here's where my confession comes in. I told him I would bring you to have lunch with him today. Only if you are willing and have nothing else planned.' He finished speaking rapidly, raising his eyebrows questioningly.

'Of course! I'd love to meet your grandfather,' Cristi answered without hesitation, unable to disguise the relief and enthusiasm in her voice.

'I know we still have a great deal of business to get through, but I think you'll find it a lot easier to deal with if you know a bit more about your family and how you came to be here.'

'I really am interested, but there is something I need to know, and I don't know if you will have the answer.'

Now, it was his turn to look wary and concerned, his dark brows meeting in a frown above his incredibly blue eyes.

'My mother,' Cristi began. 'Do you know where she is? I mean, do you know where she is buried?'

'Not exactly, I'm afraid, but I am sure we will be able to find out. I believe your grandparents settled farther north when they returned, so I shall ask my researcher to make some enquiries.'

'Thank you. I feel so guilty for taking up so much of your time.'

'There is nothing that can't wait. Nothing urgent. Giulia will deal with things here, so don't worry. Let's go and have a coffee. You can tell me more about your school and your family. By the way,' he added, slipping into the jacket of his suit, ready to leave, 'I'm sure you'll like my grandfather. We are very much alike, as you'll see.'

Chapter 22
Signor Luce

Lunch was a simple meal served outside on the terrace under the shade of a tiled canopy, which ran the length of the house. The table had been laid beautifully for three people, and yet again, she felt relaxed and quite at home.

They had arrived in bright sunshine just after midday, but instead of going up to the large door at the front, Seb led her down the side of the house to the rear. This, she realised, was where the view was. As they came around the corner of the building, the panorama of fields and mountains opened up in front of them. The scenery was breathtaking, stopping her in her tracks to take in the beauty of it all.

'Fabulous, isn't it?' his quiet voice broke the silence. 'I never, ever get tired of sitting out here and drinking it all in. What you see, of course, changes with the seasons. The light, the textures, the colours. We are very fortunate,' he said, more to himself than to Cristi, his eyes fixed on the distant hills. 'It looks as if Marina is ready for us,' he went on briskly, moving towards the table.

'Who is Marina?'

'My grandfather's housekeeper, driver, secretary, nurse. You name it, Marina can do it. I'll go and tell them we're here.'

He left her standing, still gazing at the immaculate garden. The house itself was substantial, built from stone the same colour as the coffee she had ordered earlier. Mature yellow climbing roses helped to mellow and soften the rough edges at each corner of the house, and pale green vine leaves fluttered along the edge of the canopy, casting dappled shadows on the white tablecloth.

'Cristi!' The voice startled her. 'This is my grandfather,' Seb said, standing aside so that the man behind him in the doorway could walk through. Whatever she'd expected, it hadn't been this. The old man was shorter than she was with a shock of thick white hair neatly trimmed just above his collar. Signor Luce's face was tanned with few wrinkles, his mouth wide and smiling beneath the same shaped nose as his grandson's. He too had deep blue eyes, a little dimmed with age but still striking.

'*Signorina,*' he welcomed her, both hands palms-up outstretched towards her.

'*Buongiorno, Signor Luce,*' she replied, taking one of his hands and shaking it firmly. He was wearing a black, open-necked, short-sleeved polo shirt with cream trousers and soft, tan leather loafers. He looked confident and affluent, and she was glad she'd decided to leave her casual, holiday clothes in the wardrobe.

On the way up from the town, Seb had told her that his grandfather would be eighty-eight years old at the end of the year and that she needn't worry because he spoke five languages fluently, English being his second language. It had been his grandfather who had first set up offices on both the east and west coasts of the United States. He had then left it to his son, Alessandro, to extend the family business in other countries.

'My father and one of my sisters and her husband do most of the travelling, but we have good people in all the offices. You'll have no trouble chatting with him, I can assure you. He loves meeting new people, especially young ladies, and his eyes positively lit up when I mentioned you,' Seb had enthused.

'I can't imagine why, but I'm looking forward to hearing more about the da Calvis, especially from someone who actually knew them.'

They spent the rest of the journey in comfortable silence. Cristi had been totally absorbed in the beauty of the passing scenery.

'I'm delighted to meet you, *signorina,*' the old man enthused, his eyes alight with pleasure and a touch of curiosity. 'Please take a seat. Marina will bring our drinks.'

Cristi sat on the high-backed chair facing outwards, while the younger man took his place at the end of the table to her right, his grandfather to her left. No sooner had they sat down than Marina arrived. She wondered fleetingly if the short, plump, homely-looking Marina had been loitering in the shadows, waiting for the exact moment to appear.

With a kindly '*Buongiorno, signorina,*' she placed a large jug of iced water and three tall glasses on the table, disappearing as swiftly as she'd arrived. Without asking, Sebastiano poured each of them some water, put the jug down then leant back in his chair sipping his water slowly. Marina appeared once again, carrying a platter of cold meats and slices of melon. Small bowls of olives and sundried tomatoes were already on the table together with a basket holding slices of home-baked bread.

'I suggest we relax and enjoy our lunch first, then I can speak to you about your family,' the old man said, refilling his glass with water.

'Thank you, I'd like that,' Cristi replied, smiling at the man who just didn't look his age. Idly, she wondered if this was what the young Sebastiano would look like when he reached the grand old age of eighty-eight.

'Please serve yourself, *signorina*. Shall I tell you what the meats are?'

'Yes please,' she said, thinking, in her ignorance, that they were all a different take on salami. He pointed out the pale slices of *mortadella*, then *prosciutto crudo* and the almost-transparent slices of Parma ham.

'I shall try a little bit of each one, I think,' she said, helping herself to the meats and a slice of juicy melon, not noticing the smiles exchanged between her two companions. She was happy to savour every mouthful while the two men chatted in rapid Italian. The water had been replaced by a crisp, white prosecco which was perfect on such a warm day.

The antipasto was followed by a small bowl of green spaghetti. Seb told her that it was pasta mixed with pesto, the basil and the olive oil produced by his grandfather. She enjoyed every mouthful, and Marina's homemade lemon sorbet completed a perfect summer's meal.

'That was really excellent,' she commented after finishing the last mouthful. 'Thank you. I enjoyed everything.'

'We'll have our coffee on the comfortable chairs, I think. You can bring the wine, Seb,' the old man instructed, not noticing Cristi's look of surprise at the use of his grandson's abbreviated name.

It was just before five o'clock when Seb dropped her off outside her hotel in Montegrano, with the promise to come back to collect her at eight-thirty. He wanted to take her to a much smaller restaurant where she could try some simpler, regional dishes.

After the early afternoon lull, the *piazza* was slowly waking up again as she walked into the hotel. Only two old men sat outside, waiting no doubt for the rest of the "gang" to arrive. Back in her room, she put her bag on the chair, kicked off her sandals and released her hair, leaning over so that the thick, heavy waves swung from side to side, enjoying their release from confinement. Straightening up, she tucked her hair behind her ears as she walked into the small bathroom, remembering that the "C" for *caldo* on the tap meant "hot" not "cold". She opted for the tap marked "F" and splashed her face with cold water. As she patted her face dry, she realised that instead of feeling weary after hours spent in the warm sunshine, she felt surprisingly energised and excited. The old man had shared so much information, her mind was alive and buzzing.

She stripped off and crawled under the sheet which she wrapped around herself before propping up the pillows so that she could lean back against them. She rested her outstretched arms down by her sides, palms flat on the bed, tilted her head back and closed her eyes, ready to relive the afternoon in her mind's eye.

Once settled on the comfortable chairs and wine glasses refilled, the old man began with a question. 'Seb tells me you know very little about your mother or her family. Is that so?'

'To be absolutely honest, I don't know anything about her or her family,' she replied truthfully to the sympathetic rather than critical tone to his question. 'My mother died just before my fifth birthday. My father remarried, and I was brought up by Gillian, my stepmother. I have two lovely half-brothers, and we get on really well. Yet, somehow, I've always felt that my mother belonged to a different time, a different life.'

'I know for certain that my father is still emotionally attached to her, especially when he looks at me,' she smiled sadly. 'I look so different from my half-brothers, you see, and Dad sees her in me, but just cannot bring himself to speak about her. Perhaps he feels he'd be betraying Gillian in some way by sharing memories of his first wife, even with me. So, I stopped asking about her a long time ago.'

'OK. I'll tell you what I know, but there will be gaps. As soon as I start to bore you, please say so; don't be polite. Seb will tell you I like the sound of my own voice, and I do ramble on a bit.' Turning to his grandson, he asked, 'Are you staying?'

'If Cristi doesn't mind,' Seb replied, looking in her direction.

'Of course I don't mind, don't be silly,' she said quickly.

The older man looked from one to the other, and nodded imperceptibly, pleased with what he saw.

'In that case, I'll start at the beginning. Where else?'

The old man spoke perfect, accent-less English, and she found herself hanging onto his every word, his soft voice mesmerising.

'This village,' he began, 'is typical of villages all over Italy. Most of the families have been here for generations, so we are, if you like, all part of one another's history. Some think it's a good thing, others not so good. Secrets are almost impossible to keep,' he laughed quietly to himself.

'When I was a boy, everyone knew their place. Here in Passo Santino, on the one hand, you had the workers, mostly farm labourers—the da Calvis among them. I don't suppose you know this,' he continued shaking his head, 'but in those days, the workers were not allowed to own their own land. Then, on the other hand, you had those who had a profession—the doctor, the teacher and the lawyer—our family. The priest was a law unto himself, of course, and then, at the top of the pile here in Passo, there was Fioretti.'

'I suppose, in England, he would be the called the "Lord of the Manor". Virtually all the land around Passo and beyond was owned by the Fioretti family. We only ever saw them at Mass, at the *festas* to celebrate the harvest or at the *raccolta,* the grape harvest. In our case, it was when we were summoned, my father and I, to the *Palazzo Piceno* on legal business that concerned the village. Have you seen the *palazzo* yet?' he asked her suddenly.

'No, I haven't,' she replied, not noticing the swift glance that passed between the two men.

'I'm sure Seb will take you to have a look before you go home,' he added. 'Drink up,' he gestured to the other two glasses. 'If I start to ramble, just stop me.'

'Don't worry, we will,' Seb said jokingly, leaning forward to refill the glasses.

'Not for me,' Cristi said, moving her glass out of reach. 'I don't want to fall asleep in the middle of the story.'

The terrace, although shaded, was warm with a dry, still heat. A very gentle breeze whispered past, leaving the whole house cocooned in a soporific silence.

'I knew the da Calvi family well,' the old man continued. 'Ernesto and Elena had four sons. Andrea was the eldest, then Giorgio. Giuseppe was the same age as me and one of my best friends. Ennio was the baby of the family. Did you know that your great-grandmother on your mother's side was not Italian?' he asked, forgetting that she knew nothing.

'I would have guessed that she would have been a local girl,' Cristi said, not really knowing what to say.

'Not so,' the old man went on. 'Ernesto, your great-grandfather, met her at a family wedding and spent the next two years trying to convince her parents to let her leave home, marry him and move to live here, with him, in Italy. Your great-grandmother was Greek!' he announced in a voice which suggested he had more surprise revelations in store for her.

'Very surprising in those days. Italian men married Italian girls, usually from the same village or at least one nearby. But not Ernesto da Calvi. The family wedding was somewhere down south, near Brindisi, I believe. Elena was very beautiful. You have her hair, *signorina*,' he said, the compliment implicit in his voice.

A little embarrassed, she asked, 'How on earth do you know all this? It must have been way before your time.'

'The same way I know about most things that go on around here. I listen to gossip, but Ernesto da Calvi and his Greek bride were the talk of the village for quite some time. It was a story often told to young couples planning their marriage. I suppose it was held up as a prime example of determination, commitment and love. Anyway, the family was very close, which made future events very difficult for Ernesto and Elena to bear.'

At this point, he stopped talking, his mind somewhere in the distant past. Neither Cristi nor Seb considered breaking the silence. They just waited until he was ready to continue.

'Giuseppe was my friend, as I said, so I got to know the family very well. Their house, I remember, was full of energy, noise and laughter. There always seemed to be delicious food prepared for anyone who happened to call, no matter what time of the day it was. All the brothers helped Ernesto on the land, but there was one big difference between them and the other farm labourers. Elena could read and write, and she insisted that her sons, all of them, should be able to do the same.'

'For one hour each day, they broke off from their work and returned to the house for their lesson. By the age of seven or eight, they were all literate. Even Ernesto tried, but he found it took up too much of his time and was too difficult so, he gave up, much to his wife's displeasure, I recall. No one thought to ask how Elena could teach them so well in Italian when her own language was Greek.

Only later did she admit to studying each lesson herself just before the boys arrived for theirs.'

'A remarkable woman,' Seb commented.

'Oh, yes. Remarkable and so beautiful, but I feel that in the end, being able to read about what was going on in the world made the older boys dissatisfied with their lot on the farm, and this eventually contributed to the breakdown of the family.'

Before Cristi could comment or ask a question, Marina appeared with a large tray bearing a jug of fresh, iced lemon juice and a plate of almond biscuits. The old man fired a few questions at his housekeeper, which she answered in rapid Italian, nodded and smiled at each of them, then retreated once again into the house.

'She has agreed to take me to play cards tonight and to collect me later so that I can have a few more glasses of wine,' he said, explaining his exchange with Marina. 'Please help yourselves to juice, don't wait to be asked. She makes the biscuits herself. Much better than the ones from the bakery. Not so hard. Now, where was I? Ah yes. Clever boys, the da Calvis, but I'm afraid the Second World War was on its way and about to burst the bubble we were all living in, especially here in the centre of Italy.'

Sebastiano hardly drew breath. He was a good storyteller but seemed afraid to pause, in case he lost his train of thought and missed something out.

'Giorgio idolised Andrea and followed him everywhere. So, as Giuseppe was my best friend, I found myself tagging along with them as well. Andrea didn't seem to mind. In fact, I think he found it amusing rather than irritating. That's how we came to find ourselves at the back of the meetings that Andrea organised, either in the public gardens at the far end of the village or in the bar on the *piazza*. The meetings in the gardens needed a lookout, and as young boys, we found the whole thing really exciting.'

'Andrea was an activist, you understand, and so dissatisfied with the government's treatment of the farm workers, he eventually decided it was the right time to do something about it. I remember standing in the doorway of the bar one evening, listening to him address the crowd. The place was so full, I couldn't get further than the door. Giorgio was leaning against the wall to one side, his eyes fixed on his brother.'

'Andrea was standing on a table, feet apart, his arms and hands orchestrating his words. His black curls bounced lightly across his forehead as he spoke, his dark eyes compelling the audience to listen to what he was saying. A scarlet kerchief knotted loosely around his neck was the only splash of colour in an otherwise dark and gloomy room. His voice was firm but not loud. He spoke to them in the language they understood. He didn't insult them by showing off but had their full attention and wanted their support. It was all thrilling and exciting, especially as I shouldn't have been anywhere near the place!'

The old man put his head back and closed his eyes. 'I can see and hear him now as if it were only yesterday. Much later on, when I was much older, I realised how clever Andrea had been. He knew exactly what to tell his followers, but more importantly, he knew what to leave out. He knew they wouldn't understand terms like corporatism, syndicalism and expansionism, all key elements of Mussolini's fascism.'

'He didn't mention the organised violence or *Il Duce's* powerful propaganda machine. The men of the village didn't know about the attacks that had been made on socialists and Catholics as far south as Apulia and the burning of their headquarters. No! Andrea spoke to them in the language they understood. His voice was clear and firm with conviction—he had no reason to shout.'

'He told them about the Public Works programme, the proposed development of the public transport system and improved job opportunities for all of them. He explained in simple terms how important it was for them to develop a sense of nationalism and move away from the restrictions and the suffocation of traditional regionalism. He encouraged them to feel part of the new Italy, thankful that the government was investing in the countryside at last, and that their dissatisfaction had been noted and acted upon.'

'"Already", Andrea insisted, "improvements that started in Milan have been witnessed further south in Bologna and Ferrara. Improvements, my friends, which include a fixed minimum wage, an eight-hour working day for all workers, the development of our railway system, and",'—Sebastiano paused for effect—'"voting rights for women".' Saying this, the old man opened his eyes and looked directly across at Cristi, a wide, mischievous smile on his face. 'As you can imagine, *signorina,* this last statement was met with shouts, whistles, boos and much laughter. The whole place erupted. Needless to say, there wasn't a single woman in the room, so all the men felt quite safe with this outburst. Andrea joined in momentarily, but then raised his arm. Silence rippled back from the front of the crowd until he had their full attention once again.'

'I can still hear his words clearly. "Let us all be clear about this", Andrea had spoken sincerely. "We have all heard about the Battle for Grain".' Sebastiano chuckled. 'Most of the men in the bar that night hadn't a clue what he was talking about, but everyone nodded, not wanting to appear ignorant, and seemingly oblivious to the lack of response to his statement, Andrea went on, his right arm lifting and falling to emphasise a point.'

'"Five thousand new farms have been set up, and five new agricultural towns have been built on land reclaimed from the Pontine Marshes. Valuable resources have been diverted to us to support our grain production. We owe it to our leader to give something back, to show him our support. Do we want to continue living as we are?" he asked the crowd.'

'"No!" many of them shouted back.'

'"Do we want to continue labouring night and day for little return?"'

'"No!" came a more positive response.'

'"Do we want to exist in our small world of work and poverty? Or do we share *Il Duce's* dream of making Italy a nation that is great, respected and feared?"'

'"We do! We do!" They shouted.'

Sebastiano Luce had looked at her, gauging her reaction. 'Once again, *signorina*, voices were raised, building to a crescendo bordering on frenzy. Andrea had them all exactly where he wanted them. He could relate easily to their struggles and was about to offer them a way out. They trusted him, but did they have his courage?' The old man shook his head.

'"I leave for Milan at daybreak", Andrea announced dramatically. "Any one of you is welcome to join me. *Il Duce* needs our support. We must take action ourselves and not wait for others to tell us what to do. Are you with me?" he demanded, looking out over the heads of the crowd. He raised his arm and shouted, "*Se avanzo, seguitemi. Se indietreggio, uccidetemi. Se muoio, vendicatemi.* If I advance, follow me. If I retreat, kill me. If I die, avenge me".'

'And of course,' Sebastiano nodded, 'all those except the old and infirm shouted out their response. They were fired up, excited, carried along on a wave of nationalistic fervour. Apart from me, only Giorgio and Giuseppe remained silent and still. They couldn't believe what their brother had said. I felt sorry for them both. They looked so desolate, but I think I knew, at that moment, that at least one other da Calvi brother would be on the road to Milan at dawn. I remember praying selfishly, that it wouldn't be Giuseppe, surely, he was much too young.'

The old man stopped speaking, seemingly back in that crowded, smoky bar, the images still vivid in his mind.

'There was no choice, for me, you understand,' he went on, his tone more matter-of-fact. 'Like Giuseppe, I was far too young. The members of my family were not labourers. I didn't feel so strongly about what was going on in the rest of Italy. Looking back, I was, I suppose, very selfish. My life was comfortable, and it was expected that I would follow in my father's footsteps, and that is exactly what I did.'

'So, what happened to them, the two older brothers?' Seb asked before Cristi had the chance.

'In the end, only fifteen villagers joined Andrea on the journey to Milan,' his grandfather replied. 'They were all about the same age, maybe a couple of them were a bit younger, but all were idealistic, young men who believed they had no real future ahead of them the way things were. Every so often, we would hear vague rumours and reports from the north, but finally, two men from the next village came back with the news that in late 1940, Andrea had been killed, ironically in Greece. They returned some of his papers and his red kerchief to his parents, Ernesto and Elena.'

Recalling the look in Signor Luce's eyes as he'd recounted this last piece of information, Cristi found it difficult to swallow the lump in her throat and couldn't release the tightness clamped around her chest. Her hands clutched the crisp, white sheet close to her hips, and tears hung in the corners of her eyes, suspended, waiting to fall as soon as she blinked.

What must they have felt like? she asked herself for the umpteenth time, taking deep breaths to try and relax. Earlier, she had managed to keep her emotions in check as the old man had carried on with his story. Although he had expressed sympathy for Ernesto and Elena, Cristi gained the impression that Sebastiano Luce believed it had been Andrea's idealism and rash, cavalier behaviour that had got him killed so far from home, and that but for a quirk of fate, his brother Giorgio could have been killed in the same battle.

When Signor Luce spoke about Giorgio, his whole demeanour changed. He had kept his eyes open and sat up straighter in his chair.

'Are you sure you want to hear all this?' he asked, just getting into his stride.

'Of course,' Cristi answered immediately, 'as long as you're not too tired.'

'Tired? Me? So many of my generation are no longer with us. I have no one to reminisce with, to share memories with. You, *signorina,* are a da Calvi. What better reason do I need to remember? You will be able to pass these stories on to your own children one day. Have some more lemon. I'm afraid it loses its chill very quickly in this heat.'

Cristi leant forward and refilled the three glasses. Light rivulets of condensation crept down the outside of the heavy glass jug, obscuring the opaque lemon juice inside.

'So, what happened to Giorgio?' she asked the expected question.

'Ah, Giorgio,' Sebastiano said, with genuine affection. 'My best friend's brother could never make a decision,' he laughed. 'He did whatever the other boys chose to do and was happy to have no responsibility. He was much shorter and slighter than Andrea. Many people thought we were the brothers when we were boys. He was quietly intelligent, and yet, full of life. He had an opinion on everything. Giorgio, Giuseppe and I talked more than anything else. Sometimes, we'd kick a ball around, but most days we'd take the path up the side of the hill, sit under the shade of our favourite olive tree, and just chat.'

'What did you chat about?' Seb asked.

'Everything and nothing. Just idle boys' chat. Giorgio was the second son. Giuseppe, who came after him, was completely different. Very difficult to say why, but Giorgio preferred to spend most of his time alone. Even when they were working on the land, he would choose a job away from the others. Sometimes, he'd go off for days wanting to be on his own, so they didn't worry when he disappeared in the spring of 1939. Only this time, Giorgio didn't come back after the usual three or four days.

'The whole family fretted, and people in the village searched the area, just in case he'd had an accident and was lying in a ditch or field somewhere. Giuseppe took it very badly. In spite of Giorgio's funny ways, the brothers were very close. Andrea was big and forceful, a law unto himself. Ennio was just very young, but Giorgio and Giuseppe got on really well. So, you can imagine how betrayed Giuseppe felt when he realised that his brother had just taken off without him. And before you ask,' Sebastiano went on, holding up his hand to halt the question hovering on Cristi's lips, 'I'll tell you what happened to Giorgio.'

'It seems that during one of his more recent disappearing acts, he'd travelled north as far as Milan to get a work visa to go to England. Looking back now, I suppose he was what you'd call a pacifist. He had become increasingly worried about how the political situation was changing, not only here in Italy, but in the rest of mainland Europe. Fascism under Mussolini was rife and spreading south. Even teachers in schools and universities had to swear an oath defending the fascist regime. *Il Duce* was pushing to take charge of all Italian business, enforcing wage and price controls. Even newspaper editors had to seek approval from the fascist party before publishing their articles.'

The old man shook his head and sighed resignedly. 'Funny, really,' he went on, 'how two members of the same family, both intelligent, both exposed to the same information, could interpret a situation completely differently. Andrea saw Mussolini as some sort of saviour. Giorgio saw him for what he was, an aggressive bully and dictator. I would like to believe that his decision to leave Italy was not a sudden one. His dissatisfaction had been building up for years, and although I had been present at the table when the family had discussions, I hadn't realised how strongly Giorgio felt about what was going on.'

'We seemed to be so far away from everything. He asked me once, I remember, if I knew about the Italian forces fighting and subduing the Abyssinian army in Ethiopia, forcing Haille Selassie to flee. I didn't have a clue what he was talking about, and neither did Giuseppe. Then, a few months later, Giorgio was incensed because Mussolini had intervened on the side of General Franco in the Spanish Civil War, support that was to last for three long years. For Giorgio, the final straw came when it became clear that Mussolini's relationship with Adolph Hitler was much closer than what he'd led people to believe.

'Although Giorgio went north with Andrea, he broke away from the group before it joined forces with the fascist units just south of Milan. Apparently, he then made his way west, but how, or even if, Giorgio got to England, no one really knew. In the end, as Seb here found out, his decision was not a good one.'

Signor Luce stopped speaking. He looked sad as he sat up straighter in his chair.

'Forgive me, *signorina*,' he said quietly. 'I have gone on a bit too long about Giorgio, but I think you needed to hear about him to understand my friend Giuseppe and what he decided to do some years later. You may not be aware, but most Italians will shorten the name Giuseppe to Peppe. But not him. His mother always insisted he be called by his full name. Like me. I call my boy here Seb,' he said, leaning over and squeezing his grandson's forearm, 'but I have always been Sebastiano.'

Once again, the old man settled himself more comfortably in his chair, his hands resting loosely in his lap, his legs outstretched, crossed at the ankles. Not for the first time, Cristi admired how elegant he was and so at ease with himself. She knew he was enjoying every second recounting his memories, even the sad ones.

'After both sons had left, the atmosphere in the family home changed. Andrea's absence hit the family hard. He left a gaping hole that could never be filled. Ernesto worked even harder. Elena seemed to age very quickly, and Giuseppe became much quieter. We'd still meet up now and again but would sit in long silences whereas before we'd talk ourselves to a standstill.

'He once told me he knew how it felt to be an only child. Ennio, he said, was still a child, running across the fields, playing in the river and climbing trees without a care in the world and not yet old enough to do the hard work. Giuseppe had to make up for the absence of two labourers, and he found it hard and tiring.'

'Sometimes, *signorina,* I felt guilty and uncomfortable. I did no manual work at all, and I knew that within a matter of months I, too, would be leaving to go to university in Urbino. Anyway, without going into all the details, we survived the war. Giuseppe stayed on the farm, and I went away to study. We'd meet up during my vacations, and despite our lives being so completely different, we still found plenty to talk about. We were true friends, *signorina,* true friends.'

Cristi didn't move or say a word. She watched as Sebastiano shook out a perfectly clean white handkerchief and wiped his eyes behind the pretence of blowing his nose.

'That's better,' he said. 'Please excuse me, *signorina*. I'm a silly, sentimental old man. My only excuse is that Giuseppe and I were like brothers. I'd even go as far as to say that I was closer to him than his own. Anyway, in the end, I qualified as a lawyer, and Giuseppe took the decision to go to England himself to look for Giorgio. He was convinced that someone, somewhere in the Italian community in England would know where he was. We met up again just before he left for London, and I left for New York. It was many years before our paths crossed again, and then only briefly.'

While Sebastiano had been speaking, the mid-summer sun had sunk lower in the sky and had lost some of its ferocity. She sat with the two men, comfortable in their company and totally engrossed in the slowly unfolding story. She still had no idea where she fitted into the scheme of things but was quite content to sit back and wait. She knew that he would get round to it in his own good time.

Marina appeared once again, said a brief '*Scusami,*' then asked a question in, if anything, even more rapid Italian.

'*Si, si,*' Sebastiano replied, smiling. '*Grazie, Marina. Sei molto gentile,*' and turning towards Cristi, explained, 'She asked if we would like coffee, so I said yes. You might prefer tea, *signorina*, but I wouldn't recommend it.'

'God, no!' Seb added, horrified. 'Marina's tea tastes just like. . .'

'Thank you, Seb. Let's just say that her coffee is a hundred times better.'

'Has Marina been with you a long time?' Cristi asked.

'Do you know, I can't remember a time without her. Remind me, Seb, how old is your father?'

'Fifty-four. He was born in October, and it was Marina's mother who came to help *Nonna* look after the new baby.'

'That's right, so in a way, she has been around for over fifty years but took over the household and me when your grandmother died more than twenty years ago.'

'I don't know why she puts up with you,' Seb teased.

'Two reasons. I let her think she's in charge, and she loves me!' Sebastiano burst out laughing, a deep throaty laugh of genuine delight when he saw the look of astonishment on his grandson's face.

'I'm sorry, *signorina*, but it's true. Marina and I live happily together, but to put your mind at rest, she treats me like a doting father, so you can both put any improper thoughts you might have out of your mind.'

She felt herself blushing, so she just smiled and shook her head at him.

The coffee was excellent as promised. Fortunately, they served themselves, so she could take more milk than usual to weaken the very strong, dark liquid. The aroma of coffee beans was intoxicating, and she breathed in deeply through her nose, held her breath for a few seconds then breathed out slowly through her mouth. On the tray next to the small, dainty coffee cups and saucers was a plate of thinly sliced, apricot flan decorated with small sprigs of redcurrants.

'This looks absolutely marvellous,' Cristi enthused. 'Don't tell me Marina makes this as well?'

'Oh, but she does, and the apricots are from that tree over there just below the cypress. We always have too many in one season, so she spends her days either making jam or bottling the fruit for desserts and flans just like this one.'

The sponge base, dusted lightly with icing sugar, melted in the mouth, and the sweetness of the sliced apricots was to die for. Cristi hoped she'd be offered a second slice even before finishing the first. Signor Luce finished his coffee in two mouthfuls but didn't have a slice of flan. Instead, he pushed his cup and saucer away from him, sat back and took up his story where he had left off.

'Giuseppe was a bit like Giorgio in that he found it difficult to make decisions. In English, you would probably call him a "ditherer". Yet, while I was away studying, he made, probably, the two most important decisions of his life. The first was to marry a young lady, Maria Leone, who worked in the bank on the *piazza*. Everyone was delighted. At last, Ernesto and Elena had something to celebrate; for a short time, at least. The second was to leave the farm and go to England to search for Giorgio. But then, I suppose, in a way, they lost Giuseppe, although he did come back for a visit I was told, with Maria and his beautiful little daughter, Maria Cristina, who must have been about four years old. I'm not sure exactly.'

For the first time, Cristi reacted instantly, remembering the photograph in the suitcase.

'Did you say Maria Cristina? But that was my mother's name.'

Her outburst was met with silence, giving her a few seconds to process the information she'd just been given.

'So, are you telling me that your best friend Giuseppe was my grandfather?'

'That's exactly what I'm saying, *signorina*. You are a da Calvi, and it gives me great joy to have Giuseppe's granddaughter with me in my home.'

He repeated the gesture with his handkerchief and spontaneously, she got up from her chair, walked over to the old man and laid her cheek against his, her hands on both his shoulders.

'Thank you, thank you,' she whispered in his ear, choking slightly over her words. Straightening up, embarrassed by her actions, she smiled at him affectionately.

'Slowly but surely, I'm finding out who I am,' she said quietly, and turning towards the younger man who had sat silently watching her as she'd listened to her family history, she held out her hand to shake his. 'I have to thank you for all your hard work and for arranging this, she smiled. 'I can't thank you enough.'

'What I'd like to know,' Seb said teasingly, holding her hand in both of his, 'is how come he gets a caress and kisses on his cheeks, and I just get a handshake?'

'Oh!' Cristi said quietly, drawing her hand away, feeling the heat invade her cheeks once again. Totally embarrassed, she returned to her chair, her eyes fixed on the tiles of the terrace.

'Take no notice of him, *signorina*. He's only jealous!'

'Please call me Cristi. Everyone does,' she said, desperate to move on from the harmless, light-hearted teasing. 'My full name is Cristina Elena.'

For a few moments, they just sat without speaking. The afternoon had passed into early evening, and only birdsong fractured the enveloping silence. She sensed that her charming host had come to the end of his story. Now, she would have to find a way to fill in the rest, as she was sure there was much more to come.

Only when Marina came out to remind him that they'd have to leave in fifteen minutes did Sebastiano bring his mind back to the present. The young ones had left some time ago, but he hadn't felt the need to move from his chair.

So much had happened in such a relatively short space of time. Once again, he cast his mind back a couple of years. Francesco had come to see him first, then Ennio, then Massimo. Of course, those events had started with the letter from South Africa. He hadn't been into the office for months, but Seb kept him up to date with what was going on, and the lovely Giulia called in at least once a week for a chat over a glass or two of their favourite *Conero Rosso*.

After Seb's visit with that letter, and the request for his help, he remembered feeling re-energised and excited, sensations he thought he'd never have again. He didn't really miss his work and the inevitable stress, but the prospect of researching and dealing with a case from way back in his career had made his stomach churn and his chest flutter.

The juice in the jug on the table in front of him was slightly warm but he poured some into his glass anyway, gave it a swirl, and took a couple of sips. Marina reappeared, carrying a tray. She looked at him and opened her eyes wide, raising her eyebrows questioningly.

'*Sono quasi pronto, Marina.* I'm nearly ready,' he assured her, pulling himself slowly out of his chair.

As he watched her clear away the remnants of the late lunch, he decided to put his thoughts about the Fioretti case on hold, at least until he was alone later in his room. He still couldn't believe that he'd spent the afternoon with Giuseppe's granddaughter, a lovely girl with Elena da Calvi's hair and eyes.

She'd looked happy to be in Seb's company. Dare he hope that at last, the boy had found someone special? Not Italian, but as near as dammit.

'*Andiamo!*' he shouted out to Marina. 'Let's go!' He didn't want the card game to start without him.

Apart from the pleasure of being in the company of his best friends, the evening had not been a success. Sebastiano hadn't won a single game, and for once, he'd been relieved when Marina arrived to take him home. Looking around the table, he'd had to smile.

Tommaso Caponi, his best friend, was short and fat; there was no other way to describe him. He was completely bald, his cheeks looked like two ripe, red apples and his neck had slowly but surely disappeared between his shoulders. His considerable paunch grazed the edge of the table each time he leant forward and put his arm out straight to play a card. The large signet ring on the little finger of his right hand was high-quality gold, as was the narrow chain nestling between the folds just below his chin. Tommaso was good company, always had plenty to say, and had an infectious laugh. He was also very intelligent and had built up a successful architectural practice employing innovative and highly qualified young architects, designers and *geometri*. *He'd know all about Fioretti's properties,* Sebastiano thought to himself, as he'd been involved in the conversion of the Palazzo many years earlier.

Salvo Zaninelli sat opposite him as usual. Looking at him, Sebastiano could only smile even more. Salvo had lived and worked in Passo for more than half a century, and yet, he was still regarded as *Il Siciliano*. Like many of his contemporaries, he had left the poverty of his island for the mainland and had travelled north to find work and a better standard of living. After working hard to pay for his education, he eventually qualified as a doctor and established himself in Passo at about the same time as Sebastiano took over the legal practice from his father. They had been good friends ever since. Unlike Tommaso, Salvo was slight with olive skin and a shock of thick hair, which owed its rich darkness to the fortnightly visit to Enzo, the barber on the *piazza*. Salvo's surgery had expanded over the years, and his son now coordinated the large, modern medical centre which served not only the town, but most of the surrounding area as well.

'*Tocca a te,*' Sebastiano. 'Wake up! It's your turn!' Guido prompted him.

Guido Menconi was the only one at the table not to have had any direct dealings with Silvano Fioretti in person. Guido was a reputable accountant, which was no mean feat in modern-day Italy! But Fioretti had kept all his financial affairs far away, preferring to engage an accountancy firm in Milan. This arrangement, Sebastiano knew for certain, had created a great number of problems and complicated legal issues when Fioretti had died. Perhaps Guido had had a lucky escape, although recent events had changed the situation completely.

Slapping his cards down on the table, Sebastiano finally gave up. He had played badly, his mind constantly wandering away from the game. As he took a final glance around the table, he confirmed to himself that each and every one of them, including Guido to some extent, had been touched in one way or another by Silvano Fioretti.

Marina kept up her usual flow of chatter on the drive home. She insisted, as always, on driving in the middle of the road, claiming that she had plenty of time to pull over when she spotted the glare of oncoming headlights. Sebastiano was never convinced, but as he was still alive he couldn't complain. He'd been particularly quiet during the fifteen minutes it took them to get home but had been fully aware of Marina's sideways glances, eventually telling her to stop looking at him.

'*Sembri stanco e pallido!*' she'd remonstrated.

'I'm tired and pale because it's late and it's been a long day,' Sebastiano replied defensively.

'*Non hai vinto, eh?*'

'No, I didn't win. *Non riuscivo a concentrarmi.*'

It was true. He hadn't been able to concentrate, his mind full of da Calvis and Fiorettis, his grandson and the delightful Cristi. His grandson hadn't been able to take his eyes off her.

Once safely back at the house, he went straight to his room. He needed some time to himself, so he left Marina with a brief '*Buona notte, a domani.*'

His room was cool and welcoming. In here, for some reason, he always felt calm and at peace with himself. He'd had quite a day, yet in spite of his weariness, he couldn't stop the memories scurrying across his mind. Where had the last two years disappeared to?

He could still recall feeling delighted when Seb had asked for his thoughts and opinion on the letter from South Africa, and as things turned out, when he'd arrived at the office the following morning, he'd found that everything he required had been filed away in the cellar just as he'd anticipated. All the legal documents and certificates had been easy to find, and within half an hour of arriving, he had been ready to start work.

Giulia had been delighted to see him and had produced coffee, just as he liked it, in record time, black and strong. A desk in one of the smaller interview rooms had been cleared for him, and on a small side-table, she had put a bottle of water, a glass and a small bowl of pink roses.

It had taken him just under two hours to get through the paperwork, still amazed at the financial acumen of Silvano Fioretti. On the other hand, the man's son had done nothing apart from leave all his father's business and investments in the hands of those who knew what they were doing, and in whom he put all his trust.

Francesco was coming home. He'd asked specifically for him, Sebastiano Luce, so whatever the issue was, it had to be serious. Armed with as much information as he could keep in his old head, he remembered he couldn't wait for the appointment with the Monsignor.

Francesco had been as handsome as Sebastiano remembered. The face was that of an old man, but the eyes were those of a young boy. Although polite, the *Monsignor* hadn't been interested in idle chat. He wanted to deal with things as swiftly as possible as he had a flight to catch from Rome to South Africa later that evening. He had been more than happy for the younger Luce *avvocato* to sit in on the meeting and was pleased that what he wanted to do could be accomplished very quickly, if he was prepared, yet again, to put his faith in the two lawyers in front of him.

'I have no choice in the matter,' Francesco had declared when told he would have to sign the bottom of some blank documents as there wasn't time to have them drawn up before he had to leave Italy.

'Just give me the papers and I'll sign.'

'Giulia, my secretary, will countersign if you agree, *Monsignor*.'

'Anything you say, *Dottore,* and the name is Francesco.' The old priest had smiled. 'I have my own pen.'

Midnight came and went. Remembering was tiring. Reluctantly, Sebastiano undressed and crawled into the big, empty bed. Why did everything seem to come at him all at once? Francesco, Ennio and Massimo. He'd retired more than twenty years earlier, and apart from a small number of consultations he'd managed to stay away from the office.

Some weeks after his visit to Ennio, Massimo Sauro had requested a meeting, and he'd found himself listening to the story of yet another da Calvi brother. Sebastiano closed his eyes. He was tired, but somewhere in the back of his mind, a little voice was telling him that he was the one who would draw together the threads of this one family, and today, in his own home, the final beautiful thread had come to take its place in the da Calvi tapestry.

He woke up with a dull, thumping headache. It was still very early. The birds were singing loudly in the cypresses. There were no sounds coming from the kitchen. His legs had seized up overnight, so he exercised them gently under the sheet before attempting to get up. At least, he didn't suffer from arthritis, he consoled himself. He just needed more and more time these days to get going in the morning. He knew he should drink more water. He felt dehydrated. His own fault. So he would have to suffer the regular hammering behind his eyes and the nauseous feeling at the back of his throat.

He filled the mouthwash glass in the bathroom and gulped down the cold water, only pausing to refill the small glass three times. The clock on his bedside table showed five twenty-three, much too early to get up, so he got back into bed, covered the lower half of his body with the cool, white sheet and reflected on what Massimo Sauro had told him. Fortunately, the old man's account had been factual and to the point. There had been no long-winded anecdotes. The subject matter had been far too serious.

Massimo had been one of the few young men fired up by Andrea da Calvi's words during the meetings in the bar on the *piazza* more than sixty years earlier. He had made his way north with the others, but unlike most of them, he had managed to return. None of them had had any idea about what they were letting themselves in for. Their idealism had blinded them to the daily realities; the hunger, wet clothes and boots, lack of sleep and mile after mile of trudging through the countryside. They had not been prepared in the slightest, a ragged bunch of men calling themselves soldiers but unarmed.

The equipment was sparse, shared out between them. They had been sitting ducks. He went on to describe the massacres he'd witnessed, comrades dying in front of him with little or no chance of fighting back. Why he'd been spared he couldn't understand, especially when his leader, Andrea, had been shot down as they'd pushed forward. Why hadn't any of the bullets hit him? He hadn't even been wounded, at least not in body only in his mind and he had lived with the guilt ever since.

'I still see the look in his mother's eyes when I brought home Andrea's red scarf. I wake up most nights hearing the sound of gunfire, but it's her eyes that I can't get out of my mind, *Dottore*, her eyes.'

He had let Massimo talk, asking no questions nor making any comment. He just waited and listened until the storyteller ran out of steam.

'*Scusa mi, Dottore*. I've had no one to speak to, to tell these things to, but the time has come for me to put my house in order. I met Ennio da Calvi some weeks before he died. He had come to you to make his will. Now I want to do the same. My will is quite simple, *Dottore*, but before I leave, I want to pay you for the time you have spent listening to me today.'

Compared with Ennio da Calvi, Massimo had very little to show for a lifetime of hard work. What he did have was left to the sister he hadn't seen for more than twenty years even though she lived a matter of hours away in Perugia. He paid the fee for the meeting before leaving the office, but Giulia was given instructions to deduct the amount from the final charge for drawing up the will.

Just after six o'clock, he heard Marina on the move, so he got up, showered and dressed ready to face the day. Francesco, Ennio, Massimo and now Cristina—so much in such a short space of time, he thought again, and he knew that there was even more to come. In his search for the beneficiaries of Ennio's estate, his grandson, Seb, had also found out what had happened to Giuseppe, and to Giorgio. By the end of the day, he would have all the information he needed to complete the da Calvi story. He knew that Cristi had quite a shock coming to her.

Part Five
The Legacy

Chapter 23
Cristi

Cristi gazed out of the window as the earth fell away and the aircraft climbed steadily from Ancona's Falconara Airport, out over the Adriatic, taking her away from Italy, and more importantly, she realised, away from Seb. The last twenty-four hours had been a whirlwind of activity and information overload. As it flew into dense cloud obliterating her view of the glistening waters of the sea below, she cast her mind back to the final business meeting in Seb's office.

He had suggested an earlier start as there were so many official papers to consider and get signed. As usual, she made sure she was on time and, after a surprisingly swift greeting from Giulia, she had been shown immediately into the now familiar office. Seb had walked around his desk, and, for the first time, without hesitation, had welcomed her with what she recognised as a very continental greeting, a swift kiss on both cheeks, his hands on her shoulders.

'Let's sit on the comfortable chairs,' he suggested in a very practical, business-like tone. 'We have so much to get through this morning. I would have dealt with some of this during our previous meetings, but there were still one or two small details, pieces of important information not yet in my possession. So, first things first. I need to bring you up to date with the da Calvis.'

She just sat back and listened, at the same time noticing that, as always, he was immaculately dressed. His voice when he spoke was quiet but confident, with just a hint of accented yet perfect English. *She had never met anyone remotely like him, and never would again,* she thought.

'…So, if you are happy to do that, I'll proceed,' he said, unaware that Cristi had not been listening.

'Of course,' she replied, having missed completely what he'd been saying, daydreaming instead of concentrating. 'I thought you said that Ennio da Calvi was a simple farmer, so I assumed that there wouldn't be much of an inheritance.'

'That was the case precisely up until two years ago. Everyone considered Ennio to be exactly as he appeared—a well-known local tenant farmer who kept himself to himself. Then, in a matter of weeks everything changed. We received a letter from Johannesburg, requesting an appointment with my grandfather for a Monsignor Francesco Fioretti. My grandfather recognised the name immediately, of course.' Seb smiled as he said this. 'Francesco wasn't only Ennio's best friend but was also the son of the local landowner. Many years ago, when they were boys, they had both been told repeatedly by their fathers not to play in the stream that flowed through the valley at the bottom of the fields. I'm sure you can imagine what being told not to do something meant to the two nine-year-olds running free in the countryside.'

'That stream must have been like a magnet to them,' she laughed, thinking about a few of the likely lads in her class back home.

'Exactly,' Seb went on. 'But unfortunately, on one, very hot afternoon, while paddling in the stream, Francesco slipped and fell, cutting his head very badly on the sharp stones. Ennio had the presence of mind to run home and fetch his father, who pulled Francesco from the water and carried him home—quite a distance, I might add.'

'Needless to say, Francesco's father was furious with his son, but at the same time, grateful to Ernesto da Calvi for saving the boy's life. To cut a long story short, Silvano Fioretti rewarded Ernesto very generously, giving him ten extra acres of land together with the farmhouse, the da Calvi family home. Of course, there was a condition attached to such a generous reward! Silvano Fioretti never did anything for nothing.'

'Ernesto had to agree to keep Ennio away from Francesco. They were never to meet and definitely never to play together ever again. Fioretti demanded that Ernesto decide on the spot whether to agree or not. It only took a few seconds for Ernesto to weigh up what his decision would mean to his whole family, to have the extra land, the farmhouse and not have to pay rent. Elena and his other sons would have a secure future. It was an easy decision to make. He agreed to the condition. Somehow, he would make it work. Ennio would have to do as he was told.'

'How sad,' Cristi whispered.

'I agree,' Seb said, 'but in the end, after thinking it through, Silvano Fioretti realised his demands were unrealistic and impractical. He had acted impulsively. The boys were bound to see each other in the village and in church, even under supervision. After the accident, Francesco was kept indoors for weeks to recuperate from concussion and for the deep cut, which had required stitches, to heal properly. When it was considered that he was well enough to travel, he was sent away to be educated in a school far from home. Silvano Fioretti got his wish. The boys didn't get to see each other again for more than seventy years, that is, until Francesco arrived to see Ennio for the last time and to finalise his will, here in this office two years ago.'

'Isn't life strange?' she'd commented. 'How did they manage to be apart for so long? I can't imagine it, especially when modern-day travel has become so much easier.'

'Circumstances, I suppose, and a deep-seated reluctance on Francesco's part to return to a place that, to be honest, held nothing but very unhappy memories. His father had been cruel. No one told Francesco when or where his brother or his mother had died, so he never felt the urge to come back until he needed to tie up all his business affairs and to see Ennio before he passed away.'

'So how does Francesco's visit fit in with my situation?' She'd asked tentatively.

'I hope you are ready for this,' Seb said seriously. 'In his will, apart from a few South African charities, Francesco Fioretti left all his assets, and I quote, "to Ennio da Calvi—my soulmate and best friend in the whole world". Those assets, *signorina*, in turn, have been bequeathed to you as Ennio's only living relative.'

She had no idea what to say. The account Seb gave her had given her goosebumps. She couldn't believe what she'd just been told. He gave her time to think about the possible implications of what he'd said.

Taking a deep breath, she said slowly, 'Let me get this straight. Many years ago, Silvano Fioretti gifted a farmhouse and some land to Ernesto da Calvi. His son Ennio lived in the house and worked the land. Then about two years ago, Ennio's boyhood friend Francesco came back and left virtually everything he had to him, and now, in turn, Ennio has left everything to me. The two friends died within months of each other—still thousands of miles apart. Am I right in assuming that, as a priest, Francesco abided by the vow of poverty so didn't leave a great deal?' Cristi asked.

'He certainly abided by those vows in his own way of life, leaving what he inherited from his father in the hands of business people who knew what they were doing. Francesco took very little or no interest, but finally arranged, in detail, for everything to be legally signed over to Ennio. Now it is my turn to sign everything over to you.'

'What exactly do you mean by everything?' Cristi asked nervously. Butterflies were fluttering madly in her stomach, and she felt that panic itself wasn't too far away.

'In simple terms, Francesco had two thousand two hundred and thirty euros in his bank account,' Seb explained.

'Well, that's a sum I can manage,' Cristi said with a sigh of relief.

'I'm sure you can,' Seb said smiling, 'but there's more, much more, I'm afraid.' Without looking up from the document he was holding he continued. 'You also inherit three tenant farms—the houses and the land. Then, there is a very successful agricultural machinery company employing two hundred and fifty workers. Last, but not least, there is the *Palazzo Piceno* my grandfather mentioned yesterday, which is now rather an exclusive boutique hotel, spa and conference centre. As of the end of trading last night, Fioretti investments stand at over six million euros, but of course, that figure fluctuates on a daily basis.'

Finally, he looked up at her, recognising the look of horror on her face which had drained of colour. She was obviously overwhelmed by what he had told her. Reaching out his hand to hold hers, he said encouragingly, 'I can see that this is totally overwhelming, but before you panic, everything is under control, of course, just as it has been in the last two years before we found you. The farms are run well, and the machinery company has two very competent, trustworthy directors, although you now become the largest shareholder. The *Palazzo Piceno* also has a first-class management team.'

With these words, Seb got up and walked to the door and out of the room. Cristi could only sit and stare at the chair he'd vacated. Within minutes, he was back carrying a jug of chilled water and two glasses. Without asking, he filled both and handed one to her. Sitting down again, he said, 'We do not have to rush all the paperwork; in fact, we don't have sufficient time today to complete everything that needs to be done. All this must come as such a shock to you, but I need to know if you can make arrangements to come back in the near future to finalise everything.'

Cristi just stared at him. Still speechless, she nodded, thinking about what she'd been told and trying to visualise all the commitments she had back home. There were only a couple of weeks left before the start of the new term, and she was going to be the Acting Headteacher. Her time was not her own until October at the earliest. What on earth was she going to do? Did Seb consider two months to be the near future?

'May I make a suggestion?' he interrupted her thoughts.

'Of course, please do. I need all the help I can get.'

'Apart from the few legal papers we can deal with quite quickly, I thought you might like to visit Ennio's home which, of course, is now yours. I have the key.'

'I'd love to do that. Thank you. A good idea.' She suddenly felt that a break away from the office would help to clear her mind.

'We could share a light lunch somewhere, then go on to the *palazzo*. It's only five minutes away by car. If you are happy to do that, I'll give Gianni, the manager, a call to tell him we'll be calling in. We went to school together, so I know him well,' Seb smiled. 'He'll be happy to put a face to the name he has already seen on the deeds transfer papers.'

'I'm more than happy to do that. Meeting face-to-face is always a good thing.'

'Good. Perhaps before I take you back to your hotel?' Seb asked tentatively.

'I think you have just described the perfect morning. Thankyou.'

The *strada bianca* leading down to the da Calvi farmhouse from the centre of the village had recently been resurfaced by the *Comune,* Seb told her, and the hedgerows cut back. He knew exactly where he was going, and after what only seemed like a few minutes, he turned into a wide, open parking area behind what looked like a very substantial stone farmhouse. Yellow roses in full bloom intermingled with juniper bushes and low-lying lavender. Getting out of the car, she just stood breathing in the air enveloping her—the scents of rosemary, thyme and oregano vied for supremacy with the perfume of the roses and jasmine. Everything around her was so beautiful.

'This is all so incredibly beautiful,' she said quietly to Seb.

'This is the back of the house,' he replied. 'Wait until you see the front.'

They walked down the side of the house past external stone steps that Cristi assumed led up to the first floor, but she didn't have time to wonder any longer as the view that met her at the front of the house took her breath away. From a well-tended garden, swathes of land fell away from the house into a valley below. The hillsides directly opposite shone out in blankets of bright yellow.

'The sunflower crops,' Seb said. 'Unfortunately, you have missed the poppies.'

She could make out the rooftops of a few houses on the skyline, and, as if on cue, a distant church bell rang out the hour.

'And all this is now mine?' she questioned.

'It certainly is, at least, the house and all the land down as far as the stream in the valley. There are also two fields on the opposite side of the road, and one more rising up behind the house from where we've parked the car.'

Seeing the look of concern on her face, he went on hastily, 'All the land is contracted out to a local farmer at least for the next three years, so you need only concern yourself with the house and garden for the time being. I shall arrange for your name to be put on the contract and for you to sign on your next visit.'

'And is that a vineyard?' she asked, pointing to neatly planted rows of vines to her left.

'Yes, it is, but then again, there is an agreement in place with one of the locals. He tends to the vines, picks the grapes and bottles the wine. He had a gentleman's agreement with Ennio, who could ask for the number of litres of wine he wanted, and the winemaker could keep the rest either for himself, his family or to sell on. In the short term, you might like to carry on with this arrangement. It would take another responsibility off your shoulders.'

'I really don't want to rush into changing anything,' she said. 'I need time, and lots of it, to get to grips with all this, not to mention all the changes I'll have to make when I get back. May I have a look inside Ennio's home?'

'Of course. Would you like to have a look round on your own?'

Cristi glanced at his profile, amazed at how considerate and thoughtful he was.

'Thank you, but no. I'd like to have you with me,' she said, smiling at him. *In fact, I want you with me all the time,* she thought to herself.

Seb unlocked and pushed open the heavy, wooden door. For a few seconds, she stood on the threshold before stepping inside. It was cool and dark until Seb opened the shutters. She felt as though time had stood still in the da Calvi household for more than half a century. Yet again she wanted to cry, this time for all that had been lost by her family. Yes. *Her* family. Standing in the middle of her great-grandmother's kitchen, Elena's kitchen, she could feel the presence of her great-grandfather and his four sons. It had been such a powerful, yet at the same time, such a tragic household.

Apart from a well-used wooden kitchen table and two chairs in the middle of the room, there was a cast iron range against the far wall with a variety of pans sitting on top. Along the wall to her left was a very old settle with a fraying floral cushion along its length. How many years had that been there, she wondered?

She wandered slowly into what, at home, would be called "the parlour", but here there was only one large armchair, piles of books on the floor, and an old-fashioned radio. No sign of a television. So, this was how Ennio lived. How she regretted not knowing him. She felt instinctively that they would have got on really well.

For the moment, she had forgotten Seb. He had kept himself a little way away from her, giving her space and time to absorb her surroundings.

'The upstairs is empty, but we can take a look if you like,' he interrupted her thoughts.

'No, thank you. I've seen enough for the moment and, if anything, I've felt even more.'

Running her fingers along the back of the armchair, she looked directly at Seb. 'This house speaks to me. I love it here,' she said, her voice full of emotion.

He just smiled and nodded, finding any further comment unnecessary. 'If you've seen enough for the time being, perhaps we should have that light lunch I promised you, then drive over to the *palazzo* and meet Gianni.'

With one last glance across at the sunflowers, she left what was now her very own property.

The light lunch turned out to be exactly that. Seb bought some pizza *"al taglio"* from the kiosk in the park. They ate the large slices sitting on a bench surrounded by colourful flower beds. The gentle sound of cascading water from a central fountain provided a musical accompaniment to their food.

'I think you could do with some time on your own this afternoon to think about everything I've told you. I'm sure it must be overwhelming, but somehow, I also know that you will deal with it all in your own good time,' Seb said, after taking time to bite into his slice of pizza.

'I don't really have much choice, do I?' she replied, sounding quite positive even to her own ears.

They finished eating in companionable silence with Seb lounging back on the bench, his legs stretched out straight, ankles crossed, his face tilted up to the sun, his eyes closed. She had taken this brief opportunity to study him at close quarters. He was so handsome with long, dark eyelashes resting lightly on the tanned skin of his face. She stared at his mouth, his nose and his thick, slightly wavy, black hair finding absolutely no fault with any of his features. She had the overwhelming desire to reach out and touch his face, but at the same time, inexplicably, she wanted to cry. She was so physically close to her perfect man and yet, in practical terms, so far away.

So engrossed had she become in her own thoughts, she hadn't realised that, although he hadn't moved, Seb had opened his eyes and was looking at her intently.

'You seemed to be so far away, Cristi,' he said quietly.

'So much to think about and so little time,' she answered, wondering how long he had been looking at her.

Pulling himself upright, he held out his hand towards her. Hesitantly, she had put her hand in his, and, smiling, they had wandered back to the car.

The heat inside his car had built up intolerably, so, instead of using the air conditioning, Seb drove with all the windows open. It was lunchtime, so the roads were relatively quiet, and the wind in her hair brought her the feeling of intense contentment.

'The traffic won't build up again until late afternoon or early evening,' Seb informed her, 'when it gets a bit cooler, but at this time of year, you don't really notice the difference. Shops and businesses stay open much later here than where you come from. We open earlier and close later but have a really good break in the middle of the day when the sun is at its highest point.'

'Do the schools do the same?' she asked.

'No. Schools start much earlier, and here in Passo Santino, they close at lunchtime. Some of the older pupils might return in the evening, but that depends on the subject teachers.'

She had a problem imagining such a system working in her school, far too many variables surrounding transport and childcare. The continental day, it appeared to her, belonged right there, on the continent.

Within minutes, Seb turned in between two high stone pillars and drove up a cypress tree-lined driveway ending in a semi-circular parking area in front of the entrance to a very grand residence. Before she had the chance to take in the full impact of the building, a very tall, tanned, dark-haired man appeared in the doorway at the top of the steps, both arms outstretched towards them. He was wearing an open-necked, pristine white shirt, and beautifully tailored black trousers. His soft leather shoes looked handmade, but jewellery, even a wristwatch, was conspicuous by its absence.

'*Sebastiano, mio amico,*' he greeted Seb in a loud voice.

'*Ciao, Gianni,*' Seb greeted him, shaking his hand. 'This is *Signorina* Cristi Jenkins,' he continued, his hand held gently under her elbow.

'*Buongiorno, Signorina* Jenkins. *Piacere.*'

Cristi shook the hand held out to her. '*Buongiorno, Gianni,*' she said quietly. 'I'm sorry but I don't know your surname,' she apologised, smiling at him.

'Gianni is fine, *signorina.* Please come inside. A cold drink is in order, perhaps, before you look around.'

'That sounds perfect,' she agreed, as they followed Gianni across the beautiful marble floor of the entrance hall. For a split second, she forgot that she actually owned the place and, as crazy as it seemed, that Gianni was one of her employees.

They sat outside on the rear terrace with a panoramic view of the surrounding, rolling countryside. It was so peaceful, the only sound coming from leaves rustling in the warm breeze. A young waiter appeared with a tray bearing a selection of fruit juices, cordials and iced water. The beautiful glasses matched the cut-glass of the water jug.

After they had chosen their drinks, Seb started the conversation by clarifying Cristi's position relating to the *palazzo* and its future. 'As you are aware, Gianni, Cristi has inherited the *Palazzo Piceno.* The buildings and grounds no longer belong to the Fioretti Foundation. What is important for you and your staff to know is that, for the foreseeable future, nothing changes apart from the name of the owner. As long as you are happy, everything will continue as normal, and of course, you can call on me at any time if there is a problem.'

'As I told you on the phone, Seb, my staff and I are delighted to hear the *signorina's* plans and are more than happy to maintain our high standards here at the *palazzo.*'

'I think a conducted tour will have to wait, Gianni until Cristi's next visit. Our time is short today, but I'll be in touch again early next week.'

Taking this as her cue to finish her drink, Cristi complimented Gianni on the immaculate appearance of the gardens and told him how impressed she was by everything she'd seen so far.

'We have an excellent team working here, *signorina.* We pay well so we can recruit the best. On your next visit, you must stay here and really get to know us.

I am sure that Seb will be more than happy to make the necessary arrangements,' he finished off with a broad, knowing smile in Seb's direction.

'That would suit me fine,' she replied, as Gianni escorted them back to the car.

Once on the road again, Seb apologised for cutting the meeting short. 'I thought you might like to have a few hours to yourself this afternoon to process all the information I've given you this morning, and I know that one of Gianni's conducted tours would have taken hours.'

'I'm quite happy to go back to the hotel. Apart from everything else, I have to pack ready to leave in the morning.'

'Ah, yes. About that,' Seb said hesitantly as he pulled the car over to park just beyond the terrace outside her hotel. 'I believe your flight leaves at twelve-fifty, so to get to the airport we need to leave just after nine o'clock.'

'What do you mean, "we"?' Cristi asked, turning towards him. 'Anna has offered to book a taxi to take me out to the coast.'

'Surely you didn't think I would leave you to make your own way back to the airport? I have cleared my schedule for most of the day tomorrow so that I will be able to wait with you until you go through departures.'

One look at the determination in his eyes told her it was futile to argue.

'Nine o'clock it is, then, but as it's your last evening here in Italy, you definitely can't spend it alone. I would very much like to spend the evening with you, perhaps for a light meal here in the *Ristorante Centrale,* so no driving. The pasta dishes are simple but delicious, and you can walk back across the *piazza* afterwards. What do you say?'

'As usual, you seem to have thought of everything perfectly, and I would love to spend my last evening with you—anywhere.'

'Ah, just one slight addition to my plan I need to mention,' he went on looking straight ahead rather than directly at her. 'If you prefer not to go, please say so, but I told my grandfather there was a chance I might take you to see him briefly before you leave. Perhaps just for an *aperitivo* before our meal this evening.'

'How could I decline such an invitation? I'd be delighted to see your grandfather again, especially as I now know my place in the da Calvi family and my relationship with his best friend.'

'Go and enjoy your afternoon, and I'll be back to pick you up at seven o'clock. Half an hour with my grandfather should be quite enough, then we can come back here to eat.'

'I don't know how to thank you for everything,' she said, opening the car door.

'Just agreeing to spend time with me is enough, I can assure you,' he answered, and Cristi could tell he meant what he said.

'See you at seven.' She smiled at him as she got out of the car, closed the door and walked into the hotel without a backward glance.

Cristi decided to wear the same outfit she had chosen for her father's anniversary celebration. Although this would be their second meeting, she still wanted to make a good impression on Seb's grandfather.

He was waiting for them on the terrace where he greeted her enthusiastically with kisses on both cheeks. He looked delighted to see them both.

'Thank you for indulging this old man's wishes. *S'accomodi.* Please sit down, *signorina,* and make yourself at home.'

No sooner had she sat down than Marina arrived with drinks and glasses. Bowls of nuts, olives and mini-crackers were already on the table.

'As you don't have a great deal of time, Marina has kept it simple. What would you like to drink, *signorina?* We have prosecco, Martini, Campari or perhaps a glass of wine?'

'Prosecco is fine for me, please,' she said, choosing to stick to a drink she was familiar with.

The time just flew by. Thirty minutes turned into an hour. The two men took it in turns to go over everything they knew about her inheritance, but more importantly for her, more details about her Italian family.

Eventually, leaving Seb's grandfather on the terrace, she realised she had never felt happier. She now knew more about who she was and where she came from…*and belonged*, her inner voice added.

As promised, the pasta dish in the *Ristorante Centrale* was delicious. They both decided not to have the antipasto, and both chose the spinach and ricotta ravioli in a buttery sage sauce. When it arrived, she couldn't help but smile. There were two, large, filled pasta squares on her dish. At home, she had only ever had the tinned variety—numerous small squares filled with some sort of minced meat and smothered in tomato sauce. Quite a difference. In front of her was obviously "the real deal".

They chatted comfortably about their own local traditions and a great deal about their work, especially about how different their daily routines were. Seb was a good conversationalist, but all too soon after enjoying a *limoncello,* and a raspberry *semifreddo* dessert, she walked slowly back to her hotel, very conscious of Seb by her side.

'Thank you for another lovely evening. I enjoy your grandfather's company so much,' she said sincerely.

'Not only my grandfather's company, I hope,' Seb said mock-seriously, frowning slightly.

'I would have thought my enjoyment of being with you is more than evident,' she replied, reaching out spontaneously to hold his hand. His grasp was warm and firm as was his '*Buona notte, Cristi. A domani, alle nove.*'

'*A domani.* I'll see you in the morning at nine,' she replied automatically, before pulling her hand away reluctantly and walking into the hotel.

Chapter 24
Seb

Seb had really enjoyed his evening with Cristi. There was something indefinable about her that appealed to him. He couldn't believe that in a matter of a few days, his life could be turned upside down so completely. As far as he was concerned, his life was just perfect. He was fit, healthy, enjoyed his work and a lifestyle he could easily afford. His apartment in the old part of the town was exactly as he wanted it, furnished to his taste and very comfortable.

He also loved his car. It made him feel good every time he slid onto the soft leather seat and heard the purr of the powerful engine when he switched on the ignition. The body of the car was not flashy. He had bought it for the quality of the engineering. He felt that he and his car complemented each other nicely.

He dressed smartly yet conservatively and had an excellent brain. He hadn't told Cristi Jenkins he spoke five languages including Mandarin, and that he had been the top student in the year he had spent at Harvard. With her, he hadn't felt the need to promote himself. It had not seemed necessary or important. She had accepted without question that he knew what he was doing and was working with her best interests at heart.

Of course, taking her to meet his grandfather had been a masterstroke. Sebastiano could charm the birds out of the trees, but even he had reined in his charm offensive. The old man and the young lady had shown each other a deep mutual respect which Seb had recognised from the sidelines.

He had been brought up surrounded by females, and strong females at that. His mother, the chic, glamorous Giovanna from Milan, had floated in and out of his childhood, often leaving him and his sisters in the care of a nanny while she travelled around Europe and the States. His father, Alessandro, was rarely at home and it was not until he was much older and studying law himself did he understand why. The provincial town where they lived was too small to hold his father Alessandro, who felt that the family law firm would benefit greatly from having offices outside Italy.

Seb's father not only had an excellent legal brain but also a sharp business brain. He had wanted to stretch his wings and not get trapped in the backwater where he had been born. Gradually over the years, Alessandro extended his own father's legal practice with medium-sized offices in Rome, Bologna, Milan and Venice in Italy, and then further afield, in London, Oxford and Manchester in England. There were also smaller offices in New York, Washington and Montreal.

Seb's father supervised and monitored every office and employed the best lawyers he could find. They were all paid well and treated fairly, resulting in strong company loyalty. Alessandro had been allowed, by his father, to work to his strengths, and in turn had granted Seb, his own son, the same courtesy.

When his mother had spent some time at home, Seb had found her delightful. She would play quite happily with him and his sisters, her hair tied back with any old strip of material or an elastic band. Her clear olive skin would be free of make-up, her nails trimmed short and unvarnished. She spent every day in shorts, T-shirt and flat comfortable sandals.

They would cycle for miles down the valley and picnic on the small shingle beach beside the lake. He had been happy surrounded by the women in his life. They teased him mercilessly but had taken great care of him at the same time. Like most Italian men, he loved his *mamma* and would feel bereft for weeks whenever she left again to join his father somewhere far away. His sisters would do their best to occupy him, especially during the long school holidays, and looking back, he conceded that they had succeeded for most of the time.

As he had grown older, he'd accepted his mother's absences more readily. He travelled extensively himself and spent longer periods of precious time with his grandfather. Girlfriends came and went. They always seemed to be far more enthusiastic about him than he ever was about them. Far too often, they bored him. Being pretty was not enough. Being intelligent was not enough, and more often than not, being pretty and intelligent was not enough either. There was always something missing. His mother, sisters and especially Giulia were desperate for him to find a nice Italian girl to marry, settle down and have a family with, but he kept telling them that he would know when he had found the right girl.

Amazingly, without warning, she had appeared in his office three days ago.

Chapter 25
Cristi

The pilot's announcement from the cockpit broke into her thoughts and brought her back to the present. Twenty minutes to landing. Italy as far away as ever. She had packed her t hings the previous afternoon before her meal with Seb, so once back in her room, she had cleaned her teeth, stripped off and fallen straight into bed. She intended to travel in the same clothes she had arrived in and had left room in her suitcase for what she'd worn to the restaurant.

After a fitful night's sleep, Anna had had a cappuccino and a freshly baked almond croissant waiting for her when she went downstairs carrying her luggage just after eight o'clock. She wanted to sit outside and absorb the activity on the *piazza* for a while before Seb came to pick her up. True to form, he was there on time but not looking particularly happy.

'*Buongiorno, cara*,' he had greeted her before picking up her case and stowing it in the boot. 'You have a beautiful morning for your journey,' he added casually, holding the passenger door open for her. Just for a second, she looked directly at his face, but for once, she couldn't determine his mood.

Traffic on the dual carriageway out to the coast had been light, and even the A14 motorway wasn't particularly busy. She had sensed that conversation between them was stilted and, for the first time since they'd met, she felt uncomfortable. Signs for Falconara Airport appeared a few miles north of Ancona, and on arrival, it hadn't taken long for Seb to find a parking space. Before getting out of the car, he had explained that the airport had had a number of different names: Ancona, Falconara and also Rafaello Sanzio, named after Raphael, the High Renaissance artist.

'Unfortunately, these days, after the expansion, the airport is just known as Marche Airport. Not so interesting.'

'You don't have to wait with me,' she had felt compelled to say, even though she wanted more than anything for him to stay with her. He had said nothing, just got out of the car and, after opening the passenger door for her, had walked round to collect her suitcase.

'You don't get rid of me that easily, *signorina,*' he'd said, locking up the car. 'I'm with you until you go through to the departure lounge, and I can no longer see you.'

She had nodded and smiled at him, not really knowing what to say. It had been a short walk to the terminal building, and there had been only a few passengers in front of her in the queue at the check-in for London Stansted. The whole procedure had only taken a few minutes, and she had felt a twinge of disappointment when told that her flight was on time.

Seb had waited for her at the coffee bar but had drawn her to one side away from all the people milling around on the concourse.

'I know that the last few days have been emotional and overwhelming for you, but everything will be sorted out, I promise you. It will take time,' he'd said earnestly, moving to stand very close to her, his body shielding her from all the other passengers. 'You will come back to me, won't you?' a note of desperation in his voice.

'Of course!' she had replied without hesitation, looking directly into his eyes.

'You turned my world upside down when you walked into my office, and it hasn't righted itself since.' He'd smiled broadly, looking into her eyes intently.

Instinctively, she had cupped his cheek in her hand, and stepping in even closer, said, 'I think we can agree that we both feel the same way.'

The kiss, when it came, had been intense, yet soft and gentle at the same time. They fitted together perfectly, and a wave of calm had settled over her as she had leaned into him.

'I must go through now,' she had said, slowly pulling away reluctantly. 'I'm sure the time will fly by, and then, I shall be back,' she added confidently. In her mind, she had already worked out exactly what she needed to do once she'd left Italy.

'Call me to let me know you have arrived safely. I'll be waiting to hear your voice.'

'It will be very late,' she had warned him.

'I don't care. Whatever the time, I'll be waiting.'

She had joined the end of the queue to go through security and had then glanced back before going into the departure lounge. Seb had still been standing where she'd left him, his hand raised. A solitary figure among a horde of travellers.

The whole journey from boarding the aircraft in Ancona to arriving outside her cottage had been tedious and very tiring. Although the flight had landed at Stansted fifteen minutes ahead of schedule, baggage reclaim took more than an hour. The Stansted Express into Central London Liverpool Street station had been crowded, and then she had to take the Tube to Paddington.

Fortunately, the Elizabeth Line ran every five minutes, so she didn't have long to wait. Needing to focus on signs and timetables, she had little time to think about Seb and his parting words until she settled into her seat on the train heading west, back home to Wales. There was still one more connection she had to make before the final leg of her journey.

She had taken no interest in her fellow passengers, just staring out of the grimy windows, not registering the names of stations as the train passed through at speed.

Her connecting train in Carmarthen was twenty minutes late, but by that time, she couldn't care less. She took the time to ring for a taxi to pick her up at her destination, mentally preparing the answers to the questions she was sure the local driver would ask. She was bound to know him and could predict that he'd want to know where she'd been, who with, for how long, and whether or not she'd had a good time.

She was well aware that whatever answers she gave, the information would be all over the village in less than forty-eight hours! As far as the driver was concerned, she'd been to visit friends from university, the weather had been fabulous, and she'd really enjoyed herself. But as always, she told him, it was great to be home. Only she knew that this time, it was all a lie.

Huw George, the taxi driver, dropped her off outside her gate just after nine-thirty.

'Thanks, Huw,' she said, as he handed her case out of the boot and took the twenty-pound note she handed to him. 'Keep the change!'

'Another scorching day forecast for tomorrow, Cristi,' he said, 'and high tide by eleven. Perfect for a morning dip.'

'I'll think about it,' she called over to him as he got into the car and drove away.

For a few moments, she just stood and stared at her cottage. In fact, she acknowledged, that she seemed to have been just standing and staring quite a lot recently. It felt as though she had been away forever, not only a few days. The small, stone building had been her safe haven for years but, for an instant, the image of another stone building came into her mind, much larger but just as welcoming.

On the train, she had decided she would tell her father that she had been left the farmhouse and the land. There was no need to go into details about the rest of the legacy—that would come later when she had come to terms with the situation herself. She would resign from her position at the school as soon as the new term started. This would give the school governors time to find a replacement. She would arrange for a local agent to find a tenant for her cottage and manage the tenancy. Last but not least, she would find an Italian class and settle down to learn as much of the language as possible in a short space of time. She would return to Italy at half-term, fully intending to move there permanently as soon as she possibly could. The prospect of spending Christmas with Seb was more than appealing.

She pushed open the gate and walked up the path, carrying rather than dragging her suitcase. She fumbled in her shoulder bag and eventually found her keys. As she turned the key in the lock, she glanced at the carving on the door in front of her: *Cartref*. 'Home—but not for much longer!' she said out loud. Then, grinning broadly, she walked into her cottage and closed the door behind her.